In The Woods

S.E. Smyth

Paperback ISBN: 978-1-915905-28-4

First edition, Spectrum Books, 2023

Discover more LGBTQ+ books at www.spectrum-books.com

Contents

Each and every person has something.

PART I

Chapter 1

Michelle opened the front door of her mom and ma's house and screamed. The hollow air suddenly became full. A neighbor across the road quickly pushed the curtains open and then closed them. A squirrel lay before Michelle, its head shot clean through with some sort of projectile. It startled her in more than one respect. *It's not a present.* She shook her head and shut the door.

She scoured the house one more time for a person, an explanation. Still, she knew if she found a person, they wouldn't be able to give her one. Just as it had been the day before and the day before that, Ma was gone, and Mom was nowhere to be found. Michelle, in the past week, religiously, had visited every day.

When Ma told her, "I want to make things better, I honestly do," and her eyes filled with tears, Michelle buckled. When Ma asked her, "Will you help me make things better?" Michelle agreed. She would do nothing short of pledging, swapping blood, and signing a contract. Another week went by, Michelle coming to the house every day to fulfill her end of the agreement. Ma wouldn't answer her phone.

Michelle sat on the lumpy couch and remembered the moments as they came to her. She opened her journal. It was a step she took often, as a way to hold on to the happy thoughts. She would use it to encourage Ma to be the best she could be for them all, for the long term. She wrote down the episodes, the times they all got along, the good times. Those moments might escape her in favor of the terrible memories, the horrible overpowering moments that Michelle's ma so easily created. She certainly was unpredictable, but she never went a week without answering the phone.

Hours passed, and Michelle bided her time. She clicked the end of the pen with her nose until memories came through. She scribbled remembrances down. When she found Ma she could share her efforts, cheer her up at the very least. Mom opened the door, looking unaware of her surroundings. She had grocery bags cradled in her arms.

"Did you see it, Mom?"

"What?" Michelle gestured and Mom looked down at her feet. After a sweeping motion, kicking the squirrel out of sight, she hopped into the house. "Eww. Gross. Where did that come from?"

"I don't know. Where have you been? I haven't seen you or Ma in a week. I'm worried about Ma."

"I said. I answered your texts. I was with Mick. Right, honey? It's all so new. You'll have to forgive me if I spend some time away from you both." She kicked off her shoes and swished into the kitchen as if nothing was wrong. "Let's clean up this mess. Who would ever?"

"Not fully. You incoherently typed something about her camping. I'm still unclear. Where is she?" Michelle clenched her fists and her head lurched forward.

"Oh, Ma? She's at the cabin. In the woods. Can you believe it?"

Chapter 2

Thumbs wrapped around her hip belt loops, Jamie leaned back for a stretch. Yellow caution tape surrounded the house with a generous forty-foot buffer. The storm couldn't have destroyed the cabin, their second home, at a less opportune time. Her location situated her one hundred and fifty feet past the structure. She huddled by the fire ring. She stood still, passing the time as best as she could with calisthenics. Jamie's life had toppled over onto her shoeless feet a few days ago, so here she sat occupying space at a cabin in a clearing at the top of a mountain. The cabin was one of those people spy as they pass by in cars at the base of the intersection of hills along the Appalachian trail—a place where one can't imagine a road leads to the spot. No one could get to her in the Swiss Alps. *Everything,* her mind echoed, *will find a place.* Jamie left the family home, shook by statements and then requests Ellen made about divorce and separation. She came to live on their other property with a cabin. But she camped outside in the rough.

At the start of the school system's Winter Break, the family had often made the trip. Entering through the most direct route to get to the tree, the children bounded in first. A bold red front wood slab clapped when their small family entered, ready for Christmas. The skylights on the steeply pitched roof were likely impressive to their neighbors, who walked by sometimes on an expedition. They would stare for a long while between hard pulls on their beers.

One year at Christmas, she had heard the people in the cabin next door comment in unison, "That's a big house for two women and a girl." They stared at her through the window. Her face with its subtle masculine ridges and rounded corners, she knew, gleamed in lighted glass.

The neighbors likely admired their guns and ammunition. In the same regard, Jamie and her wife—almost ex-wife—worshiped their cabin. In her blue-green eyes, Jamie's home, similar to their guns, came to be a trophy. The family somehow shared the woods with neighbors, those casing the place by moonlight and making a ruckus with bullets and tin cans. The area of cabins butted on the north side of the Blue Ridge Trail and set against game lands to the west. A stream ran parallel to the east end of the family property. A person could scream or call out and a few birds would flap their wings. Nothing else made a noise.

Blinking away the memories, Jamie focused on the present and strained her eyes looking at the window. The window beckoned her, and she walked toward the opening. Yesterday the window exhibited only a missing sliver. Now a ragged-edged hole covered most of the pane. She grabbed a long length of caution tape from the ground and moved toward the window. After placing the tape across the ridges of cut glass, she paused. All became content. After she made the change, she returned to her makeshift home.

Jamie had lifted weights every other day a year before, pulling weights knee to chin, repeatedly, repeating. In the makeshift gym in the basement of their everyday home, she had gathered herself up on a pull-up bar, proving her strength to herself and no one else in the damp dark place, a single bulb shining on her accomplishments.

She had lifted, had started herself on a kick, to heave herself out of a depression, occupy herself. The grunts she had emitted when the weight held her down, too heavy or the reps were too many, did, in fact, take her mind away, make her concentrate on the task before her. She could no longer drift, and the tears had dried in the harsh light, wrapping shadows around her and casting others onto the floor.

In fifth grade, she had learned to play like the boys, hit hard and with purpose. While girls learned to pass and work as a team, she learned like the boys, how to be an individual player, supporting the team by attacking using aggressiveness in every action. Those traits now seemed unsavory, selfish, confrontational, and controlling.

The weights she lifted reminded her of teenage years. She always just made the team. Her powers of dexterity and concentration on the game lacked a little too much. So, she lifted, stayed after school, trudged in before basketball, early in the morning in the summers before volleyball. Months ago, she tried to draw herself out of a similar rut, build up strength to satisfy her ego, her happiness. She realized physical activity never had made her happy back then. She got a little better at sports, at self-confidence, and then she collapsed. Her more recent athletic efforts produced the same results.

Now a flopped mass on the orange inflatable mat—in a figurative crime scene of a tantrum, she wailed, beating her fists against the ground. She realized in that moment satisfaction eluded her. Her mind grew weak, her concentration focused on the piece of lead in her hand. She never exuded happiness as a child, and her efforts only brought her again, interminably, to that state of being. Persistence reared its head for naught. Her sexuality was fine.

She dropped cross-legged onto the mat outside the tent, much as a twenty-something hippie would do, even though lines now grew at the corners of her eyes and the skin on her cheeks sagged a bit. Her joints crackled with the swift pressure. She thought perhaps it would be less damaging if she moved slower. She could keep the same movement. Her test of life without a cell phone differed for someone thirty years younger. Neither was her evaluation of unemployment. She relaxed, stretched often, and picked with liberty and often from her travel sized bag of granola mix. She had made the nosh herself with Rice Krispies, peanuts, almonds, and a bag of dried apricots. The ration, more reasonable than items for sale in the gas station, allowed her to coast on economical purchases for the time being. Low-priced go-to foods included items stored in the cabinets at her primary home. The food registered as her wife's groceries. The cabinets were her wife's.

The sole thing Jamie took was a sweet note from a long-lost friend on the trip to the house in mid-August. She burned the paper in a pit of fire, after she let the sentiments rest with her one last time. Slowly, the remnants turned to ash and flitted away in the wind.

Bitterly starting an assembly line, she shuffled about putting snack bags in order this last day before moving on. Her ex-wife labored away at work. The dire situation had developed weeks before; they nodded together when it was decided she would go. When her wife left the next morning for work, she had gathered her things.

In a reach for something authentic, she bagged the mix, feeling the campfire and not the rain. Visions of squirrels and nuts sat unsettled. She wouldn't train animals, she thought. She had no ideas about circuses, but she confidently proclaimed she could coax the squirrels closer. One by one, she dropped vitamin waters into a trash bag from a height a little higher than necessary. She smiled loosely at the idea of nutrition. Beef jerky, peanut butter, and other non-perishables all tasted yards better as she rolled their scent over her tongue. Expiration dates and hollowed guts drove her decisions. While wondering if she could eat canned soup cold, Jamie gathered up more than she believed to be required.

At present, Ellen checked up on their grown child and took care of the house. She woke up every morning with something to do and she had admitted only swift memories of Jamie passed through her head. This act had called for a break in her now normal pattern.

Jamie slumped into her crossed legs and smiled. She bent her chest to the ground, trying to make herself feel younger. She laughed to herself until despondent. The despair rose in her through the laughter and when the noise came out, it seemed perplexing, unfitting. Jamie didn't have to care about making minor efforts to keep the apocalyptic arguments and struggles at bay. She didn't have to start the repetitive "discussions." She knew they drew these out, unresolvable, and minor. The arguments kept going until they were both too tired to continue without explosion. The debates: Who's schedule is better for getting groceries? They shouldn't have a dog. Who would do the dishes in a particular week?

Ellen spoke passionately about any issue, all arguments, and most actions once she decided an ordeal amounted to Jamie's fault. Ellen threw water on a dry skillet to make the smoke rise and agitated the metal by adding greasy ingredients, cooking with flair. All this percolated under the hood of the new stove. Right now, likely at this exact moment back at their house, she was teasing, spitting oil and cursing Jamie before throwing the meat on to fry.

Memories, caringly absent, said, "You're welcome," for the past few years. Nothing would haunt her. Blanketed truths held. They were both devastated and satisfied. They had told each other as much. She was this person. Daily routines created friction. Energy didn't mesh. Anger never resolved. She didn't fit with her.

Jamie knew and held to the fact that Ellen, soon to be her ex-wife, shouted while making any weekday dinner, the same as when she made it before guests arrived on any evening they entertained. When she looked at Ellen and when Ellen was not there, she conjured up this fact, this truth. Washed recollections heaved but kept the anger at bay. The tension drilled into her temples and now, when the screw untwisted, there was release. The woods covered her and smothered her in comfort, disguise, in a place of respite and calm. She rested under the canopy of a small aspen, biding her time, picking at her Krispies one by one. She bobbled her neck and cracked her jaw because she must be free.

Chapter 3

The drive up the mountain top weaved in and out of trees. A berm of fifty feet of brush crowded toward the road, hiding the runoff that flowed for miles to the mountain base. This trip, one almost as laborious as the two-and-a-half-hour drive from her house, taxed Ellen. The beautiful landscape, the water's edge, the cabin in the woods, she owned half. Jamie claimed the house now as her own. For this, satiation existed, even if that feeling required a three-hour hike of a drive up to the top of a mountain.

The fall air slipped in, about to cut. With her window open a crack, she could feel the temperature drop throughout the rise in elevation. She thought about how she could smoke a cigarette. What most thought was an effort to be cool or patient was, in actuality, a prescription for anxiety or frustration, a bit of a relief. Ellen knew this much, even though she only had smoked occasionally in college. She counted to twenty and then lost count. After she bought twenty packs, the same error occurred. When she realized she had lost touch with the extent of the habit and the money she could've spent elsewhere, she stopped. But she never forgot the crackle in her brain, the frustrating one letting out tension, letting the anger dissipate. She inhaled the fresh air and wondered about the freedom her lungs held, even though she never took up running. Although mild at the base, the summit turned wistfully chill in the shade of the trees. The fall, then the holidays, would be upon them soon. The scene at their joint family cabin would not last much longer. The cold would see to the end of it all.

Ellen stomped up the driveway, angry. No surprise. She brought noise with her. As she moved toward Jamie, the things she held onto waved about unconsciously. Her boots planted down harder than they rose, so much so if her steps had been on a thin wood floor, hollow underneath, she might have gone right through. The same anger surfaced; what she had after she chucked a slab of meat onto the raw skillet. "Well, well. Still here, huh?" She smirked. She was now proud, with a sense of angered ownership over their years of failed marriage. The dissolution was all but complete, now a tangible, discrete thing, their summed-up accomplishment now named divorce. As a tornado does, her feelings bounded in powerful and suddenly dissipated. The high winds and churning ruined their last shared asset. She also thought she did not have to split. At least she wasn't on the sounding board this time.

"There's no reason for sleeping out in the woods. I don't know what your tantrum could accomplish," Ellen said. She waited, showing Jamie should not respond. She stood and stared for a minute. "Why are you up here? I can't find the sense in your behavior," she said.

Jamie smiled blankly.

"You could get an apartment. What are you trying to prove?" She swept by her and felt the same ownership over this place as their divorce. Standing still, she leaned into her left foot and lifted her hands to her hips, still holding plastic grocery bags. She didn't know where to put anything.

Jamie answered, "I'm fine up here, entirely a-okay. No sense in trying to help me. Don't even try." She picked at a scab on her left forearm. The mark, a minor scrape, could've been from a rock or branch. "I can get anything I need. Look, we're divorced and having you around doesn't help. I need time on my own. Isn't this where we had been going for time on our own?" Jamie asked. She winced, but then grinned broadly.

Jamie swished dirt with the toe of her boot in the pause. Folding in on herself, she stretched, grabbing her toes, relaxing her elbows. For seconds, then minutes, she reached and stretched, not looking up. Jamie's side-eye glance reached Ellen while Jamie's arm extended over her head toward her opposite toes. Ellen jumped to speak.

"We have been going here for time on our own," Ellen said mockingly. Her word lacked effect. "Look, this is ridiculous. Where's your car? This is childish. You think you're alright? Mick thinks I should take you to the hospital, you know. He thinks your attitude is unstable and not at all a good example for Michelle." She placed a new rolled-up mattress pad tucked up under her arms next to the tent. The grocery bags still hung from her hands.

"I'm fine. I'm fine. The air is peaceful here. I'll stay until after the inspection, until we put the house on the market. Life is stress free. No traffic to give you a headache. I mean—no cars. This quaint place is relaxing. Look around... be quiet with me," she said. Jamie lifted a finger to the air. She might have looked a little like a Greek statue, Ellen thought, if she had been washed over with plaster. She smiled a bit.

Ellen smirked. She knew she wasn't ever in the mood. The plastic bags still dug hard into her hands. The left one now seemed notably more weighted than the right. She warmed, counterbalancing the weather. Her actions could be considered more than words. She put forth effort. With an articulated stretch, making herself tall, she careened down the hill, stopping her feet into the ground, but not leaving even a dent. She couldn't see through to next week.

Ellen slammed the car door and sat waiting for Jamie to come check on her, to see why she hadn't left. She picked at the cuticles on the sides of her fingers. Happily assuring herself, she tilted her head back and forth and mumbled to herself she was better than this. Holding her phone in her hand, she tapped at the metal sides. If her daughter needed something, she'd pick up the phone. Bobbing the phone between two fingers, up and down, she came to—the phone didn't have any additional information. The day would be better without more news or alerts, highlights of events, or people's thoughts.

She had teeter-tottered with Michelle years ago, at the playground right before they bought the cabin. Michelle had been ten years old when they bought the place. Ellen rocked her phone up and down on the fulcrum, her finger thinking about the conversation. Michelle's glowing locks were already cumbersome. She had cried to have short hair like Jamie. She wanted to drive the car like Jamie. Pestering Ellen, she complained she didn't have cut-off jeans, couldn't drink beer, or couldn't hike for hours on end in the wilderness like Ma. Jamie.

Michelle sat down opposite Ellen as she popped up and down and held the bar tight, both cognizant that their actions were the only way to make the see-saw work. She only talked about Jamie though. Jamie this. Her hero, that. Michelle left Ellen behind in her adorations. She merely called her the mother. The person who listened, took in, and reflected with her about the love, the characteristics, and the greatness was Jamie.

Ellen shifted now in her car seat, still waiting for Jamie. Jamie never appeared. After ten minutes, with a swift movement, she turned on the ignition. The car they had bought together a few years ago came alive. She pulled out, window still down, listening to the loose gravels spit and chuck in various directions. A pop made her think Jamie might've put nails down to trap her up in the mountains with her.

Strand her on a mountaintop. Strand anyone to capture them with her in her loneliness. Ellen wished she had. Pulling the steering wheel around, after a soft three-point turn, she coasted down the drive to the road that fell swiftly into the valley of the working world. Leaves left their trees, littering the ground. They would be slippery if wet. If Ellen returned after the rains, she would have to be careful. She would need to move with awareness.

On the drive back, Ellen remembered the times. The times they had together. Her mood swiftly changed with her partner's absence. Remorseful, she remembered the good things. She forced herself to see the pictures, look through the images in her mind, the photo book she had never put together.

Jamie hadn't always been erratic. She could see the past actions in her mind.

Their twisted lives had been filled with goodness, day after day, until a few years ago. When the lashing out started, when Ellen did anything and everything, including issue anger, Ellen screamed at the top of her lungs. They had been together a long time, since their twenties. Longevity counted for something. Longevity bleeds comfort, bleeds the permission to yell. Ellen struck her head up from the wheel, pleased with herself and the way she had handled the visit.

Their fights brought out childish anger. She had always tempted fate with an outburst. Michelle always responded in kind.

Chapter 4

"I'm only dropping shit off up here. All I'm doing." Mick shrugged. "Then, I'm leaving. I don't know why the hell you're up here, and I don't care. I'm doing this for Ellen because I love her," he added in between choppy, gasping shouts, some words split in half to accommodate for clouded draws. He paused and leaned his hand on his knee. He rested his body on his elbow and barked out, snorted. Mick, Ellen's new boyfriend, reached the peak of the slope, mouth half closed, spitting air out of the corners of his mouth.

Jamie muttered something that wasn't, "Thank you." She knew she should feel flush and embarrassed, except she didn't give a damn. She turned her back and said, "Shove it."

No one else was out here to witness, so whatever Jamie told everyone would have actually happened in their minds. No one would carve words on a piece of slate way up the top of a mountain for everyone to come and behold.

Mick pulled his chin back, showing he thought he and Jamie were different people; His face blanked out. Jamie looked at a confused Mick. He exhaled and made his way up to the setup.

She eyed him warily. Mick worked as a warehouse manager and frequently equated project management with the idea of, "the taller you are, the harder you fall." Even though Jamie wasn't a project manager anymore, he still treated her like one. He bullied someone with an occupation, to make sure they knew what was what and who was who.

His tight cropped jet-black hair covered his sweaty head, greasy likely from oil and muck from cars. Even though he was a manager, he still "checked out the undercarriage" as he liked to phrase it. He smelled slightly musty, never of cologne, but Ellen had said she wanted a raw man. That person was him. He wore a polo and khakis and combed his fade back every so often. Staring at her blankly, he clearly searched for something to say.

What could she see in him? This son of a bitch is anything but redeeming. He's built for an entirely different life. His life runs on the fumes of the good people he's screwed. He'll never know her the way I do, the way I love her.

Mick held a few canvas bags full of odd kitchen supplies, which he might have gathered in a rush from Ellen's kitchen. The paper towels unrolled out of the package. He held the half empty dish soap by a detaching pump.

"I stopped at the grocery store on the way and picked you up munchies. These fire jobs you like. If you don't want them, that's okay. I've got some friends coming over to watch a football game this weekend. I'll be using your couch and chair." He threw the bag and contents all down like a pile of junk.

Mick was a dick. Jamie knew he was worthless inside and out. His words always held a tinge of sarcasm, a tinge of hatred. He tolerated Jamie, her emotional hurt and anguish. He barely knew the angst. At one point, he had quipped about having threesomes with Ellen. His words bit hard when he spoke. "You're the only baggage we'd have to bring along and take home afterward. You think Ellen's still in love with you, but I'll cut you if it's true."

Mick didn't know how to use words gently, and each one amounted to a guttural bark, erupting with frankness. Jamie left herself to his will. He enjoyed figuratively pushing her to the floor and giving her a kick. He didn't care about the history between them, and no reasoning could position her otherwise.

"You know, she'll go back to women," Jamie said. "She loves women. I see the notion in her eyes. You'll never truly satisfy her."

Mick stared hard and long, beading on Jamie's feet. He gave one swift kick to the ground. Nothing was in the vicinity, nothing to launch forward, and only some bits of grass and dust issued forth. "I'll fucking cut you. You know that Jamie."

Jamie moved toward her fire ring, keeping Mick at her back. She left the groceries flung to the ground; the contents spilled out of the bag. No one spoke like that to her face. She still held shreds of dignity.

Halfheartedly Jamie paced about, keeping her back in Mick's direct view. Odd bits of clothing, a lantern, and camping gear sprawled out around her. She never had to clean before. The wind the night before had carried trash out of the trash bags, strewing garbage here and there. As soon as Jamie cleaned up the disarray, some other item would appear. Some of the trash still littered the area. Jamie wanted Mick to tote some of the junk down for her. Odd food wrappers, attempts at rigging for a garden, and a leaking air mattress all needed a more permanent home. The mattress only stayed inflated for half the night. The slow leak resulted in her losing half a night's worth of sleep. She had to be extremely still to get the most out of the flattened pad. Ellen had bought the key camping accessory. Jamie had no qualms about throwing the mattress away.

"Look, I'm going," Mick said. He turned as quickly as he came. Jamie didn't have a chance to ignore his comments and questions like expected. She twisted slightly, apprehensive and disappointed.

Because she uttered no response aloud, Jamie would appear to be drifting. She guessed her quiet would still give Mick something to report. As much as Jamie wanted to provoke a fight, she only watched herself hurl the bags of trash down the hill in her mind.

So, Mick barged out as swiftly as he had come. Jamie dozed in an inextricable daze, as if Mick had punched her or slipped a roofie in her drink. Jamie buckled. She darted her head to the side and avoided his sight. He had come and left in an instant.

Jamie lay on her one-inch air mattress, her relaxing mattress, outside of the tent during the daytime. The lime green mat, padded enough to hold aching joints above the rough ground, provided much needed support. She drifted into a gentle recline, moving almost musically into a horizontal position. Within that, she grew sleepy. Mick's sucker punch put her down for the count—almost as if an overwhelming stress or more like a concussion makes a person pass out. Despite not wanted to sleep, Jamie let go, letting her thoughts leave with the wind.

Chapter 5

Leaving behind *Margaret Mead Made Me Gay* on the seat next to her, Michelle exited her car and slammed the door. She'd rather Ma know she was coming. Michelle climbed and summited the driveway's hill. This was not the first time. Stopping at the top of the hill, she sought to find energy to move forward into the scene, her ma in the woods. She stared hard, squinting with a little more anger after several seconds passed. The time being after five o'clock, the sun flirted with taking away the day. The camp setup passed muster, though perhaps narrowly so. It was more her Ma's behavior that made her eyes narrow.

Ma sat huddled around the fire. The weather had grown colder. Temperatures dipped into the fifties at night now. Michelle thought she saw a few leaves fall from the trees. The more permanent chill of fall came rushing through the campsite. Michelle watched Ma, with stirring, crazy eyes, look for an extra blanket. No one had brought her an extra blanket. Ma picked slowly at a branch as a few leaves serendipitously dropped from the tree and onto her lap.

As Michelle approached the scene, she was sure her Ma could hear her voice, and so she expressed her full concern.

"Don't you tell me about having a tough time? You figure your issues out, Ma. I have no time to straighten out what's going on with you," Michelle called out. She grunted because the sound felt good. She said what she meant.

"Listen now; it's not so bad. You want some nuts?" her ma said. She smiled sheepishly, giggling a bit, just audible.

Michelle saw the grin all over her ma's face. "I'm not sure what you think you are doing here? Can't you get a hotel room till you're set up?"

"This land is perfectly free, except for the taxes. I might as well use the wilderness as I can. You remember when we used to set up a tent out here, right?"

"Yeah, we had good times. I wish you and Mom could be friends. Pat's parents are friends. They still take each other to doctor's appointments when they need a ride and discuss things civilly. They even grab dinner now to catch up," Michelle said.

She had told her Ma a few weeks ago, before she came up here to commune with nature, that Pat had asked her to move in with her. Michelle had said not just yet. She had gotten a new, better job and was throwing herself into it and simmering. The master's degree in international business had paid off. Ma had sat back in the easy chair, the same one she slept on, but hadn't offered advice. Mick had told them the day before that he would move in at the conclusion of the week.

Michelle fussed with the string extending from the critical points of the tent to the ground. *No one ever puts up these strings. They don't give a lot of extra support.* Ma did. Her Ma kept things tidy, mostly. An empty Cheetos bag lay on the ground. Two pots set one on top of another next to a fire pit. They seemed only used once. Michelle drew up some strength, and her body rose.

"Do you need a gun, Ma? I can get you a gun."

"It's fine honey. The lights from the neighbors' houses. The light is enough to scare animals. I pack up the garbage. I might have some you can take. The garbage is beside the house. If the wolves come to get me, that'll be a glorious death," her ma said.

"Ma, you can't even. A fire's hardly enough."

"I don't make a fire often."

"Exactly," Michelle responded.

Michelle met Ma's eyes. They wobbled similarly. Michelle tried to find Ma's stability and composure. Michelle's eyes did not break through with tears, but the melancholy was deep. *Was Ma, in a way, going here to die, to be herself one last time, before she grew up?*

"Look, honey, I can't explain what I'm going through. I'm looking for something out here. I'm going to find the words to vocalize what I'm in, and I'll move on." Ma choked out a cough. "There's no sense in feeling sorry for me. I want to be here. Hopefully, I will find the reasons, the answer, before the seasons change. That's all I can add. Other than a few snakes... And I think I heard some howls last night. This camp is safe."

"Ma, I don't wanna—"

"Maybe one day, you'll know. It would be nice if the cabin were fixed up and usable by then. I'm not saying you have to camp."

Michelle watched Ma roll rocks under the sole of her shoe. Her eyes had cast down and never returned to exchange looks with Michelle.

"I wish you'd wrap this episode up. The only thing you'll find out here is how long a person can go without a shower or running toilet." Michelle let her shoulders hang loosely.

"I want you to have this cabin. You'll come up here like me one day and try to remember. Or. Or find something. You know, by being by yourself." Ma appeared to tense up.

Michelle watched Ma fall into herself, retract and become introverted. Ma fiddled with a twig stripping the bark from the outside. In swift movements, she trimmed the single stick with her thumb nail alone, whittled down the branch, pruned the excess. Then she flicked the pieces of bark, still gooey and alive on the inside, one by one, into the dusty fire pit. When the pale center of the stick was all that was left, it too went into the pit. Then, a new twig took its place, grabbed from a pile at her side.

"Well. My issue is the bipolar disorder acting up." She flicked another piece. "Characterized mainly by a depressive episode at present." She sniffed in hard with a single breath. Her cheeks fluttered a bit as she did. "Delusional, something, something. Doesn't matter. That's all there was, really. Except we weren't sure about the something, something part. Then, this week, he told me the ailment was borderline personality disorder. He gave me a final diagnosis."

Michelle lifted her toes and set them down. Her knees raised her hands, and she shut off parts of her brain. *This wasn't happening.* "Ma. We know how hard this is for you. Everyone has something. We'll... you know, get through things. If the doctor's right, if you're falling in again, this isn't the best place to be."

"You don't need to know. The issue is mine. I know you don't understand, but I can't... I don't intend to share this with you." She wobbled on the log. For some unknown reason, she had switched from throwing pieces into the fire ring to throwing them over her back.

"Ma. Why are you..." Stumbling to a halt, she tried to order her thoughts. She meant to say, "Why are you having so much trouble? What can I do to help?" but her eyes beaded on the bits of branch cascading over Ma's shoulder.

"It's good luck. That's what I tell myself, at least. Why not, if I believe it, why wouldn't it be?"

"Ma. You have shared this with me. I have some issues; I know depression, and I'm moving forward."

"I... I don't know. There's so much up here. Getting myself here... is hard for me."

Michelle felt the distant memories too, but she didn't choose to be there. She bent over to come down to her mother's level so they could look each other in the eye. Michelle's empty words were going on a walk in the woods. Her anger melted to sadness and welled in her eyes. She fidgeted with her hands, then clasped a hard fist.

Michelle spent another two hours above the world on the hillside with Ma. She asked about her comfort and reminded her of soft bath towels in hotels and apartments. Her words showed her frustration and disdain. To coax her mother out of the wilderness required something beyond Michelle's powers. She stayed for a bit, creating cairns even though they never rose much higher than eight stones. Each of them took a turn until the stack fell. The largest rocks were the bases. They saw the piles like this on the trail but had never built their own. They only stood back to stare and went on their way.

Michelle never lasted longer than two hours when she visited her family. She liked to show her face and keep a consistent record, but she always needed to get out of there before they could tear apart what she wanted to keep as a wonderful moment. Waving to her Ma even though she knew she might say, "I love you," she said she would be back with the jugs of water she had forgotten to bring.

Chapter 6

"This isn't your best life, my friend." A person in a black trench coat took Jamie by the hand and looked at her square in the shoulders. "I'm Gerry's soldier." They gave Jamie a big hug, wrapping their arms around the breadth of her back, pulling her in and holding for several minutes.

"If it was this much love they wished to give, Gerry should've come themself." Jamie pushed them back and looked at them with the same squareness she had received. They looked healthy. Their teeth were clean. They were shaven, though bits of rough stubble came through. They rubbed at the protrusions with a full hand. Jamie knew too much to give them full commendations. If Gerry, and this person in front of her who seemingly had come to give a hug, were still stuck in the world of crime, a dark world in a country with rules all its own, at least they were taking care of themselves.

Jamie remembered acutely the day Gerry came to her room, a posh hotel room in Bern, their hands covered in blood. Gerry rushed in and, as Jamie approached to hug them, they held up the backs of their hands simply because the palms held too much blood. Jamie nodded, and Gerry went to the bathroom, lathering and washing for what seemed like an hour. An additional hot shower lasted at least a half hour. Gerry got dressed, and they ducked out. No one uttered a word that night. Jamie knew not to bring the departure up when they met again, but she didn't want to know. She didn't want to spoil what they had, and particular words most certainly would have.

Jamie had loved Gerry when they were together and after for many years. That didn't mean she would've risked her job while they were together. At most, Gerry relayed a few pieces of information about their jobs, the assignments given to them through a criminal organization in Switzerland. Jamie believed the activities to mostly revolve around money laundering.

Ironically, Jamie's plight included being mixed up in the same things in the United States. These things kept Jamie from ever being with Gerry, ever thinking it would be anything more than simplicity. Jamie knew they would never be together because she didn't have the guts.

"Handle. Pleased to meet you." Handle paused so as not to startle Jamie. "I saw Gerry with you that day in the bar. I knew the bartender. A son of a bitch. That's for sure. Or all three of us would be together—still." Handle rolled their shoes on rocks at the base of their feet. They meandered around Jamie's home, or camp as it may be, and then over to the broken cabin. Now and then, they darted their head back toward Jamie. They whispered curses, heads up into the air, about this place they were in. Some words were in German, but Jamie could make out *"fucking place"* and *"where the hell."* They kicked holes into the ground with deep blue steel-toed boots outside the side of the house, almost as if to say, *I could kick this cabin just as easily. Knock the house down in one motion.*

"You're starstruck lovers, you two?" Handle asked.

"I'm not sure I know what you mean?" Jamie itched at her forearm.

"Gerry said you were in trouble. Somehow, he knew."

"Gerry?"

"Transitioned, yes."

"Gerry knew you were in trouble. He sent me to get you. To bring you back to him. He said about unfinished business, but you must know already if you are both psychics."

"Oh, hardly," Jamie said. "I must've. I dropped a note off. He, ah, he sent me a cryptic postcard unexpectedly. He said he loved me, but the way we'll always be in love." Jamie laughed a loud, popping laugh. "I told him I gave up women. My god, Gerry."

"Well, I'm here. Let's eat dinner and then we can leave. I have two tickets for us."

"I can't. I can't just leave. The action is beyond me. I haven't told anyone. I can't just..."

"It's all taken care of. You can simply leave. You can."

Jamie moved to grab a pan. She still had some bread from the grocery store she could warm up. She hesitated as she grabbed the doughy bag and led him to believe they would go.

"You're not going to go, are you?" Handle centered on her hesitation. They could tell as she smiled in the corner of her mouth. She tried to tell them she couldn't go.

"I just can't. I have a life here. Oh, I love Gerry. There is no doubt about that. But I have a life, and it's good. It's in pieces, but the shreds of it I'm picking up are still good. When Ellen... I'm not sure." Jamie looked into the distance, mumbling to an almost stranger she didn't even know. She wasn't sure if the words were too vague for them.

As they nodded their head in agreement, Jamie looked back. "Gerry said not to push?"

"That's true."

"Stay here for the night. I'd love to have you in this, my makeshift place."

Jamie and Handle spent the night naming tunes they could both hum. One of them would key up the rhythm and the other would chime in. They discussed their favorite American and Swiss sayings. Handle's was "better off dead."

They drifted to sleep, Handle in a blanket, and Jamie in the regular sleeping bag, debating the redeeming qualities of American cheese or Swiss cheese. The arguments included—Swiss provolone is better than American provolone. Later—Swiss American was better than any other cheese. Handle started snoring and Jamie didn't know if he meant a particular cheese or the Swiss version of American. Either way, Handle presented a never-ending argument. They would never let up.

In the morning, Jamie couldn't find Handle.

Chapter 7

If it wasn't her girlfriend's house, she went to the grocery store. That's the only other place Michelle had been going. Pat's apartment sent inviting chills down her spine. They lounged together and apart in the spacious open living room and quiet nooks of rooms. Michelle's gluttony surfaced as spending the weekend in bed, only leaving to cook eggs and bacon before the other half woke up. TV series ran over and over, binged. Pat whispered hot words in her ear as they drew closer together in the evenings, eventually starting what they both expected.

"Listen to me, your lips are like clouds."

The words resounded. And they found out how many things they agreed on. That's what Michelle and Pat had been like before Mick and Mom, at least, before Ma went to the woods.

Now, she picked at a box of eggs, opening the lid but not finding the energy to turn each one over. She surveyed the shelves, wanting to return as quickly as possible.

Michelle didn't go to many other places, besides her Ma's fort next to the old family cabin. She gathered up some more supplies with only a slight notion of what she might want. This trip was the first time she had traveled to the grocery store solely to stock Pat's house. They sanctimoniously killed time together. Last month and the month before, she selected a few things, and then a few other things, taking them specifically over to Pat's house for snacking or when she stayed over. Pat said she would stock up, but Michelle began getting extra things to take over, things they both would like.

Pat and Michelle set up a fort at Pat's. They joked about the unhealthiness so early in their relationship. Pat mentioned the U-Haul place down the road, and Michelle choked, mostly because of the urge to check rental costs on her phone. Pat hung ropes and chains and various other scary bondage type of decorations around the house for Halloween. "I'll trap you here," she joked, acting like a witch or Dom. Michelle rolled her eyes playfully at the comment. She wasn't sure which it was. She scratched her chin with a thin finger, nails groomed, as always.

At the register, she stopped before moving forward to the conveyor. She had forgotten the bread. Glancing over at the cashier, she knew she'd lose her spot. The snarky glare said she understood. She got it. She'd seen this before. Peanut butter with a spoon then.

Michelle unloaded her groceries, tenderly placing them on the moving conveyor. The cashier jolted the platform forward and stopped, jolted, stopped. Pears wobbled, bobbling without directive. The cashier perked up and aware, grinned and then looked down. Michelle tensed her lips together but didn't intend for the cashier to see her unamused. When she looked sidelong back, Michelle rested her basket on the conveyor, her last stand.

Michelle's hands shook, and she dug her nails into her palms. She called herself into action early, fists up. This cashier's soft hair and supple skin dated her as young, too young to understand. Michelle wouldn't let her misunderstand her. Michelle barked back with her glares. She took dramatic sidesteps up to the credit card keypad, bowing her head and smiling. She had lined the items up like soldiers. The cashier wantonly unloaded and scanned, unloaded, and scanned. A reckless toss into the bag caught Michelle's tongue. She moved no further, but she nodded and opened her side-satchel for a card. Her gaze drifted back behind her, three registers down.

Mick's back and his slicked back, overgrown crew cut, took form in Michelle's pencil thin black glasses. Mick, Michelle's girlfriend's father, was anything but kempt. His demeanor struck Michelle a certain way as well. He regularly spouted his feelings, actualizing his self-involvement. He talked about being brave in the world and what particular hard rock lyrics meant, and what his deepest, darkest secret would do to the family. Not that it would ever come out.

Michelle wouldn't ever call him dad. She decided this through and through. If he asked her, because he struck her as a person who might, she would in fact not use the words. She would feel uncomfortable. She wasn't quite stable enough to endow him with parental posture.

The divorce was inevitable. The marriage would come along next. She loved Ma and Mom together. They were her parents. She knew no others. Her dad was absent, had grown increasingly absent by the time Michelle was sixteen and drinking consumed his life. She saw a bit of her dad in Mick. His crafty sentences. The way he leered and gave a quick smile. He picked at his teeth when bored, but he wasn't ever bashful about shaking someone's hand. A modern cowboy, for sure. His M.O. allowed him to show up to events whenever he wished and leave on errands amid dinner. He hid his daily activities and presented as bluntly straightforward in demeanor.

Yes, Michelle and Pat whispered back and forth, exchanging confused glances. Three months ago, their parents started dating. Michelle's mom was bisexual, and even though she only ever remembered her mom with Ma, Jamie, that didn't mean Michelle didn't know she could have feelings for a man. She had talked about her bisexuality in casual sentences every so often when they were getting coffee, or after she and Ma had a big fight. It seemed to Michelle, in her humble opinion, that Mom thought everything would fix itself, life would turnaround, if she dated a man.

When they met, Michelle's mom and Mick hit it off right away. Michelle's mom met all Mick's harsh responses with intrigue. Mom questioned Mick, trying to find out more about every topic. Everything was foreign and new, and what she called his "biker sex appeal" had her captured. They meshed, and Ma was absent, off in another world. Michelle couldn't blame Mom for going with him when he swooped her up.

Pat thought it equally odd. Both agreed things might fizzle out and they shouldn't let others' emotions affect their relationship. They were, despite all the parental drama, falling into a deeper affection. A jolt in their relationship. They tried to put affection out of their minds at the very least, and hope it dissolved or severed.

They could be stepsisters. Michelle drew back and wobbled a bit at the thought. She and Pat would've moved in together if the cleaver hadn't been inserted by their parents, together, into their lives. The inconvenient attraction suited them, and they didn't realize quite like the would-be sisters they were offbeat in their passion. Mick and Mom's coupling might sever Pat's and Michelle's relationship. They both knew that. But who could splice true love if that was, in fact, what Mick and Mom had? Michelle and Pat waited their parent's relationship out, hungry to see if their bridled passion could become more in proper circumstances.

Michelle looked back, not wanting to see the things in front of her, and her mouth gaped out of relief and anxiety in equal parts. The table upset, she looked for more answers to confirm.

Mick sat dumbfounded, unaware of Michelle's glance. But when a woman in a green shirt and dark green skirt tucked her arm under

Mick's waist and gripped her hand under his belt, he jerked up in pleasure. Public affection in the grocery store clearly made him smile.

Mick leaned in and whispered in her ear, and she let her arm go loose. He squeezed her arm as he leaned in, giving her an affectionate kiss on the cheek. The woman in green grabbed his butt and let the hunk of skin go, both confirming and hiding in plain sight from their involvement. Michelle's eyes were off the clerk; She couldn't care less about her sucker punches at the moment.

Michelle's head now jerked up and down. Two poses: seeing and unseen. The woman in green cradled a pineapple like a baby. The prickly fruit rocked back and forth. They wouldn't put the mass in the bag, motioning toward the bag and then away. Her hand jerked off the fruit as she came upon something sticky. The woman in green cradled the baby back and forth, while Mick gathered up five plastic grocery bags. Around the corner, out of earshot, Michelle could see them talking but didn't know the words. The bags, almost too many, bobbled and crinkled in his arms as he adjusted and meandered in his way, awkwardly, in the opposite direction of Michelle.

Michelle ducked out of the store. The card swiped, the bags gathered, the strides lengthened, then they were gone. She would voice several questions but never an affront. She wouldn't meddle as her mothers had, parent to child.

Chapter 8

"Wow. Over there. Such a nice one! An A-frame. Jealous. Honey, when are we getting a cabin?"

Jamie heard the woman's booming voice coming from a path that connected with the road. The trail bent around behind them, extended, and then continued around a corner. They detoured off the main trail onto the property, lurking before ascending over the crest of the hill. Tromping up the hill, they stopped to stare at her. She probably looked quite the sight. Her hair was tangled together, unbrushed. However, her expensive hiking boots and Gore-Tex jacket might've been what let them know it was okay to speak to her.

"Oh, hi. You don't have a bathroom, do you? I am not prepared to use the woods. Sorry, I'm Elsa, and this is Edward," she said. "We're freshly here from abroad. We're moving and hoping we might take up a spot in the woods, besides our home in the suburbs."

"Well, we have the caution tape up," Jamie said, holding onto the frying pan and thinking about cooking. "Look, I guess it's fine. I think the bathroom is actually fine." She motioned for them to follow her through the caution tape and led them up to the house. She turned the key to let them inside and pointed down the hallway.

When they returned, they found seats in the dirt around the fire ring. The cinders stuck solid to the ground, dampened several times. Dusting off their pants before they sat down, they committed to sitting where they probably normally wouldn't. Their awkward winces came through as the hardness of the earth dug in. They adjusted and scrunched up their faces, looking back and forth at each other. They made small talk, edging on conversation.

"What's the caution tape for?" Elsa said.

"Oh, geez," Jamie said. "A tornado blew through, and the inspectors are coming to look at the house. See the downed trees over there?" Jamie pointed. "They're worried the house is structurally unsound. They've got to check it. I'm living out here for now. Everything's fine, really."

"The house seemed okay when I went in. Unless the problem is the foundation? You could probably stay in there," she said. "I enjoy camping too, but cabin comfort is what I want at this point in my life." She held her knees to her heart and hugged.

"It's our dream to buy a cabin. We've been thinking about buying for the past several months. A cabin is something we have in common, our dream from childhood. Didn't we?" Edward looked at Elsa.

"We have a two-year-old and a five-year-old. I'm sure we'll also camp outside," Elsa said. Then she paused. "But I like having a bathroom option. Do you live here full time?" she asked.

Jamie said, "I live here now. I own the place, so to speak. But this place, especially outdoors, still feels like my family lives here." She stared off into space, thinking about the twenty-year-old greenhouse of memories. She slowly let out the steam. "We, my family... I mean, my wife and me, are getting a divorce."

She looked at the distant trees, silent for a moment, absorbing this.

Finally, she said, "I'd sell this one to you, but the place is full of my good thoughts about the past. Sorry if I'm wearing myself on my sleeve." Jamie couldn't see past the thick, overgrowing vines. She almost didn't remember planting them so many years ago. She paused slightly and broke through, indicating paperwork is always such a hassle. "And the house needs the inspection, of course," she said. In actuality, the house only had a few minor blemishes.

Elsa hummed a sigh and Edward beamed, holding his head tilted high in the air. He looked stoic and ready to please. In one instant, their eyes twinkled together. They got up and dusted off before they turned to head into the trail. Edward gave Jamie his card.

***

Jamie ran down to the woods sometime later. Slick, green, and slimy leaves shuffled under her feet. During the time on the recliner, sometimes she relaxed and smiled, happy not to be moving. She grew an extra paunch, even though she didn't eat. A desire to fix things brought her off the recliner into the woods. She had energy now, a spark in the ignition, a reason to live. She needed to resolve several messes. The effort to clear up the disarray would be costly.

She had enough of the chaos and the madness of living outside. She nested here to look for a feeling, find the memories, and find the people who mattered. If she could only bring the people, their essence, back into her soul, she could stand up and be who she was, lift out of her depression, the low.

In a dip of the ground, almost a sinkhole, she collapsed. Her head bounced off a branch. Her body collapsed. She gave up hope for a minute. She could see the next hour. In the vision, she didn't move. Her arm skidded in the mud; she wiped a thin line of blood from her forehead as she strained, lurching upward. She gave out and lay as flat as possible, kneading her shoulder blades into the ground. The sinkhole would swallow her up. Though collapsed into herself, she attempted to rise and picked herself up. She squinted her eyes for one last breath and thought about herself, a travesty.

The stump where she and her daughter had carved some rudimentary lines resembling letters laid in front of her. She rolled the heavy object into view, touching the incisions. Petting the worn wood aged, picked at, and rubbed by the weather, Jamie could make out one or two places where the gouges held firm. The day was entirely different with different weather. She remembered the temperature to be the same proportion of warmth and sun. She thought she had deceived herself and they were new marks. The place was a musty family photo album. Jamie was trying to walk away from her memories of this, her long walk in the woods. The air, the memory, was much more palatable than being alone staring at the overcome night sky or looking, eyes rolled back, at a dry fire. Dry autumn air descended, and light slipped away. She knew she would not be long. At most, she would count the family as done.

After a rest, after what could've been a full hour and a collapse into resignation, she gathered steam once again. She rolled her body from the muck, the place that wasn't quite a sinkhole didn't quite consist of quicksand. She found solid ground. With all the thousand aches and pains that came with her atrophied, recliner body, she rose up. Centering the energy in and pulling it up and out, her body rose. They might forget her here.

Jamie meandered up to the location of an almost forgotten bridge. The bridge had collapsed after a big storm, becoming a playground. The two by fours, mismatched or sideways and half crisscrossed over a small patch of dirt, were a mess. Jamie remembered her daughter would meander, crossing legs one over the other, watching the wood fall in unpredictable directions. The next week, the wood would be in a different sequence. She had never seen the area covered with mud as it now felt it could be. In its place, a brand-new crossing extended across the mud, with fresh stained and treated logs linked next to each other. Hikers had picked up the trash. The pulsing bump on her head subsided. The cut no longer bled. Smears of mud were nothing but scars of battles with the memories of her daughter, her wife, their life together.

The eggs spoiled in the cooler; the ice had melted days ago and the cooler now served as an airtight trashcan. Putrid fumes escaped despite everything. Jamie dragged the thing over next to the cabin. After she raised the lid of the mucky bin, she dipped her fingers in the tepid water and tended to her cut, the smears of mud rubbed deep into the right side of her face. She had battle wounds from her emotional illness, deafened ears from her pending divorce, and now actual scars brought upon her while she looked for memories of happy times. Now alone in the woods, she was sure no one had as much mortal damage.

Chapter 9

Dr. Prince walked in and out of the orange tape, trying to get closer. A trail wrapped around into the back and then over towards a set of woods. The light subsided with the day. A kitchen sink and several pieces of PVC piping lined the ground, tripping hazards. People dumped junk in the woods. The items, car parts, toilets, were so big the trashmen wouldn't be able to pick them up. The things were too far from the junkyard.

"Ah, Michelle. I remember you. You were much smaller. Oh, gosh, you've grown." His eyes glazed and his lids lowered. He smiled emphatically.

"You looking for my Ma, Dr. Prince?"

"Yes, indeed, yes. She's nowhere to be found. How is your mom—Jamie?"

Dr. Prince wore deep blue pants, Dockers. Michelle guessed this was a weekend outfit. Usually, he wore a distinctive suit. Usually, his outfits were much more reserved. The style could've been from the eighties, in Michelle's conception of that era. The pleated pants dated his style decades behind the time. Some people don't buy a lot of weekend outfits. This one looked leftover from the 1990s. It might've been from even earlier. Awkward as he might've been in a tweed jacket, Michelle might've let him leave it there if he had taken the coat off and forgotten it. If he were a mite closer to her family, she'd have asked to borrow it.

"Crazy as ever. Ha," she said. Michelle waved off some bugs and squinted at the doctor as if he were far away. His muted intentions to question her further stopped. He didn't pry into her life too.

"I rarely make house calls, or cabin calls should we say," Dr. Prince said. "But for Jamie. We all know she's important to so many people. To you. How are you, Michelle?"

"Oh fine. Yes. This is a lot."

"You should be angry, right?" Dr. Prince leaned in, pulling at his chin with an index finger and thumb.

"Yeah. I know. She does things. I get angry, but I want to get everything straightened out. You know. I can't be too angry."

"You have a right to be angry, dear." Dr. Prince tilted around with his weight on one foot, surveying the area, apparently looking for damage and evidence. "I'm angry." He said. "I'm angry. We all try hard for her. I rarely make cabin calls, you know." It was now a joke he could recite for his amusement.

Dr. Prince investigated the scene, pulled junk from a pile, clearly trying to decipher her ma's actions from the debris. Michelle had done the same. He held tight to a large metal square, attempting to pull it to the side so he could see what was below. A sharp and rusted edge sliced his hand as he ran his palm down it. Blood dripped to the ground. The square dropped with a thud.

"I think it's a fire grate." Michelle knew he was out of his element.

"God. Dammit." He wiped his palm with a dirty paper towel lying next to the cooler.

He lifted the top of the cooler and then jerked his head away from the stench and adjusted his body to leave. In a display of audacity, he doubled back and lifted a carton of eggs. "These eggs are no good."

Instead of putting them in a plastic garbage bag, he dumped them right back where he got them.

Michelle looked on, wondering how this helped her Ma's brain, her mental state. The doctor thoroughly rummaged through everything, looking at camping implements and common sticks with the same regard. Michelle kicked dirt. Thinking the better of herself, she kept quiet.

Dr. Prince jumped back as blood streamed from his hands. He lifted it to show her and backed away. "I'm part of the crime scene now." He chuckled a laugh and wiped his hand, looking afterwards at the metal he removed and the rest of the objects in the pile. Unabashed, he took his index finger and pushed a few more things out of the way so he could see. Tipping his head to and fro, he looked through the gaps in the assortment of random building materials, wood, parts, and pipes.

"Well, my wife... She wanted me to check up on her, you know. Do you know when she'll be back?" He rubbed his fingertips together, then tapped on the cut on his palm. "Doesn't look like she's killed anyone. I'm sure she'll be fine. I'll catch her another time. One of these times, she'll—" He stopped.

"I couldn't tell you, doctor. This is all new. The jury's out where she'll be any day in the future. It seemed like she'd be here all the time. No car. No place to go. I'm not sure if she's left." Michelle stopped herself. "I mean—Or, she could have moved to a hotel. I did tell her to get a shower and a warm bed. The nights are getting cooler." Anxiously, Michelle tapped her finger. She wanted to get a bearing on the fabric in his clothes, how many years the threads had seen.

"Michelle, your mom seems unstable?"

Michelle wouldn't bite. "She's fine, doctor. Just a little loose in the actions these days. She'll be alright."

Dr. Prince eyed the scene, turning a three-sixty to view the place and the surroundings. "What's over the hill?"

"Oh, the woods. There's a path down to the bank. I yelled down there a minute ago. She isn't down there." The corner of Michelle's mouth rose. "Really, she's been in this spot constantly. Always here when I come to visit. I mean the several times," She changed the beat again. "I'll tell her to come see you, if that's why you're up here. If you think she should have an appointment. It's—" Michelle followed the doctor, scanning the environs, looking at both him and his line of sight. "She's been here religiously. She might've left."

"Well honey. Give your mom our best. Jamie will turn up. I'm sure of that." He said the last bit matter-of-factly, as if using his degree to make a statement. His assurance didn't help.

Michelle sensed a tinge of inevitable doom in his tone.

***

Michelle relaxed into Ma's spot, crossing her legs, and warming herself by a fire that wasn't really there. Michelle had called them both mommy when she was ten. When she first met Ma, she called her mommy right away. They were, as she told them, going to be one big, happy family. She welcomed Jamie, Ma, so quickly, knowing she had needed it. She had needed a place, a family. The place was now amok. The air felt like stagnant mayhem. Still, Michelle persisted. This was her place. Ma would always be her Ma. The same as it all began, she worked to make them a family, intent on bringing her to be at home with Mom and her.

Chapter 10

At her mom's house weeks later, Michelle leaned back in the recliner, built for one and a half bodies. This made the chair comfortable for sleeping. Her ma had soaked all her sick sweat and gritted every grain of resolution into the chair. The chair didn't fit her ma's character, especially the plastic handle. A bill had showed up on the joint credit card days later.

After getting kicked out of the bedroom, her ma had little recourse. She had driven to Sofas Plus or Dave's Furniture and bought the thing.

Strong worn-in men, with their wives at home, put the hunk of fabric, metal, and plastic in the family room. She used the thing for four solid months. After work, after she lost her job, and through the night, there she had been.

"I'll be in the family room," she had said. She used short abrupt words, and her face tugged at the bags under her eyes.

Long ago, at twelve, Michelle had felt Ma's cool breath cascade over her body as she hushed her to be calm, to stay strong. The black and blue mark on her body had been a result of the hard, inhospitable world of strangers who knew her name. Ma patted the bruise to suggest the wound didn't hurt badly, but Michelle remembered wincing all the same. Her ma reiterated the desire to harm others lived deep within and it sometimes surfaced, accidentally or purposefully, almost longingly. Either way, Michelle's attackers would remember it differently than she would, and it would plague them as adults to their deathbed. Ma had underscored how Michelle should not harm back. She then blew on the wound, the single visible mark of her trial by fists. Michelle knew, though, that she had lost and the ice wouldn't help.

Ellen entered the room as Michelle sat, gaze toward the ceiling, remembering and reacting to the feel of the ghost of Ma in the chair. She gave Michelle a thick postcard meant for overseas travel. The paper could be bent slightly but confidently without losing its form. The edges revealed the postcard had traveled some distance. Everything obscured the pleasantness of the postcard and what she was also saying in the ink.

"Will miss Christmas. The search is on for Heidi's hut! Love, Ma."

Her handwriting used confident, angular, and bold pressed marks. There was no return address.

Michelle flipped over the card. An image of a Swiss flag shown on the front beneath a glossy surface, and a man with a traditional alphorn puffed his cheeks. A small passage defined an alphorn in the upper left of the card before the hand-scrawled words. A light pencil line drawing mimicked the image on the front. The postmark, barely made out with light ink, bore the name of a nearby town.

Michelle's Ma had hiked seriously twice in her life. Even those treks had only comprised a few days in the woods. She had never quite met the goal mileage and always came home happy, never defeated.

Crazy people leave the country without notice. As Michelle grasped to question Ma's departure and as she felt herself scolding her ma, now countries away, it didn't matter. *This is what it feels like for a parent to wait up late on a Saturday night for a teenager to come home.* Perhaps this was her idea of role reversal. Though what did it matter, because Ma couldn't tell her.

Michelle lifted her gaze back to the ceiling in anguish, not anxious fondness. A few cobwebs set in the corner. Neither mother cleaned. Michelle cursed the ceiling. She cursed the whole affair. She wouldn't know what to say to Ma in return to thank her for blowing on her wound many years ago. She couldn't cradle her head and say the black and blue would go away because it hadn't. All those years, all the times up and down, the words hadn't worn off or rubbed away. Over and over, the wound reappeared, and they all witnessed it. Mom had a stiff upper lip. She might not return. *She might not tend her wounds with us.* If Ma was left to her own devices, Michelle couldn't imagine where she went or what she did, just as much as they couldn't conjure the feelings she often expressed, an articulated madness that affected them all in a multitude of ways, each collecting their own special shrapnel.

In the afternoon, Michelle drove back up to the cabin to see if her note was a joke. She thought her ma was lonely or feeling neglected. A week and a half had passed since anyone organized a trip up there. It was true. To some, it could've appeared like they were giving up on Ma. Life became less dramatic, drawn out, and stale. Last time Michelle saw her, her ma said she would make a trip to town to wash up and get groceries. She firmly wanted to walk. She would take an Uber if absolutely necessary. Michelle doubted she would go up to the cabin. Instead, she thought about Ma's fond recollections of Switzerland. She remembered the photos of the Swiss Alps on her ma's computer. The place, likely now quite chilly, was so far away.

Michelle pulled into the lower driveway at the cabin and the familiar sound of gravel shifting below the tires caused her to slow down. Despite her hurry to get up here, she didn't need to upset Ma if she had come back. On the ground, drifting in the wind, a piece of yellow tape swept by her. Swooping up what appeared to be a streamer, she held the yellow tape in her hand and rubbed until the plastic stretched a bit. Both the yellow and the black had faded with the elements. The tape had seen wind and rain, just like Ma. Out here in the woods, everything got more than a mite dirty, a tad worn in. Ma and the tape were not to be excluded.

With the window mended, the cabin sparkled with newness. Two people moved around the front door, in and out. They yelled back and forth to each other, happy and spilling laughter. Michelle approached them. Both had Merrell hiking boots and blue coats that matched slightly but were distinct brands.

They sashayed and set up kitschy things at the door, a tall wooden sign, some fake antlers. Then they spread some pine twigs around an empty pot below the doorbell. Their laughter overwhelmed Michelle. The foreign noise foreshadowed the impending sad news.

Michelle looked over toward the fire ring and saw there was no tent. An empty bag of nuts littered the ground, but everything else was missing. She caught herself imagining there might be more ashes in the fire pit than last time. There weren't. The couple were almost unaware of her until that point. Consumed by laughter purportedly too loud to hear the churning gravels, the slammed doors, her Ma's silent screams for help.

"Oh, hi!" the woman said.

Michelle relaxed into an awkward conversation. The woman, Elsa, and her husband, Edward, had bought the house. They picked up the keys two days ago and had planned to move some stuff in soon. "We were lucky the place was move-in ready," they said. "Brand new almost, is what they said. Only four years old, but we were especially satisfied with the look. Do you live up here?"

"No, no. I knew the person who used to. I hadn't realized they sold." The cabin was over twenty years old.

Their grins subsided a bit at her understated words.

They chatted; Michelle nonchalantly held their position against their energy to complete their tasks. She picked at a stem from a limb that had fallen from trees on their property. She did as much damage, in anger, as she could.

Their kids loved the tire swing out back, they said. Michelle champed at the bit. Ma hadn't been at the closing.

Michelle trailed off down the hill. She hadn't ever wanted to go back when her ma camped outside the house. Now she wouldn't ever go back. She pictured her ma by the fire ring with her overgrown hair, trying to have a spiritual awakening, even though she'd never, ever been what you called relaxed for even a moment.

Chapter 11

Ellen adjusted the ice in the ice bin. The refrigerator doors hung open while Jamie put the groceries away. They danced a bit, with the doors still ajar. Cheesy love songs played on the radio. The February day in 2010, with the dampness of yesterday's snow, left a bit of dew on the outside of the window. Jamie touched the window with her index finger and pulled it down the window's glass pane. A long-drawn-out move was finally over, and they were setting in for the winter, hibernating together, bonding. During a pause, Jamie lifted her arms and wrapped them around Ellen's neck. Ellen took hold of Jamie's soft hips. In an instant, they knew they would not let go. They swayed to "Just Like Heaven," and Jamie whispered in Ellen's ear.

"This is the life. Isn't it?"

Ellen nodded in slow, even motions, and her breath matched the movement.

Jamie pulled her in and let her fall out and twirled her under a raised arm. Ellen collapsed in again and held Jamie tight at the waist.

Ellen revealed so much about her past to Jamie in the first few months of their relationship. They both were open and ready for commitment. They got to know each other so thoroughly and quickly, and there was nothing that could separate them.

Jamie listened to stories from Ellen's past with open ears. Right after Ellen graduated, in an act of indiscretion, she had slept with her now ex-husband and he got her pregnant and demanded her full attention. The asshole had ordered her to come home directly after work and wait on him over the weekends. He had wanted Ellen to wash the towels every day. He used three a day. Mounds of laundry gathered and so did her to-do list. He bought her jewelry only to make her repay him somehow. She had felt suffocated. Ellen had said it was the deep inhale of Jamie's sweet cologne that had made her relax again. Ellen had brushed her lips against Jamie's cheek after she had said it.

Ellen and Jamie had met two years ago, after Ellen's divorce. They got to know each other, and some might say they rushed into marriage on a whim. Ellen and Jamie hitched up in Vegas. They brought Ellen's daughter Michelle, ten, with them. Jamie told Ellen about her sometimes erratic behavior. And she knew the Vegas proposal could've been her displaying her irrational nature. An impulse move she should have recognized at that point in her life. But they talked about it, and Ellen was convinced of the positive impact Jamie had on Michelle. Ellen told Jamie in her vows she couldn't see herself with anyone who needed and cherished her love more than Jamie, except herself. Jamie belonged to her person and though they formed a close attachment quickly, they felt true love like Jamie had never felt before.

They returned freshly married to Ellen's apartment. Here they were, less than twelve months later in a beautiful house, as beautiful wives.

Ellen looked under the sink and found a dripping pipe. The need for a decision surfaced.

"I'll look on YouTube. I'll figure it out." Jamie paced, pressing her fist to her chin. She would tear the house apart to find a wrench to find a tarp and a bucket. Ellen could see her planning the things she would need as she paced. Her tension rose and Ellen got nervous as well. As simple as owning a house might be for some, they envisioned there would be missteps and learning. Learning would be part of the process.

In all their time together, they always got through arguments. They built a constant optimism between them. Jamie needed the devotion to the relationship. They never rolled over in bed upset or turned to the other side. They faced each other with one kiss, or fourteen sweet kisses, before closing their eyes.

Ellen got the phone out. "Honey, it's fine. I'm pretty damn sure we don't even have a wrench. Fixing the leak would take up the whole day. Turn the water off. Let's do what's easy. We have the home warranty we can use. We'll get through this."

"Ouch." Jamie looked for a valve under the sink. "I could do this." She bumped her head again as she tried to twist the stiff valve, which was covered in rust and gunk. The motion made the task seem more daunting.

The kitchen fan spun circles, pushing wind gusts at Jamie in a direct line of propulsion. As she rested onto her butt, outside of the sink cabinet, she caught the blades turning in the edge of her eyes. The light turned on with the fan. An easy fix. Pull the cord on the fan so it doesn't turn on automatically.

Jamie scratched at the nape of her neck as flowing air grazed her skin and gave her a chill. She warmed the skin with her hands. What were stubbly pricks at her scalp previously were now reaching toward the end of her neck. About three weeks had elapsed since her last haircut. Ellen would remind her to find a barber close by, someone near the new house.

The house, not quite lived in yet, cost over a hundred thousand hard-earned dollars. Jamie and Ellen signed the deed jointly, but most of the down payment came out of Jamie's savings. Jamie bought streamers and house-theme balloons for Valentine's Day. She tucked them away in a closet in the spare room. The house's kitchen tiles still smelled like a new car, but a bit more like plastic. Not much work needed to be done on the place. They were ready to call the house their own. They installed some new curtains, bought some comfortable furniture. The past several weeks they put toiletries in the right spot, made sure all Jamie's work files and Ellen's jewelry were still there, and figured out which cabinets and closets to use for what.

Jamie's job with Tradger's paid well, but she aggressively sought a promotion. She couldn't help feeling slighted every time a younger employee got a high-profile assignment. The way she tracked projects in Excel caught management's attention more than once. But instead of laudatory commendations, they simply spread her spreadsheets and techniques quietly to junior staff. She told Ellen about the acts of sliding her work under the table and how it infuriated her. She was talented, but even when she prepped herself and practiced speaking her mind, when it came down to it, she would inevitably fail to stand up for herself.

She admitted to Ellen she sometimes acted out. The pent-up drama from coworkers, her ideas about certain workers, and snickers she heard or imagined. It didn't matter which person expressed sentiments. Everything spoken behind her back dealt blows to her well-being. She tried to cope, but sometimes would find herself in the bathroom, albeit only to whimper. She shed no tears. At one point, a coworker heard her. Jamie hadn't realized she was listening. As she wiped her dry eyes, the coworker exited the stall, washed her hands promptly, and left. As she told Ellen, at work, she shouldn't engage on issues with an emotional basis.

She brought the drama home to Ellen. Ellen welcomed her with kind words and open arms. "There is no need to worry," she would say. "You have this. You got this," she encouraged. Ellen emotionally supported her and stood by her side, stood in for any family Jamie ever had. The bolstering worked, Jamie trudged on to work, confident and relaxed. She could rule the world.

"It's nice to be with you," Ellen said.

Jamie blushed and threw a quick smile. She warmed inside. The feelings rose and fell swiftly. Jamie knew about the balancing of emotions. If Ellen complimented her too much, she swelled with love. But inevitably, her highs and lows surged equally in many respects. A negative comment days later would send her into a feverish terror, paranoid, unloved. The comment might decimate any confidence she had. The words would affect her at work. Jamie knew better to let her heart flutter too much, to avoid the reciprocal emotion when a trigger came her way.

"I love you too," Jamie said.

She tempered her sentence as her therapist said to. Don't get too involved, keep a little distance. "If you get too close, you'll lose who you are," he had advised.

***

They cuddled in the small bed, covers pulled up as the sun rose, and its accompanying breeze sent chills inside the chinked log walls. This was their vacation, their life. Alone in the woods, traveling far enough away to fall in love with each other, albeit not as much as with where they were.

When they got married, they traveled to local campgrounds on weekends. They did this on Ellen's ex-husband's weeks with Michelle. They shared custody. Even Ellen needed a break some weekends and she was glad their distancing relationship had a little room left, enough to coordinate their daughter's well-being. She still needs a man in her life, Ellen would say, to pad his ego and get him to stand up and take responsibility. He fell for the ploy every time. Well, I guess we can go to a ball game. Ellen knew she'd rather be at the batting cages with her friends. They worked tighter to keep her ex-husband's dates with his daughter out to keep any positive efforts alive.

They could afford to camp. They put money away monthly for their own cabin or a campground spot to set a camper for a season. A getaway would have to be the perfect place. Despite their best efforts, each place had something negative. The trip to the bathroom took ten minutes. Unsavory residents clamored around at all hours. Bears lurked at night. As hard as they tried to find some place in their hundred-and-fifty-mile radius, they had no luck.

"Honey, this is ridiculous. We could be camp hosts, get a free plot, you know," Ellen said.

"Oh, and quit our jobs for the summer? I couldn't get a shower in the bathrooms and then show up at work. There is inherent dirtiness in camping. I'd smell of campfires and marshmallows. When we retire, honey." Jamie picked the dirt out of under her fingernails. She made the fire the night before and remnants of the soot still gathered in her crevasses, on her flannel. In a bit, she would shower up and work at the grime. But days would pass, and the muck would still be there, somewhere she would find leftover soot. Her freshly washed shirt or ironed shirt got stained, and grass wore into and discolored her favorite sneakers. She double thought about camping every trip.

"The location is far away, Jamie. I want a scenery change," Ellen said.

"We haven't even been in the house for a year. Let's take the steps slowly."

"I know you're right. I would love to have the quiet of the woods, to read and relax. Away from the house and the city. The silence would be as good for me as the relaxation would be for you. The dream can be a reality. If we can take the leap, we should. Seize the day is what they say, right?" Ellen folded each shirt before she put the clothes away, smoothing the creases, fluffing them a bit for the return trip home.

"I'm trying to get that promotion. I'll work it out. If we had a bit more money, we could buy a cabin. Wouldn't life, our life, be nice?"

"Jamie, nice? Ah, yes, absolutely. But we can't afford the bills. For real. Christmases with Michelle. Absolutely! Yes. That's perfect. But we'd have another mortgage for decades. You already spent your savings on the house we have." Ellen chirped as she scurried about cleaning the cabin to leave the place the same as they found it.

"I mean, a camper or RV is about forty thousand, anyway. Really, we didn't even price them yet. But if I get this project management job, the logistics one with all the extra responsibility, things would be great. Yeah, that would settle our money worries for a long time."

"The stress though, Jamie, can you handle the stress?" Ellen knew about Jamie's stress. She was hyper-focused and walked around quiet in another mindset. She wouldn't respond to simple hellos. The stress would build and build in Jamie's forehead. Then she would snap. They'd fight; They'd have sex; They'd make up. The process would start all over again the next day. It might go on for weeks and then things would be normal again for a span.

"Honey, I love you. When I have a goal, I get through the issue. Yes, I have trouble sometimes with my mood swings, but my emotions are manageable. The trouble, the work, is worth doing—for us."

The thick potato cream broth still bubbled lightly in the soup pot on the stove, still on the burner. Jamie had heated a bowl for breakfast.

Ellen got up and dashed the pot to the counter. She paused, hands on hips, and stared at the cellophane. "Did you have enough?"

"Yes. You are such a wonderful cook. There is nothing I like better than doing this right now. Surveying the land, our state, and a few others, for where we might land... in a year or two. Not right now, but when our savings pot gets a little bigger."

"For now," Ellen said, "You're right. This is fine." She swung her soft brown hair back and forth. The radiant locks brushed her shoulder blades.

"Leave it. The soup still has to cool. Get in bed with me. We are going to have to cross this one off the list. The cabin is too cold. We'll have memories here at least." She pulled her close. "We'll remember each cabin, won't we, with the memories we make?"

They packed up their clothes the next morning while discussing whether they should go east to another park next month or whether it would be best to go a little south because of the cold. Jamie suggested trying out an Airbnb cabin. They could find one for rent at the right price. Wouldn't it be nice to set up a second shop, move all their books there, find a cabin, get away with a stable heat source and a private shower? They would find a place along a path where they could scamper down to a trail, bond with Michelle in the vast playground beyond the house.

"We're doing too much, honey. The gluttony is almost greedy. I know you have a respectable job, but we should save. We're freshly married, almost."

"For you... to cherish these days with Michelle. Have somewhere for her to go. Raise her right. The woods, hiking... reading. A cabin is the best place to grow a family. We'll get sick of traveling all over soon. Let's start the hunt for a new house. The place can be affordable. What we choose won't be too expensive. I'll assure you of that. And

I'm going to get the promotion. We'll have a boatload of money. We have to pull the trigger."

Jamie transferred the heavy bags to the car with two hands. Ellen always over-packed. Ellen rested them in the back seat, next to Michelle's trucks and miniature cars. The dump truck rolled under the seat. The metal toy would roll back and forth on the way back to the house. They would think of Michelle and plan for their future. Jamie and Ellen would discuss how they would raise the ten-year-old girl into an upstanding young woman. A woman with two moms, proud and capable, ready to conquer the world. She still needed to clean out the soup pot.

Chapter 12

Her ma was stuck in the rut, contemplating the worst, as she always did. Everyone, all three of them, knew what it meant when her head bowed down and she heaved in and out through cramped lungs. Years had passed by and now in the Spring of 2022, the disease, as she sometimes called it, reared its ugly head. Usually depression hit in the Fall, and the fact that it came knocking in warm weather meant it would be even more tragic. The other side of the madness had surfaced, the deep pits of despair. Something had triggered her to spiral into the black abyss, a space where no one could find her. She left clues about what she had done, but not where she traveled to emotionally or how to get her out of it.

Michelle's first guess wasn't what she had done, the tear in the family's bond. The bond had already become loose. Yelling tantrums and Jamie's erratic behavior had significantly stretched the concepts that had once tied them together. The ropes had loosened and any one of them could slip out. Michelle banked she had ruined a close relationship. Several months before, Ma had let loose on Mark Sumpton. She talked about this incident. Something she didn't always do unless it was something that really stuck with her.

Ma told Michelle she told him Mark was a terrible friend, a loser even, for not helping her find her a job. That much was true. Mark simply shut the door. He was done with Ma's repeated blunt degrading remarks, he had said. Done with her insistence, obsession, that Mark was worse off, below her. He wouldn't respond to any of Jamie's questions or apologies. A week ago, he left town or moved. None of them knew. He trashed the whole friendship, tired of being bugged about his lack of support, tired of the constant requests or erratic behavior.

When Michelle saw the gruesome act, the panties left behind, she knew. At first, she didn't need to touch them. She wanted to let them be. It would all work out. She threw the panties in the trash and put the bag immediately in the outside garbage.

Her mom noticed when she didn't put a fresh bag in the empty kitchen trash can. "That's odd, honey. You never empty the trash. I almost forgot you knew how. Trash duty was always your least favorite chore when you were young. You said, 'I don't want to be the trashman when I grow up.' That's what you always said." Her mom wanted to chat when Michelle's primary goal was to avoid all eye contact.

"No, it's... Sometimes the trash gets too full, you know." Michelle bowed her head and examined the stitches on her sneakers and patterns within her laces.

Michelle's mom may or may not have gone into the trash. She might not have thought the underwear belonged to one of Michelle's dates, a girl she didn't choose to bring home. Mom might have even expected Ma, Jamie, hid something. She fell into her head more often in the following weeks. She would stand still over the sink and bow her head, reiterating the day, words, searching for something. Mom, Ellen, even suspected something was up.

The bedroom door opened soon after Michelle parked the car, entered the front door, and quickly climbed the steps to share the good news of her year-end performance bonus. Her ma jumped up overtly buck, but some boxers, naked in the bedroom. Michelle was going to

Spain. And her ma's tryst, the woman from down the street, had left out the window, her high-heeled slutty shoes close to the side of the bed. She had caught her ma in the act. Ma barged in on her in high school in a comparable situation.

"Honey," Mom said, "she told me three days ago. Are you agitated lately? Things will be okay." The rare minute of calm from her mom required Michelle to be present.

Michelle knew about the conversation. Michelle had relaxed in the family room next to the kitchen. It was an open plan. She had waited for an outburst, flailed arms, or fist planted in a soft place. Nobody saw her, but she listened as usual, waiting for dinner, or reading a delightful book, at home in the bedroom she grew up in, making sure her mothers did not kill each other. With an eye especially on Ma, she acted like the voice of reason often, but not that day. She watched the conversation unravel. The relationship was none of her business.

"Oh, yeah. I got into a fight with Roger. You know we butt heads too. Ironically," Ma said, "We got in a fight about Mark Sumpton."

"No honey, the woman."

"What woman? From the book club. Oh, she called?" Ma spoke clearly and straightforward, the calm before the storm.

And then the emotion turned, everything rolled over. "This is no fault of mine. It's yours."

"This marriage is a thing. It's what we have."

"Pshh. Never again. That's for sure."

"So, you're going to throw everything away? You're a little jealous? This could roll off. The rain could just roll off, honey. We'd throw it out with the trash. If you're jealous, fine. But you can't let your feelings determine our relationship for the rest of our lives." Her mom's voice was venomous.

They fought and fought. Michelle's headache pulsed and made her hair stand up on end, wishing she weren't there.

"You know it is okay." Mom's voice sounded tight, like she was trying to control herself. "It's absolutely okay because I have a man. I have a little side piece as you're trying to conjure up to make you feel more like a person. But we're serious."

There was a long quiet span before her mom spoke again, sounding unnaturally calm. "The washer's not broke. I go out all day Saturday afternoons, because it's our date day. I don't want to make you more jealous than you already are. We have activities and fun and—" Her voice went high, she broke and said, "love each other."

"I won't give you a divorce." Choppy sounds emitted from her ma's mouth. Everyone could feel her hurt.

"You should see your doctor. He'll help you through the emotions. I care about you, Jamie, but there is only so much I can do."

Everyone knew bringing up the doctor, bringing up Ma's major illness, was off limits. Acknowledging she had this secret problem, that at the same time was not so secret, was a boundary. She was embarrassed about her weakness as a person. And she knew this.

"Oh, is it him? Is it him you're seeing?"

The turning point had come. Michelle knew when to intervene. If her ma thought her mom fucked her therapist, there would be pandemonium. She would obsess about this. She heard it in her voice; the paranoia rolled over and over, marinating in her head. She used the intimations of words as an excuse not to see her psychiatrist. Michelle got up and leapt into the room to diffuse the air. She thought if she interrupted, the obsession might not stick. She might still save her.

"I thought you weren't going to check up on me. That, in itself, is a breach of client confidentiality. I saw the appointments on your calen—" Ma left swiftly to ascend the stairs. The rounded wooden knob on the railing rattled a bit as she made the sharp turn on the steps.

Michelle appeared with an immediacy; a book shuttered on her index finger in a hard smack fully closed as she approached Ma. Gripping her shoulder, she squeezed, pushing love into her limbs. Ma's grip on the familiar knob tightened and then relaxed and her arm dropped. She looked at the steep stairs before her.

"Ma. Everyone has gotten out what they should say. Let's go out for ice cream and talk. You and Mom can't duke it out all day. I'm here for this. If I was fifteen, I'd think a divorce was my fault. Right now, twenty-three, I want us all to be the best people we can be. Ma, we still love you." Michelle leaned in and pulled her arms around Ma. Then they descended step by step, Michelle's arms on both of Ma's shoulders.

The turmoil had started. The following events and words, the decisions they approached each other with, would dictate the time they kept apart and together. They would try to work it out. But Michelle knew—she knew about Mick. When Ellen said she loved him, the words stuck.

Though caught in the middle, Michelle supported both parties as best she could. In her mind, the words rolled over. She was the only one who knew this was coming, who saw things unravel, what would happen. She knew Ma slept with someone besides her wife and Mom fucked Mick, Michelle's girlfriend's dad. Mom created rifts, and now, the words Michelle imagined spoken, played out, wanted to be spoken and out in the open, leveled the family, the close essential unit. Their lives, the three bound, would never have the same path.

To double things over, Pat also had told Michelle that Mick had an extra, a woman he saw four times a year. That bit of information was also neither of their businesses, yet very much was. The tidbit could dictate what mothers would do, how they would feel. Michelle could never tell her mom, because Michelle loved her mom. Because she and Ma needed to do this first.

As Michelle and Ma left the house, Michelle noticed her ma did not even glance at her mom. She had vanished from her life, never to be talked to in the same way. She moved around on her tiptoes. Michelle's mom only shifted in her spot, quiet as a mouse. Ma's face tensed hard as steel because she thought Mom would marry her therapist. Michelle could only wonder about her mom's reaction to this understanding, cold or disastrously bitter.

"It is a crime, Ma, your misgiving—you slept with another woman—is being seen as the crime, when we know, you know, mom loves someone—" She gulped because that was not what she wanted to say ever "—someone else."

"It is. That's my second crime. The first is my illness. Christ, I had to say the despicable word. And, when I say my illness, that's what I mean. It's mine, unlike anyone else's. I own the disorder and its uniqueness and permutations." She was utterly calm.

They ordered through the drive-through. Even though neither of them had tears, they didn't have the resolve or composure to enter a crowded place, with people talking, then glancing their way, then talking. They kept this time to share, talk with serious words. This time, the silence carried. They had, despite the summary ending to the day, nothing pressing to say, nothing they could say.

Jamie ate her ice cream, and smears appeared on the corner of her mouth. As much as Michelle wanted to wipe away the goo, she did not. She even covered her index finger with a napkin. She could not mother. They simply sat and ate, smacking every so often with delight. Smiles abounded. Then they left, and the quiet dissolved.

"A doctor, can you believe the thought? So much better than me."

"Ma, I don't think."

Slowly Michelle started up the engine to drive them home. She engaged the stick deliberately, almost telling her ma it was okay. This is normal. The words did not pass her lips. He had come, appeared, in Mom's life and made her way into her heart. Michelle didn't have the power to explain. She had no right.

They entered the same home just as her mom finished the dishes and was moving to go upstairs to the bedroom. She flopped down on the couch and complained about how lumpy it felt, how uncomfortable. She didn't intend for anyone to respond, even to hear the words. They were, as Ma knew, discernible by Mom.

Chapter 13

Jamie leaned back in her chair; head tipped up to the sky. No one was there and the room's emptiness overwhelmed her like a vast canyon. She blinked her eyes hard. When they tried to adjust, things got fuzzy, then clear, then fuzzy again. The world rotated once as the stress built. Ellen would be home soon.

She fixed herself a pot of coffee, letting the grounds from a freshly opened bag permeate the room. This place would seem good, sumptuous to her when she came home. Jamie reached into the cupboard to remove a bag of small chocolates, popping one, then two in her mouth, swallowing, barely chewing. The night would come, then the morning. She would have nowhere to go. A coffee shop would give her a seat for the day. She could take a computer, relax on the big, upholstered chairs. Sip away the day, coffee in handing, typing, emailing about something. Try to find a new job.

Ellen wouldn't humor her. She'd barge in the door like she had most days ready to hear Jamie complain about work, ready to tell her to stop bitching. She'd lumber into the kitchen and throw a pan on the stove, grab the olive oil, and sternly tell Jamie she'd have a meal she could eat in a half hour, but then she would see Mick. For four days, the sequence persisted. On Friday, the game ended.

As the clock ticked past six thirty, Ellen didn't show up. Jamie tapped her mug, the third in a series. The binge of java pulled a wave of anxiousness over her in a way it hadn't yet hit. At noon four days ago, her boss had called her into an office with a human resource employee. The scene had reminded her of being fifteen and her girlfriend had called her and asked her to come over. Jamie had sat beside her on the corner of the bed as they had grown to do for weeks, almost a month. She explained in words painstaking to Jamie's ears they couldn't see each other. Her mom suspected. They now went to church. At fifteen, the tears formed and dripped, running past her nostrils to the chin. She held them there, felt the saltiness on her lips before she wiped with an intentional swipe, an admittance of weakness.

In the room with human resources, a few stray droplets drifted again to the sides of her nose. She bowed her head and rubbed them in embarrassment. She wallowed in her failure.

The door slammed and Ellen moved into the kitchen. "Sorry. I grabbed coffee with Mick. I thought I'd eat here with you tonight. It's Friday and we have to decide. You know I like Mick. We are going to spend more time together. I want you to be okay with our relationship."

"Honey." The same dry throat, stinging as she failed to swallow, uttered no more words. Jamie tapped the empty mug. Anyone could see what was wrong, anyone except Ellen.

"What do you want, pizza? I... I like him, Jamie. He's for me. It's my thing." She moved to pull pasta out of the cabinet over the sink. They argued over the cabinet, couldn't decide to put pasta there, or use the space for non-food items. They had so many kinds of pasta. The most convenient storage cabinet set right above the sink, but it didn't matter whether the spot held soap and cleaners or pasta at that moment. "Honey, you better cheer up. Don't get your funk back, okay? What happened? A dog run into your car again? Whatever is bugging you is shaking the issue off. You're not sinking, are you?"

"I'm about to sink into the couch. Look, I'm going through things."

"Jesus Christ, Jamie. Not again. I can't handle the drama. I'm trying to hold my life together for Mick."

Jamie moved to the corduroy couch, lay flat on her back. Her head stuck up in the air. Not a word squeaked out. She didn't look Ellen in the eye. With the stubby ends of her fingernails, she grated the ridges, ribs of thick fabric, in an even-tempered beat. Back and forth, until she cut into the depth of the fabric, trying to rip a spot and create a hole.

"Oh, this is how things are going to be? You know you have to take a shower before work tomorrow. Don't leave out the front door without freshening yourself up a bit," Ellen said.

"Honey, I lost my job. I'm fine though because I think we should concentrate on us." Jamie chewed at her nails in anxiousness. She still had to tell Michelle.

"Jesus Christ, Jamie. This is not the time to quit your job."

"Honey—I didn't—"

"What did you do?"

"It doesn't matter. Me or him. It's me or Mick. Decide."

"Jamie. We said we'd never let someone come between us, but I'm not done. And now, what you've gone and done—"

"You didn't even hear my side of the story."

"I know enough. Know enough to know Mick might be an answer for me now. He can hold a job. Prove to me you can hold a job. That's what I need at this point. For fuck's sake. Someone will have to help pay for the groceries, the expenses, my brand-new car. I might as well take it back to the lot."

Jamie sank deep into the couch and buried her head in the pillow like a child wanting to hear the screaming stop. She could rise out of the lumpiness. Stuck in it, she would never find the light.

***

When Michelle and Jamie went for a drive to get ice cream like they normally did when Jamie called her to come over. Usually, that was a sign that something had happened. In fact, this time Jamie's worry was written all over her face.

"Ma, do you want me to call you Dad? Is that it?"

"No," Jamie said. "No, that's absolutely okay."

She fidgeted with her seat belt, which cut into her belly a little until the fabric untwisted against her. Despite the depression, the days on the couch, she hadn't lost weight. She enjoyed those moments of getting up, looking in the refrigerator for six or ten minutes, and finally choosing something. The act became an adventure off the couch. As depressed as she was, she didn't leave empty-handed. In the ten days that passed, she hadn't left the premises, her lair, the two rooms: living and kitchen.

"But you know. It's fine, right? If you want to be something else, something more, right?"

"That's not the issue. But I hear you. Last time, the issue was much more than that. I needed another body. But it wasn't a man's body at any rate. I was fine with my parts. I needed a distinct feeling, a way to be inside myself. Yes. I thought for a bit transitioning might be a possibility. But, again, dear, honey, that was last time."

Michelle clicked the end of her pen pensively. With an upbeat, reserved expression, she turned and smiled. "I know, Ma. I... I always wonder."

"I'm fine with who I am. My body, at least. Life's getting me down this time. There's nothing to be done."

"You mean somebody's done something to you?" She scribbled on the pad of paper. The pen produced ink after several scratches.

"I lost my job. Michelle, I lost the job." Jamie gave the belt a little more slack until the strap caught tight. After fidgeting with the band a bit more, it got more restricting. Once she finally let go, the belt strangled her across her chest, and cut into the side of her neck. She shifted uncomfortably, restrained.

"Aww. Ma. You'll get a new job. Is that all?"

"Honey. I've worked that job for a long time. No one's going to hire me. My exit was into oblivion. I still have a shred of respect. Fuck."

"Oh, Ma. You didn't overreact?"

"You bet I did. I'm embarrassed. Ashamed. I had to speak my mind, though. I had to tell them. Let them see. They weren't fair in my last project. The lawyer didn't fight the proposal the way he should've. Probably because I am who I am, but mostly because he knows Mick. He laughed at me, Michelle. Told me about my worthlessness. My wife wouldn't even have me. That's what he said."

"Oh, Ma. She would never. That's why you're on the couch."

"That's why I'm on the couch, honey. The end won't be long now. The darkness will take over. It always does," Jamie said. Her face was blank and emotionless. It barely moved, as if something was restricting her skin.

Three days later, Jamie reached for someone, anyone, in her sleep. She rolled over on the pillow. The sweat from several nights of bad dreams discolored the thing. Left stains. Couches weren't meant for sleeping. Only in sickness or if you were a teenager spending a late night with chips and a movie. Jamie even gave sleeping on the couch a bad name. Here she was, a typical depressed monster, afraid to go to her actual bed. Possibly, she craved the attention or the self-belief she would miss something. Either way, she hunkered down, ready for any action that took place yet displaced from an intersection or insertion with what went on. Still, nothing went on, really. The place echoed with emptiness. Everyone left. Here she sat, ready for anything, scared of the bedroom a million miles away.

This day was no different. Michelle had gone home twelve hours before. Ellen never showed up with a plate of takeout food after normal dinner hours. She stuck herself in a rut and couldn't lift herself up and out. Her atrophied muscles weakened the initiative, and the effort needed to move doubled. The place was hers. Her castle. Only she had no one to share the home with. No one to love within it. In a matter of days, until Ellen would ask for a divorce.

They had been through this before. Every three years, something would happen. Jamie's on the couch, they'd call the scene. Since they first coined the phrase six or seven years ago, she couldn't sit on that couch, the green corduroy one, and not think about it. Not know she had been there before. The weight of softening muscles and weakening limbs, weakening heart and mind, pulsed heavy then not off and on, understanding the weight would never leave.

Jamie rested her glass of water. The same one lasted her two days now. She knew she would have to get back to the kitchen. She had lain on the couch for seventeen days. An imminent move rattled in her head. Michelle threatened to take her to an in-patient hospital. Fed up, Ellen ignored it all.

"I'll go to the doctor tomorrow..." Jamie's voice trailed off. Someone spoke to her. Someone dialed on her phone. The doctor came on.

Blackness overcame her as she spit out, "Can you see me tomorrow?" Her eyes drowning in a wash of hazy vision. "Dr. Prince said something about two-thirty."

Michelle scratched with a pencil. The phone dropped to the ground. A dial tone. Sleep.

She'd go once, to get a few words in, kick start her life again. What else could go wrong? She held the phone in her grip and cradled the thing back and forth. She stared at the digits, hoping the number would dial, that she could talk.

Chapter 14

"So, you're doing 'sort of well.' Let's think on those words." He leaned into the sturdy tufted leather chair back. He moved from a hard ninety-degree angle crossed leg position to a tightly crossed at the knee position. Dropping his pencil and adjusting his notebook, he filled the silence. "That's my job, you know. To think about all this. What would you think if I were to say that?"

Jamie ducked her head and flicked her toes at the tightly knotted carpet. The window looked outside to the parking lot. Only a few cars sat on the lot. The mirror-like gray building consisted of a rash of non-fronted business operations of varying size and needs. The rectangular block of a building must've only been half full. Two therapists occupied the floor, and a web designer took another office. On each of the other three floors, four or five business occupied spaces that didn't need a formal entrance.

Outside, the turn of the century office turned heads. Inside, the business held modern but cost-efficient surfaces, such as the carpet and the basic, one groove moldings around the door frame. The window had a simple angular sill, and the window was a thin pane thick. Dr. Prince's exorbitant furniture cost hundreds, thousands, the things brought in. The desk had arching legs to claw paw solid wood feet. He might need several people to move the massive, five-ton beast. Jamie sat leaning on the arm of the leather, tufted couch. Jamie noticed its elegance only tarnished by a few too many hard sit downs in the one corner. The cushion folded in a bit more on the right side, away from the desk, than the left.

"I couldn't make it here the last times, Doc, because so much in my life is mixed-up in many directions. I resented you for a while. Thought you were a piece of shit, you know—" Jamie lost control. She wanted to get everything out, vomit her problems. She wanted to pronounce herself done and cured by the end of the session. Ellen would take her back.

"Oh whoa. Where's this going, Jamie?"

"No, no. It's... I thought you had sex with Ellen. I'm sorry. The notion stuck; you know. But then I found out she fucked Mick. Saw them together. It was good, in some weird way, to actually focus my energy on something real, someone who committed a wrong against me, you know."

The doctor held the silence by looking into Jamie's eyes, not letting her respond. "Let's not dwell on Mick, Jamie."

When he spoke, a chill ran up her spine.

"Oh, right. I know. Destructive energy. The guy's kind of, I don't know, a dick." She picked at her nails. She griped about him for the entire visit. Moving back into this situation with the doc was tough, especially after she held so much resentment, but she finally moved forward with the therapy, figuring out the divorce.

"Let's go back. You thought Ellen had an affair with me?" He popped up and back, arms splayed into the air, "Ludicrous. Right. Let's get that out of the way. Ludicrous."

"Yeah, doc. Right. Ludicrous." Jamie used a silly voice.

She threw her arms back over the chair arms in a mock of the doc's pose. "You see. I'll tell you the great and the short of it. I slept with the neighbor's wife and then found out my wife was sleeping with someone else—Mick. Of course, I didn't know who her lover was at first. I thought you could be the guy. The whole thing, the affair, is all my fault though, really. I was lusting after other women. That's probably why she turned to other people for sex."

Jamie coughed intentionally, trying to be as clear as she could about what she had been doing and thinking during the three months she failed to make an appointment.

"Have you committed a crime, though? Done anything irreparable?"

"My marriage seems irreparable." The words came out quickly and decisively.

"Right, your marriage."

What felt like minutes passed by.

"What are you doing for a job?" The doctor spoke bluntly. Psychology was over.

"Well, doc. I don't have one yet. Not having a job sucks. The recliner is my job, you know. I finally have some lift on the obsessive thoughts, the anger about it all, about the other men—man. I started... I'll start looking. Every time I get a setback, I have to wait, take a break, find myself again. You know, some peace."

"Look, eventually you won't be able to pay me. I don't mean to be blunt, but you are getting a divorce. This is what I have gathered. You need to come to terms with this, Jamie. You need to plan."

The doctor pulled another notebook from his desk drawer. The tan leather looked smooth to the touch. It was different. It seemed all the doctor's psychiatrist-enabling things were black, all black: his notebook, his pen, the frame with his degree on the wall, and even his tie. But this... Jamie couldn't take her eyes off it.

"Look, this is the name of a guy. What he's doing is not illegal. Might seem like it a bit, but it's for people who are kind of down and out, can't get a job, been to jail, you know. It's a straightforward way to get started. Maybe not to keep it going, but to get a breath of air, some money, and some work. You'll be drop shipping, but he'll tell you about it when you call."

"Then you can pay me back, at least, right? Make some money to pay me back for the tires and then, there you go, cash to win back Ellen. Hey, it's a start?"

The doctor folded his hands and looked at Jamie. They hadn't addressed the tires. They should've discussed the issue when they first sat down or when Jamie called to schedule an appointment. But here they were, and the event, the criminal act, was now awkward, moot, and somehow voided by Jamie.

"I'm sorry. I know. I know. I'm sorry." Jamie bowed her head, unable to look Dr. Prince in the eye. He ripped the apology out of her. She wouldn't be able to get up and move on with her life without them. "I'm sorry." Jamie, the expert at avoidance, slashed someone's tires and then asked them for help. "Look. I owe you; I'll do what you say."

Dr. Prince nodded. "Ahhh," he said, gaped mouth. Opening his hands and arms, he gripped the ends of the arms of the chair. "You need more. I don't need more. You do."

"I'm trying, doctor. I can't get beyond the incidents, episodes, you might say. I'll get the money, work the job. I'll act like a person. Promise. I'm ready to move on. But I don't think this is going to help me get my wife back."

She wrangled her hands as a boy whose mother told him to do something for which he wasn't quite ready. Peter Pan didn't want to grow up. "My main goal is to not let this divorce happen. That's why I came to you today; why I finally showed up here. I love her and I won't let her go."

"Jamie, at least show her you can stand up. As a doctor and a friend, I'm asking you to take some sort of responsibility, a part-time gig. Show me some thanks."

"If the job takes my mind away from her, away from looking for a way to keep us together, I'm out. I promise you that."

Jamie got up with fifteen minutes left in her session in a stupor, unsure of what time she had arrived.

The doctor looked down and quickly wrote a number on a folded, then torn, piece of paper from the leather-covered notebook. "Don't do anything rash in terms of your wife... and Mick... Be on your best behavior. That's how you'll win her back."

Jamie left through the lobby of the blocky building, glancing in on an office of workers inside the doors. She couldn't help but imagine herself back there in a cubicle, starting over. She now had a gap in employment, an unsavory severance, and a small list of misdemeanors. It wouldn't be a cakewalk to get back into a stable project management position. An entry level position would bore her. They would watch her more because of her record and appearance. It would be constraining. No long lunches. She couldn't help but bow her head and mumble to herself. *There's no place like a year ago.*

The depression set in the longer she stood there. In an instant, she took three gigantic steps and reached the door. Her arm wiped across her eyes as she left. The mucus from her nose and tears left smudges on her wool jacket. She squinted at the goop as she moved faster toward the car. *She would have to have the coat dry cleaned. How could she be so stupid? How could she ruin her jacket?* She rubbed her hands against the ooze harder, dampening her fingers and wiping as she moved closer to the car. In an instant, she hit the vehicle headlong, unaware of the mass in front of her. The slick surface of the metal captured Jamie. She looked into the mirror surface and felt her face, the skin not quite smooth like the car. Soon, a driver would appear and she'd once again be stuck without an explanation, without something anyone, let alone her family, could understand. This moment, a foray into pending darkness came, and it would surface again over the next several days.

Chapter 15

They requested Mick for another funeral. When he told his daughter he needed someone to come with him, Pat told Michelle they must go. She relayed she never missed an opportunity to bond with her father. This time, she also requested Michelle come too.

Mick, vulnerable, led the two young women through the door of the church. The church, a small, long rectangle of a church, mimicked Lutheran, other similar styles. Few details were present, some extra square columns at the corners. The posts ran higher than the roof line, but not higher than the steep pitch of the single gable roof. Four-pointed arch windows with cross panes flanked the side, four on each side. The sturdy wooden doors held the weight of giant trees and moved as if opened thousands upon thousands of times, never refreshed with grease. Inside, the walls felt thin, a cool fog infiltrated the place. The cool air gave an empty feel, with or without a body at the altar.

Mick frowned with precision when each person crossed their eyes against his—almost as if to say, "too bad." The group of three sat in the third to the last row from the rear. Mick sat in the aisle. He interacted with most of the people at the church in glances or glares. One or two received a smile. Four people passed. One by one, they whispered something seemingly religious in his right ear as he sat kneeling in the pew. Each wore matte black suits with thin ties. Their shoes shined like Pat's mom's silver.

Mick stood to shake hands with a short, portly man with a derby cap. He spoke with a rough Boston accent, and he constantly took out his handkerchief to wipe his brow. Mick grabbed his hand and slapped it into the man's, almost knocking him off balance. The man gathered up his hand and a small piece of paper rested in his palm. The object could've been a single bill or a note, but the man shoved the wad in his pocket, forgoing an examination of the gift or message. Mick patted his back and then pulled his arm around the man's shoulder, walking with him several rows up. He spoke in his ear and slapped his shoulder. The man smiled and laughed, leaned back, and then to the side, as if to listen more closely.

On the way over, the radio had blasted local news. Some dumb woman with high-ending inflections, tone bubbly, talked about a vehicle fire on Route 72 and a five days stale missing persons case.

"He was a good friend. All you really need to know. A hard worker. Grew up in the factories. He was a hard worker." He rose his whole body to look in the rear-view mirror back at Michelle. "You okay, honey? You look the saddest of all of us."

"No Mick, I'll be okay. For sure. Don't worry about me. Funerals, you know. They cut the mood."

It wasn't that she didn't like him, she didn't understand him. Her fifteen-year-old inner child said he was trying to take her ma's place. But, in no way did he acknowledge this behind-the-scenes fact, this way he could make her feel. He acted instead, as if he'd always been the man in charge, directing, demanding, steering every act. If Michelle wanted to watch Buffy, nope, on went Wheel of Fortune. Dinner that night, pizza? Nope, Mick felt like beers and fried chicken. "But we think alike. We both want takeout," he said with a wink.

"His issue was addiction." The older woman sat alone in the pew behind Michelle. She fussed with the loose clasp on her purse. "You know drugs have taken many. The whole thing is sad." A frown grew on her mouth, wilted purposefully with emotion. Her hair was slightly off blue, and she smelled like heavy foundation.

"Oh. Did you know him? Are you alone? Do you want to come up here?" Michelle offered. Then Pat coaxed her into the aisle and up next to them. Pat reached across Michelle and shook her hand with the back of her hand up. The woman pivoted at her hips, elbow in the gut, and took Pat's hand loosely in hers. Mick sat hunched over now on the seat, pointing and almost barking details in a low tone.

"I'm his aunt. It's true." She paused and waited for them to comment, but they only nodded their heads, waiting for more, the story she wanted to relay. "I seen him come by sometimes. In the night, he'd stop by. He'd come by for hours. Don't know what they were doing there. Sex, I imagine." She lifted her finger to lips as if she had burped. "Or drugs. I had to boot him out for both those things." She kneeled, folded her hands, and prayed. As she stooped, she said, "The drugs, though, they weren't my fault. I had to kick him out. You see, right?"

They were quiet for the rest of the service. The woman didn't move from her kneeling position. She did not raise her head or exchange any more words with them. Several times she moved, leaning her head in to speak, but no words came out. She would reposition herself again, solitary in her spot. Pat and Michelle functioned as placeholders, taking the place of an absent friend for a lonely woman.

The crowd ushered in as they waited. Mick talked to this person and that, offering advice, flicking his head back and forth, patting fellas on the back. All not above a whisper. The simple church contained pews and books, one like the next. In each pew, the sexton had chaotically scattered the books in various places behind each pew.

Mick dropped his handkerchief at the beginning of the service. A strange woman stooped in high heels to pick up the cloth. Mick didn't look at her once, only the piece of cloth, the germy thing. When he resituated himself and the woman rose high, they shared a glance, a moment in time. Clearly they knew each other but didn't speak. Mick shoved the cloth back into his pocket and lifted his pockets with his hands. She only nodded and moved up the aisle. She hurried to another seat.

Each time someone spoke, they tapped the microphone as they stood at the pulpit, a standard wood podium. The speakers watched and noted how each one began their speech. The next would tap as the one before. Mostly the men spoke. Each with a thick neck and a stubbly beard. Strong-armed men. He emulated greatness, they said. His honesty paved the way for others to be honest. His heart glistened of gold. Someone told a story about how he had won fifty games of bowling in a row. The man, still salty, grimaced. His goal to bowl over fifty games, win more than fifty games, against anyone to be square impressed everyone. He offered the challenge to the audience. No one responded. The stories dripped heartwarming sentiments and overly typical remembrances, almost made up.

The man they honored thus lay still. Speakers and participants showed their compassion. Something powerful men rarely do. Skeptical as everyone else, Michelle chuckled a bit until she stiffened and frowned to meet the mood of the room.

Pat and Michelle didn't go up to view the body. They didn't need to know what he looked like alive and thought their lack of actions was not a sign of disrespect. To not view the body when so many people gathered here only called for issuing him good thoughts to his grave. They whispered this to each other when the rest of the crowd moved. Mostly, the idea of shaking the hands of the thick-necked men scared them. The woman with high heels who graced the front terrified them. The two had exchanged words about her demeanor. Her ice-cold stares could kill. They didn't know these people or how to approach them. So they sat in their seats while Mick made his way to the front, spent three to four minutes with each person leaning in, reassuring, and comforting. His false compassion came directly through in his expressions and words. He truly shined in this crowd.

The pallbearers came and left with the casket. A procession to the cemetery gathered at the door and then people moved to their cars. Mick said they didn't have to go. He had seen what he needed to see. They all worked themselves into Mick's Honda Accord, a weird car for an everyday Joe, a mechanic no less, a football lover and a hardworking union man.

Mick looked at them with stern eyes and said it wasn't the stare of the dead man that scared him and that shouldn't scare them either, but the stare from the woman with the handkerchief.

"Will tear right through you. No way about it. I could tell she'd rip your guts out if given the chance. So, stay away from her, you both hear?" He eased his hands from squeezing the wheel a bit too hard. "You hear. If she ever stops you and tells you to do something, you do what she says. She told me to date Michelle's mom; would you believe that? Nah, I wouldn't tell you that." He laughed.

On the car ride back to Michelle's apartment, Pat apologized for her dad. One could describe his laugh as maniacal. He would tilt his head back with this cackle that could freeze over hell. Pat was used to it, but Michelle wasn't. She apologized over and over because she could see how Michelle shuffled in her seat. They would hide their true feelings about their parents dating and have sex later. They joked about their parents dating, but when it got down to things, they both felt strangely uncomfortable. That's why mannerisms and character resonated, rubbing each one the wrong way.

They also discussed the incident, the story the woman told. They decided unanimously Mick didn't have sex with this man. A viewing wasn't necessary. They didn't need to say yes, Mick would've done him or not. Giggles emerged.

"Could you see, no?" The vowel sound extended for several seconds.

"Absolutely no," Pat said. This, at once, retracted their glee. What was it to be irreverent among the dead?

"Wouldn't it be great to have a gay dad, though?"

"My dad is incapable for sure," Pat ended the discussion with a blunt pause and shake of the head.

What they didn't discuss was the other possibility the women had given them. That Pat's father might've been involved in drugs or drug dealing, Michelle came to guess. Not once during the long car ride did Michelle suggest Pat should check into her dad's history. Not once did she say it might be worth looking through his stuff. Michelle in no way burst out with accusations. Above all, she didn't relay to Pat her concerns about the effect on her mom, who now dated Pat's dad, and who she cared for and wanted to protect.

Chapter 16

Entering the empty saloon of a house, Michelle shut the door with a loud clap. She was having a temper tantrum in her thirties when no one was there to see it. She couldn't feel anything in that house, as if they had all died in a shootout. A breeze from the heating vent blew across her face. The house would be empty for a long, long time. Michelle's ma hadn't been hanging around the recliner recently. She had camped out in the tiny corner office on the second floor near the bathroom. Sighing at the sight of an empty family room, Michelle made her way up the stairs to the second floor.

The railing wobbled a bit. The house didn't hold the same strength as she had originally thought. As a child, she found pride in the new finishes, the basement stairs she could jump off into a pile of pillows. The stairs seemed sturdy in the past. Here, now, the railing shook. Whether her size now dwarfed the house, made it less of a powerful beast, or if the family's broken unity tumbled into disrepair, she didn't know. She hadn't seen the house become a wreck. She hadn't seen the storm door had come loose from its hinges until only a few days ago. The sink had sprung a leak, and no one had fixed the malfunction. The house, the family. Two things brand new and shiny, and now broken.

In an effort at compassion, she held herself outside of the bedroom door, quietly picking away at the wood molding Jamie had painted during Michelle's early twenties. Flecks shed easily with her nerves. She remembered a time in her teen years. The door had opened a tad, and Michelle had peered in, had watched at her peck away at the computer keyboard, switching mouse to keyboard to mouse.

Michelle had used the same keyboard for Second Life in the early aughts. Jamie had actually told her about the program. The virtual space had been a good place to hang out. Michelle recalled spending hours there hoping her parents didn't barge in. She'd found clubs, empty buildings, but most of all, people, crazy people like her.

In high school, Michelle had become reclusive. She didn't want to know anyone or anyone to know her, because then people would talk. Talk about her mother and inevitably her, their relationship, and what they both would do next. The anxiety had overwhelmed her, and she reassured herself she could, as an only child, amuse herself. She didn't need friends, only her mothers who she genuinely loved, despite the gossip and drama.

When Michelle tapped ever so slightly on the door, pushing it open a bit, Jamie jumped. She adjusted herself to make herself big and then at once, click, click, changed her browser. Her agility under pressure was astounding. In her teens, in the same situations, Michelle avoided her mom's gaze. Jamie swerved her eyes away, seemingly just as embarrassed as Michelle had been at fifteen.

"Oh, clicking away, you know." Startled at first, she gradually adjusted, calmed down.

"Ma, you finally have something to do. Your recliner is getting lonely."

"Right, the recliner, my woman," she said. "What do you need, honey?"

"Going out? Thought you'd want to go for a drive?"

"I can't. I have to meet this guy."

"Who?" Michelle knew her ma didn't have many friends left.

"Oh, you know. This sort of... person. He's helping me with the computer stuff."

They called the job the endeavor. Jamie wouldn't reveal too much, but it was okay with Michelle and her mom. They knew she showed incentive, worked at it to make money. Would the endeavor succeed? None of them knew.

Almost as if she realized something was actually happening, her eyes widened. Ma was actually talking to her. She got up and switched off the monitor. After shuffling papers, stuffing some under others, pushing them inside one of two folders, she threw them in a drawer and shut it. She placed a few random loose papers in a folder and then onto an organizer tray and then picked them back up and pulled them under her arm. She set them down again to put on her jacket, struggling with the zipper, looking to be in an anxious hurry.

"Honey, oh. You are dear." Ma kissed the top of Michelle's head and rushed out the door.

***

On the way over to the meeting spot, Jamie drew her eyes to the people crossing the street at inopportune locations. *They want to get hit,* she thought for a second. This down-and-out part of town bled coldness and dampness, as if the weather had nothing else to do but target this area, sink the landscape below the surface of the world. Muck and rust dominated more than the fallen leaves and puddles.

Jamie knew the drop shipping was wrong from the start, but she gave the job a shot, anyway. She acted as a seller on one major site and when an item sold; she sent them something from another site with a cheaper option. When the thing, car parts, stereos, furniture, sold she would find it elsewhere, on another internet platform, and then she bought and shipped the item. That could've been the major retailer having a sale, another store, or a yard sale app. She kept the difference. If she got a return, trouble ensued. She had to work some magic. The ventures couldn't be outright illegal, as far as she saw. A lot of paperwork went through Jamie's hands, though, and her motivation waned. She might have tried to argue with Kim on her tech support session when she threatened her outright, but she was vulnerable. She easily fell into the game. The idea she could make more money in an easier way tempted her. She flowed into this other endeavor, this other promise of money, because of her apathy. She slammed the steering wheel with her fist and muttered, "I hate you" to herself. It was her only act of defiance.

She was going to the underbelly, and she knew it. Her ultimatum had no other answer than, "yes, ma'am." This was her foray into something beyond her prior comprehension, all wrapped up in a cutesy bow. The perpetrator shrouded the crime in innocence, and she fell for the ploy. If she weren't tricked, would she have gone willingly? She did not know, but one thing slowed her up. Her depression weakened her, made her glance up occasionally to find an outlet, pulled her into an abyss. When she saw a glimmer of light and got sucked in, things became real. She looked for something to bring her joy, no matter how far-fetched. Her light at the edge of the tunnel had suddenly thrown her into an orbit in a somehow otherwise unimaginable space. Nerves electrified as she tried to keep calm.

The empty parking lot air whistled against the metal bridge above. Under the Reems Highway, Drogertown bridge, Jamie could only see industrial sites, a few smoke towers in the distance, and less frequented pothole ridden roads. No one took this route regularly. No one used this lot for carpooling or walked to work from here. The highway skipped an on-ramp and the exit ramp veered off the other side with only a left turn. A simple chain-link fence with sparse vines interweaving throughout the holes told those who entered about the maintenance of the place. Several wrecked cars, one with an impaled front end and another with a missing door, sat unused on the far side of the lot. A wet and stained blanket tumbled out of an opening without a door. Through a single booth with an automatic lever, Jamie entered the Drogertown South Parking Lot. A faded billboard did anything but confirm arrival at the correct location.

As Jamie drew closer, Jon, a round man, slouched and adjusted his half-cocked hat with a brim snapped to the cap. It was the newsboy cap, a hat men wore golfing at one point in history. He constantly looked left and right even as he leaned in to speak. He chewed gum with a flapping jaw. Jamie balked at the gum chewing and couldn't have imagined the act from his phone voice. Jon lifted his shoulders, presenting himself as powerful. Jamie subdued any qualms she had about the place or time. She showed up, even if she wanted to talk herself out of any further back-alley tasks.

"This is like the drop shipping. Except you're dropping off money. Well, kind of not really, but the job is a drop, and we call the task drop shipping—with Michael. He's your contact, Michael," Jon said.

A contact and a helper. They called him a friend. He never showed a temper, relaxed into every situation, and kept his grin only curled so high. He'd put his hands in his pockets and shift upward and inward, as if to tell Jamie something. Often, he'd say, "decent job" or a simple "nice work." He wore jeans and sweaters, not Christmas sweaters per se, but sweaters out of the eighties or nineties, thick knitting and slightly off-beat colors.

"I don't mean to be off-base, but this is nothing like the drop shipping I did—" Jamie found out about the doctor scam last week when she talked to Jon's cohort on the phone. Kim supplied technical support and advice when Jamie needed help. Jamie paid for advice and funded startup cash. Kim slipped about medicine deals, saying they might try to put the Vita-pills up on eBay under a covert name. Was Jamie interested in hearing more? Jamie scoffed—what in the heck was a Vita-pill? She replied in a calm and serious manner, tamping her humor.

The Vita-pills, she relayed, were at-home therapy pills psychiatric patients could use to stimulate their system. They were illegal, did not pass the FDA, and spread in networks of doctors who prescribed and took cash under the table.

They also sold Suppla-pills, which complemented regular prescription drugs. The Suppla-pills should be taken in tandem with prescribed medications for them to be effective, or as the doctor's told them—new medicine from Europe. The doctors took cash under the table.

That's all Jamie needed to know for now. Kim was now all-in on this effort, and she moved up a level. When Jamie tried to back off, she realized she couldn't. Kim set her date and time for a discussion with Jon and said if she didn't show up, they would cut her off. She hung up the phone.

"Right."

"I mean the drop shipping, on a computer, easy peasy. Keeping track of what shipped and all, is more like fraud? I'm not sure I'm ready for this."

"Jack thinks you're ready. Look, all you do is go to the doctor's and take the drops, then go to the pier when you're ready to surrender the cash. Cross check bottles, Vita-pills, Suppla-pills, etc. with amounts. You're short—well, Jack will tell you, you're short. You're simply a courier, but don't get your money mixed up. Absolutely no. And—ah, five thousand a month cash." He winked.

He moved to his glove box, slowly struggling with the door, opening the trap for him, then pivoting around the piece of plastic. Jamie could see over his shoulder through the sections of the window without a glare. When he opened the glove box, a gun flopped to the floor. He bent at the waist slowly, calmly, unfazed, and replaced an envelope with green dollars hanging out with the chunk of heavy metal.

"Here, some good will. I hear you have a lady. Buy her something nice."

Jamie moved toward the man's hand and took it, knowing full well they agreed in a handshake. She now had to do what they told her to do.

"Oh, and yeah, that was a gun."

Jamie coasted through the streets, calmer than she ever had been. She had to age-up. Things, her life, were more serious now. She had to be rational. If she made a misstep, it could be her life or her wife's, quasi-ex-wife's... Michelle's. She held in the emotion, for the first moment knowing she could bury it, not make a scene, not act out. For the first time, she felt reborn.

Chapter 17

Jamie woke to the sunlight. The rays cascaded in the usual way, illuminating both the recliner and the couch, giving Jamie alternate options. The sun peeled her eyes open with torturous brightness. Even the heavens were scolding her.

In a swift motion, she leaped for her spot, and reclined on the well rolled on recliner. As she looked back at her spot, the indentation looked less inviting than it ever had. Jamie took in a heavy whiff and swallowed sourly in a dry gulp, inhibited by her stank and embarrassment. A small gnat rose from the spot.

Ellen's birthday had come and passed. The family celebration consisted of an enormous party. A day they had always enjoyed together, and Michelle and Ellen were both absent. No one brought home a plate of food or a sparkler. They always used leftover fourth of July fireworks for Ellen's birthday, always afraid the fire would leave a spark in dry leaves. There were no fireworks anywhere in sight. She searched a few kitchen cabinets and the garage but had no luck. Were she to have had a small party by herself, she might've stayed, for the sake of the house. The one thing that accepted her unconditionally, didn't mind her camped out on the couch, and never minded about the strewn clothes and blankets. The house said nothing.

She made some pasta. Many people ate breakfast for dinner, but Jamie couldn't understand why no one made dinner for breakfast. The meal was the most important of the day.

An abrupt ring lit up her phone and it danced, vibrating on the table. Jamie shook herself normal. After a pause, she dropped her fork as casually as she had lifted the pointy piece of metal. She had yet to take a bite.

"Listen, this is it. This is your last chance. Get it or be done. And you know out is not done." Jon's voice resonated with disgust.

Jamie put the phone on speaker and set the weighted thing gently on the table. She took a bite of the pasta. The tomato sauce rested on her fork, heavy. Bits of garlic would seep into the recliner later, straight from her pores.

Jamie spoke.

Jon shouted, "I don't like speaker. Done. Do you get it? You get it." He hung up.

Everything will be fine. Jamie lifted thumb to middle finger, elbows bowed out, breaths in then blown into the world in long light exhales.

Everything would not be fine.

She pushed the pasta away and stood, dipping hands to toes and rolled her hands up her body to the sky. A stretch.

She went to her room, knowing the kitchen might take hours to clean up. She put the wastepaper basket in the center of the room and started pitching towards it. Some things fell in. Others fell short. They stuffed the can until it overflowed. She couldn't believe so many papers had littered the office. So many important papers.

Into a plastic bag. The bag wouldn't burn nicely in a campfire, but the papers would. She tied the plastic ties with intention. This leap would happen. She would be safe at the cabin. She would break free from what she got herself into.

Jamie moved to pack an old hiking pack; one she might've only used a few times. She scooped up some clothes littering the floor. She grabbed underwear from the drawers in Ellen's, what used to be her and Ellen's, bedroom. Some pillows. A blanket. A towel for washing in the creek. When she descended steps to the basement, she found goodies. Things she didn't need. A tent. A patched air mattress. Lanterns. Various things should've been in the cabin. Years old, years used. Tossed aside, when the weekend trips stopped, and the convenience of cabin life began.

***

The place down by the creek dripped with dampness as a light fog rose. Mosquitoes dwelled, dropped like helicopters onto skin. This was no place like home. No one would find her out there, through the half gate, the arched branches. Jamie smiled wryly at the thought. Was she fooling herself? Ellen at least never came down that far.

The muggy, buggy place made Jamie itch. She used paper reports and releases for starter material, gathered as much kindling as she could. When she flicked the lighter over and over, the paper barely caught, damp from the air. The sticks and kindling, leaves, and needles never took the spark. This place couldn't hold a fire, and the bugs would never leave.

As dusk set in on the first night, Jamie undressed by the creek. She lay flat on her back, her face to the sky in the gently rocking water. Grey birds circled the place as she looked up. She didn't bring the birding book and now she wished she had. A dark black bird, larger than the rest, but not a hawk or a vulture, swooped in and all the little gray birds scattered. Their time in paradise near the water, a bird bath as large as the eye could see, had ended. Jamie rolled to her front, blowing slow bubbles until her air had expired and she needed to gasp.

In the morning, she rose with hundreds of bites on her skin and dozens of new friends in the tent. The scent of creek water counterbalanced the sweet smell of the pines, and she already yearned for a shower. She would be here. In the woods. She forwent a shower. She wouldn't enter the house, a symbol of her family. The hearth of her previous life. In a way, she was outside the house, outside the family. She had not yet left the vicinity, but she was close. Driven out of the secure unit.

Jamie kicked the greenest clumps of grass on the lawn, unable to break through to the place they used to call home, now only a house, ready for sale. Only to be tarnished if someone entered, messed up the towels, strew clothes all around. Jamie would leave it to be what it once was and prevent it from ending up different, broken more.

She moved to a large swath of yard by the cabin. They would surely find her here. She didn't care. She didn't care how chilly the air felt. She clenched a key in her hand. Lowering to her knees outside the house, she lifted an angular rock and tucked the key under the jagged thing for safe keeping.

In this makeshift place, Jamie dwelled. Not a place to camp out, even really. But she called the place hers. She christened the scene her test. She basked in the safety and remoteness. These things came in so clear, so she tidied up her room of a tent and ate food for once. At first, what they could conceive of as a tantrum was for novelty. Later, she tried to get better. Sometimes, wanted to feel like she was surviving.

When Ellen would come because Jamie knew she would come, she would bring her things Jamie had forgotten. She would come home that evening, or the following day with a plate from Mick's cookout, BBQ, where Michelle had also been. She would look around, see Jamie wasn't there. Check the office. Look in her own bedroom, under the sheets. Then, she would say she didn't care. Jamie knew this was all true. She wouldn't even allow herself to wonder. She would go on with her day, go back to work, and meet Mick the next night. When five days were over, or would it be six, she'd know. Jamie's howling thoughts rambled. Jamie had them out here alone in the woods. She wanted Ellen. She wanted them together, but Jon, her new seedy job, the body Jon promised her, would all come crashing down. Plotting, she knew she needed to disappear.

PART II

Chapter 18

Ellen had wrapped up visiting Jamie. Pitiful up on the top of a mountain, she ate peanut butter and jelly sandwiches and stashed cups of fruit in her tent. They both knew full well she didn't have a can opener.

Ellen wanted to make up. Kiss and make up. If only the resolution were easy. If only she could stop dating this deadbeat, Mick. She reveled in the situation's complexity. Nothing pushed her to be free. Words had been said. More than words had been said.

Ellen hadn't been to see the doctor in this context before. She only saw him if it was about Jamie. Maybe that's why Jamie was tangled up in the idea of her having an affair. Jamie was having trouble, but Ellen wasn't seeing the doctor. She was forgetting about Jamie or trying to forget. Now she was here in a psychiatrist's office herself, here to find out who she was and what she really wanted.

In a blank parking lot, Ellen slammed the door behind her. She was the one with anger management problems, yet she had never gone to someone to manage her emotions. Still reeling from an argument on the mountain about whether to sell the cabin, she threw her coat towards the couch. It missed and fabric splayed out on the floor. Ellen planned to sort the paperwork this evening and take all the proceeds. Jamie would have nothing, she had said. Anger had brewed, anger she should've managed for years. She could never let someone see her, not angry once they had raised her temper or made her livid. Livid for life, she had said about companies and old friends.

She entered the office building. Such an odd place for a psychiatrist's office. Nevertheless, Ellen entered and made her way, glancing at a board and reacting, entering the elevator. She committed to do the work. She needed to do the work by herself first. Then she could make things right with Jamie.

He greeted her at the door to his office wearing all black with a hunter green tie. His pearly teeth glistened as if he brushed them minutes ago. Instinctively, Ellen leaned in to smell but could not. He guided her without words to a black leather chair, not giving her a second to choose with her eyes. Nervous and anxious, she didn't breathe until she sat down and took in the room and its plainness, the absence of color and character. The stolid room, with an absence of character, held four key pieces of furniture and caused Ellen to frown slightly.

"This is all new to me. I don't know how to act," Ellen said.

Dr. Prince sat back in the chair, leaning and bobbing. After a moment he crossed his legs stiffly, ankle over knee. When he spoke, Ellen sat up in her seat and focused her eyes like lasers.

"Tell me how you feel. Let's start with that this time. The time is yours. I'll listen and when there's something, anything, you have questions about, I'll address the issue."

"Well, first, let's get this right. You see, Jamie." She paused. "Now, I'd like to know everything about her, but you said—"

"That's right. We won't talk about Jamie except tangentially. I can't break doctor and patient confidentiality, even for related persons."

"Well then, the issue is me. All of it, all about me." Ellen sighed. "I guess this is kind of relieving."

"Tell me about Jamie, but I won't tell you about her. Deal?"

"I love Jamie. More than life itself. She is my world, has been my world. Every time I stop and stare at her, my love is pure. That's not what comes out, but I feel the sense in my gut, the love that is. The resounding love, pain, whatever it is, makes me cry sometimes. Other times, I push the stabbing sensation away."

"But?"

"No, that's the whole of everything. I love her, and I know what you're getting at. I shouldn't love her because she's done horrible things..." Ellen took a breath. "Or you think I'm punishing her because of what she's done... to learn?"

"Is it? Isn't it her fault?"

"Nope. It's my fault. It's all my fault. I want to fix us. That's why I need—"

"Aren't you beating yourself up about the whole ordeal though? Aren't things better—"

Doctors shouldn't have reactions like this, at least not early.

"It's... Mick—Isn't that what you're after? He's got a nice car. His daughter Pat is great, smart. Isn't this what you want to make work?" He paused, reflecting, nodded his head back at his desk, then the clock.

"Doctor. Do you know Mick?"

"No. No. I know of him. I guess."

"You do... Doctor. We certainly mingle in similar circles. Why didn't you say?"

Ellen reserved herself. She would keep information to herself from here on out. She couldn't describe the issues with Mick, her dissatisfaction with him, her realization of her childish behavior to get back at Jamie. Absolutely, she couldn't get into her understanding of his involvement in salacious activity. His accounting paperwork from the strip club appeared on her counter. When she confronted him, he wouldn't even admit he had been there. Cars would appear suddenly.

He would get something different about every other week. Some were really nice. Others were, to put things nicely, not nice. Chryslers or KIAs with dents all over them. Ellen had glared but not asked. She didn't want to know who or what shot at the car or why Mick had it this week and not the next.

"Doctor. I thought I could do this, but I can't. I won't." She conjured up excuses as she stood. "This type of therapy is not for me. And with such close connections. I can't do that to you." She tried to pull herself out of the moment all as nicely as possible.

"Ellen, sit down. I've helped your family for so long. Now, tell me... I know you and Jamie are divorcing. I know we must confront the life milestone, and I'm here to help you."

Ellen knew she would have to ease out of her relationship with Mick. She knew. She didn't know if she could discuss easing out of the Mick relationship with Dr. Prince. He had become close to the family. Now, who could she trust?

"Mick... He—He hit me. He said I was in too far to get out. He said we were bound to be together, and we would be."

Ellen bit the insides of her lips with her teeth, though no tears appeared. She gazed back, remembering her powerful statement to Mick, the anger she'd had. She had flailed her arms, proclaimed it over, before a slap came down on her face before stern words said they were meant to be together. Kisses ensued, puckered, smacking, manly lips, wet, controlling. She recounted how she knew what she wanted—to dump Mick—but he would not agree.

"Dr. Prince, really. I have to... I need to think things over if this is the direction you want to take me in—?"

"We want to go in..." His mouth gaped open, almost as if he wanted Ellen to mouth it with him.

Ellen scurried out the door she had come in thirteen minutes ago. Her eyes had veered multiple times toward the bold clock on the wall. Four pieces of furniture. As she left the room, she said, "I'm sorry."

Chapter 19

Jamie ruffled her sleeves in the oversize jacket and stood closer to her new best friend. She was incognito, on the run. No one in the crazy mild temperature place, warm enough to only need a jacket, with rocky land and winding Old Town streets, would guess her gender. She liked it and relaxed in the men's jeans that hugged her narrow hips in quite the right way. She nibbled the fingertip of a glove to pull it off and warmed her hands by the fire in the waning light.

Back in 1994, Jamie lived in Switzerland for four months. She lived in a hotel, debating whether she wanted to live there for good. Before she met Ellen, she had a particular type of freedom. Funny how she could remember the time before their marriage and the beginning of their relationship so well, but by about the third week of her and Ellen's blissful marriage, she had forgotten. She couldn't quite bring back the memories. Jarred, she closed her eyes one more time to remember, but she knew she wouldn't.

She leaned on a square column with applied strips of wood down the length. The hotel's fresh exterior paint glistened in the moonlight. The deeply recessed cobble stone streets below her feet threw off her balance. Bits of garbage and cigarette butts, tufts of grass and dirt, intermixed in the pathway. Long and flat, they wound around the town quite like Jamie remembered. The broad avenues complemented slick, maintained streets necessary for vehicular traffic.

Jamie flicked a cigarette butt toward the shopping district up the road. The area would go up a steep slope away from the lake. On Saturday night, the tourists and locals alike were shopping, buying up goodies for home and travel. She entered the hotel, kissing goodbye to the night. She wouldn't see those things in Switzerland but breathed in and out one more glorious breath of air.

Jamie had felt a spark when she tasted her first sip of beer. She never liked to drink alone. She knew too many friends who became alcoholics in their twenties. Her boss had sent her over. She had a fantastic job in logistics for a furniture company. She managed projects effectively and would receive a promotion when she returned. But first, he wanted her to go to Switzerland and live a little to get the need for freedom out of her system, as he said. So, here she sat in a swank hotel with no one else to tell her what to do. She took the whole place in. Confounding, she thought, how her company invested in her, their future.

She took long sips of the beer, holding the cold against her throat and swallowing slowly. We she went down to the bar, she didn't intend on going out into the night, and she doubted she would pick someone up that evening. She was up for conversation, nevertheless.

Light dust carried around the musty bar. Green lampshades hung over low yellow lights. The shades themselves dated decades back. Not an ounce of dust hid in the crannies. A pool table held one sole individual who played himself, moving from side to side, changing sticks now and then. Jamie, though captured from afar, an eager young professional, had decided not to stare to figure out which side of him was winning.

She ran her hands along the thickly coated wax of the bar stools, which weighed at least thirty pounds each. What the bar lacked in taste, the place made up for in quality and cleanliness. A few staff in white rounded aprons moved through the bar as the bartender held his hands on the thick slab of a bar, leaned in, and stared at them until they hurried along their way.

Two patrons filtered in and adjusted themselves at opposite ends of the bar. The person closest to Jamie yelled across the bar, "Never again." And they shook their head in disappointment.

"Who's that?" Jamie asked.

"Someone who will never be my friend again." They nodded their head back and forth and motioned to the bartender.

"I'll send him on his way if he acts up," the bartender said. Clearly, they knew each other.

With a glance at Jamie, they said, "They love me is all and I can never love them." Their words were slow and smooth, almost bubbly drunk with calmness without worry, almost as if they had no cares.

When Jamie asked for their name, she didn't know how to go about forming the words. She fumbled with a pack of matches and picked at the resin on the bar above woody curves and swirls. Her nails would never penetrate, but she picked away at several spots. "You from here...?"

"Gerry," they said. "And I am." A thick German accent came through her words.

Jamie gathered from only a few momentary expressions they were trying ridiculously hard to not have the particular German accent. They almost said with the inflections they were not German at all.

They blushed and shook their head at the beer in front of them. Finally, they looked up to meet Jamie's eyes with an imploring stare.

She turned her hips on the swivel chair to meet them. "Nice to meet you. I'm Jamie."

"I live here, you know. For a long time, this is where I have been. Are you from the United States? Oh, how I would love to pop into that place for a bit."

"Yeah. I'm here on a rest and relax order, so to speak. I'm taking a break from work."

"Your features are stunning," they said, sounding mysterious. They kept looking away and back and away.

Jamie knew her stark features never stunned anyone looking for soft curves and pie eyes, but her defined sleek and angled face held power and directness, coolness in a way. She hated to think she appeared more masculine in features.

"Bah, I'll have none of that."

"You'll have every word of it." Their eyelashes dropped three times slowly, and they sighed, pulling in their lips.

Jamie circled the glass rim with her finger. She had never. With someone she couldn't yet define. The idea rang through her soul that this place existed for finding love, sweet chocolate, cool crisp air, full when you inhaled. It was a setting pulling you back for moments, scenes from an easily imaginable historic place. The first night was their imaginable place, what they carved out over five flowing drinks. They would both remember a fullness of enjoyment unknowingly packed into the pleasure center of the brain. "I'm only here until the twenty-third of March."

"I'll lock you in. This is the key to my castle." They took the key card from the tight pocket opening in Jamie's pants. "You'll never find me in the streets." They got up and waltzed, without paying, to the elevator. "I'll hold the door for thirty seconds."

Jamie grabbed fifty euros from her other pocket and placed the paper on the table and left. Only looking back for a second or two, she accepted a nod from the bartender.

Her tryst with Gerry would last the breadth of the two months. They pulled the goodness clean, thin, gobbled it, tearing it away and emptying the pot. After those three nights, a void still remained, and they knew they had been glutenous. Gerry left the hotel, but Jamie did not. They brought heels back to the room on the second night. They danced, played, tumbled, and bayed. The brisk wind on the balcony filtered through, providing freshness with each day. Naked in the moonlight, they kissed and Jamie finally knew love.

They never talked about the twenty-third of March and Jamie didn't even know if they remembered the day, being they were five drinks under on the night they met. Each night or afternoon, or whenever Gerry showed up, they would bring a toy, a treat, a mood. They fought over the single piece of chocolate and relished it when they finally found a knife. Gerry took Jamie's wallet the day before in an act of defiance, and Jamie starved. Gerry didn't care.

Two and a half weeks in, after Jamie got her wallet back, Gerry brought only sadness. Gerry returned the wallet with tears, said they had spent all the money. Gerry lived alone on the streets, out past the circle in town. They took a room on nights they had money. On other nights, they showered here. That, they said, "is all I have ever known." With burdensome tears, they dabbed their eyes, telling tales of pickpockets and rapists, all they had ever seen in the world. "A passport cost a lot of money," they said. They had to go with Jamie back to the United States.

When Gerry left in the evening, relieved of the pressure of their real self, their real being, Jamie took time to recover. With their heartache passed on to Jamie, she felt the weight to mend it if she could. The love they shared had sewn back together only so much, but promised so much more.

Jamie went to the lobby. She had gotten a call from her employer to deposit a check for someone from the company. The check had Jamie's name, a bonus, so to speak, but she'd get that only on a successful return. Jamie got a spare key card and the envelope sent from her company at the front desk.

"Surprising to see you, ma'am. Can I recommend a restaurant?"

"No, that's fine. I'm going back up. I have to drop off something at the bank tomorrow."

On the way to the bank the next day, she couldn't shake the feeling of leaving the room and not telling Gerry. At the same point, how ludicrous they had been, their fun. Now it was time to move on, grow up. They'd have to if they were moving to the United States. Jamie laughed at her apprehension, her guilt.

***

Standing in front of the fire, seeing if she could catch the tips of her gloves on fire, she remembered depositing the two-million-dollar check in a Swiss bank, listening to every step from her employer.

Gerry would be here; she knew as much. Love lost was a tragedy. Was that how the phrase went? Jamie held a copy of the poetry of May Sarton that Gerry read in its entirety one night, entering, sitting, reading, raising, then leaving. In no time flat, the night had escaped. Their whole affair melted.

At the same elevated risk, though she was not sure what, her employer ordered her to return. "Take great care of your passport and return," her direct supervisor had said.

After waiting a full sleepless night, she rose and swiftly left the room. Returning from the bank and then sitting in a room, tapping her fingers, she waited, pining for Gerry to return. An attendant let her back into the place and gave her a fresh key. She sat on the bed and did not move. When the time was a half hour until takeoff, she rose, gathered her bags, and left for the airport. She made the flight to her chagrin.

Jamie hadn't returned. She let the past go and the almost three weeks they had together, her confinement. Love stories never end the same. This one, Jamie decided, was better left bottled up.

Yet here she was some thirty-five odd years later, looking for Gerry. The androgynous Gerry. The person filled with everything except Jamie's butch features. Their thin eyebrows and solid frame and wide neck and shaved head and big ears and gentle demeanor and loud voice. Gerry.

PART III

Chapter 20

On a blustery October night, Michelle returned to her parents' home. She visited less often now because of Ma's absence. Mom went to dinner with Mick most nights. Michelle would often show up to have dinner with her mom, and she'd be out with Mick somewhere drinking or dancing the night away. She ended up that evening, with everything happening, sitting in Ma's chair, in a lonely house, reading by a single light.

She opened her book to spend some time with her ma or the memory of her ma. A chill ran over her body as she relaxed into the recliner, pulling the plastic lever straight up. Her book slid off the arm of the chair, hitting the floor with a thump. She lost her page. In an awkward move, she managed to get herself out of the chair, which was still reclined. She sauntered toward the wall to raise the temperature. Mom was still paying the heating bills alone.

As the heat kicked in, she listened to the rattles of the fan and caught the smell of must in the ducts. The house, empty and quiet, creaked in other ways too. The faint smell of body clinging to the chair had dissipated without Ma's presence. Mom likely wouldn't be home for some time. With bottled, apprehensive feelings about snooping, she moved for the steps to see what she could find. For the memory or for the clues, she entered Jamie's work room looking for something. She didn't know if she wanted to find it.

This effort to visit the house to see her mom must've been a reason to look through Ma's things. She couldn't believe she hadn't looked around a bit earlier. The police didn't even ask to rummage through Jamie's things. They didn't ask about the sole room Ma used for her job. The one no one went into.

Michelle sat down and booted up the black, bulky desktop tower. Smudges littered the monitor. Her mom had started eating before she left for the woods, but she only ate in this room, at this computer, without other people around. The browser had links to eBay and Amazon, several other sites, OfferUp, Facebook. She assumed Ma used Facebook Marketplace. She checked out the favorites, and an extensive list of retailers, places of business from Nordstrom to TJ Maxx, appeared. Ma didn't shop a lot. She wrapped herself up in one of eight sweatshirts on most days. Days before she left for the woods, her ma in an act of humbleness asked Michelle for some money to buy a few new ones.

Michelle now poked around on the sites, looking for clues. Icons to eBay and Amazon were at the top. Ma might've added those first, she thought. None of the sites automatically logged in without a password. Someone had thrown a sweater in the corner and some empty notebooks with pages torn off the top littered the floor. When she lifted the notebooks and put them down, little scraps of paper, attempts to get every bit or the words off of a portion of an irregular tear, blew to the floor and scattered across the desk. Michelle picked up and examined one bit with a few letters, trying to decipher the madness to no avail. Removing her beanie, she threw her cap down on the floor in an act of resignation, running her hands through her hair in frustration.

In the closet's corner, a file cabinet turned at an odd angle irregularly jutted into the wall. One drawer was opened to the world. Michelle recognized Ma's trench coat jacket dropped over the main tower, but not the thick hunk of metal underneath. The drawer would not open. Firmly stuck, she could only open the jarred drawer an inch. Jamie had smartly locked the door solidly shut. Michelle didn't have the key. The drawer bent in at the rails. One ridge angled in inside over the wheel. She shoved the metal back and forth with effort, giving a slight grunt. The metal clanged but didn't give. The solid brick of a thing didn't move from its spot, despite her aggressiveness. With a grab, Michelle lifted a coat hanger from the neatly laundered trench coat; She tried to fish out papers. The first one she removed told too many forsaken tales.

The expense sheet she produced held codes such as, "R879044855–18 units–Dr. M564433." The following pages listed four sets of specifications for therapy dosages. The instructions detailed other prescribed drugs to take and specified amounts to be taken in conjunction with the drugs. Instructions listed use guidelines, as well as warnings on complications. A last attachment outlined and explained, albeit poorly, patient consent. A signature line closed out the agreement. Initial blocks littered all the pages. Michelle bellowed a haughty laugh at both the idea of off-beat therapy like this and the consent form: "I, the patient, in no way hold the doctor or manufacturer liable for complication in use and after effect from using these supplements. It is my sole opinion that this therapy will improve and aid in the recovery of my illnesses. I will not defame or otherwise speak ill of this prescription, and its use and effects." Michelle realized the overall ethic of this statement, which required a patient signature. Nothing would persuade her to sign the form. But had her mother?

When she flashed her light in the open crack of a locked drawer, she saw a wad of money. She could barely make out a deposit book with a slip-on top with an address in Switzerland.

As she regrouped, she knew she didn't want to touch the money. She didn't want to call the police, either. If necessary, she would talk to her mom on a burner phone.

She leaned back in the chair, unable to hold her stress. Michelle would contact her, find her virtually. She opened Ma's Gmail, and the account logged on automatically. There were three email accounts listed. The one she opened held a lot of promotions and some emails to friends and bill notices. No one had opened them yet. The business email seemingly didn't have anything to do with the wad of money in the file cabinet. She tried to get into the other three email accounts, with no luck. She needed a password and, though she tried several combinations, nothing worked. With a quick glance back to the original email, she pressed "Compose" and wrote halfheartedly, hoping a simple note would work. She entered the email address of the account.

Hi Ma,

Don't know where you are but love you. Of course, we are trying to find you and will keep looking for you. This isn't my only hope. Please call if you can or another postcard at least.

Xoxo, Michelle

She pressed send.

She wrote her ma emails every day sending them from her account to her Ma's personal account. None of them garnered a response. Days and weeks passed. She still wrote one a day. Simple notes about her day, what she did, or a cute thing mom said. They became almost a diary of sorts. An online archival journal only to be shared with her ma.

This email. The few lines she might send, which might be to or from a corrupt account, would be her last. She wouldn't give Ma the decency if she wouldn't respond to Michelle. Without attempting to open her personal email, trying the various passwords she possibly did not use, Michelle powered off the machine. Ma would have to contact her. They cut Ma off.

She wouldn't tell her mom about this. Michelle couldn't. She needed to find out more about the body in case her mom ever contacted her again. She needed to know who killed the man, that decomposing, twisted body. If her mom was responsible. Another search would start at the site of the breach, so to speak.

She tiptoed downstairs. Her mom had been sitting at the kitchen table looking at a lit candle, one she must've lit herself. She glanced up at Michelle and signed, smiled. The shock of seeing Mom startled Michelle, almost as if the person had been Ma herself. Calm and looking satiated, her mom rocked in the chair, hand on her cheek.

"I don't know about Mick, honey," Michelle's mom said.

"I know, Mom. I've been meaning to tell you something about him, something Pat told me." Michelle leaned into her mom and the candle. She cut the wax with her fingernail, picked some off and put it in front of her at her place at the table to roll and squish.

"What did you find out about Ma? I haven't gone up there yet. You know she's a mess as it is... her files. I don't know how she managed eight projects at once, but in her mind, all the data, the portfolio, was all there. Dates, figures, facts. Even if it looked astray, if you had a question about it, she had an answer. Such intellectual control." Mom picked off some of her own wax.

As if she had committed the murder, Michelle covered for her ma, coolly and calmly as she spoke. "Not much up there. I can't get into any of her stuff. She might've left in a hurry. A sweater appeared on the floor, thrown there. I didn't see clothes on the floor last week."

"Oh, honey. I'm sorry. It's not that I don't care. I mean, we are trying to find her. We were getting divorced. The affair is awkward.

You know Mick and all. Mick. What a treat? He is..." Ellen's words trailed off. "Anyway. Thank you for checking into things. This all is a lot, maybe too much really, for me. Me and your ma were together for over fourteen years. A lot happened at that time, but I can't deal with this. It's like stirring up a past and I'm trying to shut the door. Thinking if I want to shut the door at all."

"It's fine, Mom," Michelle wiped the glass of soda her mom brought to her with the corner of her shirt, removing a gooey smudge of food. "I know you're a wreck. You have to do the dishes now and cook. I know there's Mick and your heart is probably fluttering with new joy. But we need to find Ma. We owe her that much."

"Honey... I'll do what you need me to do."

Chapter 21

Ellen left the house in the morning as she usually did. The money flowed less steadily than it once had. She had noticed at least the groceries stayed put. Things had disappeared while Jamie gallivanted on top of the hill at the cabin. She knew that much. The crackers she bought, gone. The cans of corn she wanted to use for a proper dinner, gone. Even the carrots were missing. The incidents raised an anger, but the tension subsided with thoughts of their marriage. The times they had. At least, she could lend some food directly to the homeless, albeit her soon to be ex-wife. Meanwhile, the checks she normally sent monthly to the shelter stopped.

Ellen and Jamie had agreed to an open marriage before they married. The only recollection of a qualification she had was in a brief discussion. If the open marriage impeded their own marriage, the side relationship wouldn't come to a close. The whole thing came about because they saw other gay couples making arrangements when gay marriage became the law of the land. People hurried to get their license, thinking almost as an afterthought they were rushing into things. Years passed by and neither of them saw anyone else. They were in a second honeymoon phase, if she could even call it that.

Ellen dated someone at work for a brief period. They both agreed on the person beforehand with specific limits and boundaries. Because he had a sexual attraction, an interest in Ellen's kink about having her partner tie her up, they okayed it. Both of them had spouses. After the brief affair, Ellen insisted she wouldn't pick someone else up again unless Jamie found a third or her own affair first.

Ellen buttoned the top button of her shirt obsessively. She grimaced at her daughter going through Jamie's office. It wasn't her place to investigate. The police should do their job. She could easily skew evidence or try to hide something and the actions would backfire later. Their things belonged to Jamie. When she returned, she would want them, need them as is. *If Jamie did,* the mantra ran through Ellen's head every morning. The blow wouldn't hurt as much when the cops told her she would never return. Her daughter would inherit her office and the things within, through Ellen. So, maybe the investigation didn't matter. Michelle could play detective. Ellen smiled, thinking happy thoughts to brush off her anxiety, while she buttoned up her shirt and grabbed her bag, a gift from Jamie during a blue skies phase of their relationship, before Mick.

Ellen didn't believe in big box stores on principle, but when you had five random things to buy, that's where you ended up. Dog chow. She wouldn't get the normal brand but could check the item off the list. She needed shampoo and conditioner, a mouse for her computer, and a string for a craft project at work. That's what she recounted in her head: shampoo, conditioner, mouse, string. Don't forget the string.

The stolid gray front marked with bits of red here and there presented an ominous power. She charged into the big box store, knowing she could find all these things, scoop them up, and leave as quickly as she came. The fluorescent lights beamed down on her, somehow clouding her vision. She shuffled about, looking for a cart. A few people filtered in. No carts were in the corral. She couldn't find one in the aisle right past the entrance. She didn't need one. Ellen wouldn't go back to the parking lot and scrounge. She looked around for a basket, but nothing caught her attention.

The aisles and aisles of worker bees busy about their day overwhelmed her. Thirty feet past the registers, she stopped on a beat. She leaned into a unit of shelving instead of sitting right on the floor. Everything was too much. The day, the past months. All too much.

The chow and hair products were close to each other. *So odd, the managers or planner thought the two smelliest products could combine powers in one location and boost sales for both. Who decided people might forget hair products or vice versa when getting chow at the store?* She grabbed the shampoo and chow, filling up her one arm. With an extended pinkie, she pulled a rope chew toy for the dog. No one quite loved her as much as the dog right now. He deserved all the love Ellen could give.

She rested her hand on her face before her pressing motivation to get the shopping done swooshed her away. Her purpose was always present. She always moved forward, no matter what. In a straight line, she continued on her mission. The small bag of chow would last a week or two. She carried it like a load of laundry on her hip, as she had done with Michelle when she was little. She stopped by the cards section looking for twine or string.

She ran by the kid's section. A bin of bats and balls, all in disarray, capped the end of an aisle. The bats jutted out and Ellen almost had to turn sideways to go around the fixture. What kid played with string nowadays? She laughed. Years had passed, but Michelle could've amused herself with string. *Car parts!* She turned to look at the aisle signs. *They would have some there, maybe?* She made a beeline. There in the section's corner she saw Pat pointing at the wall, looking for something, potentially talking to herself, and holding a basket.

Pat genuinely cared for Michelle. Michelle discussed her relationship openly with her occasionally and then at once would flog herself for dishing. Embarrassed, she would slink away, never to admit she spoke of it. Michelle often said she felt guilty about being a distant girlfriend, unsure, and not ready to make the next move. Ellen had seen Pat was timid most of the time, which let Michelle have full control of the relationship.

"Hi, dear. How goes it?" Ellen peeked from behind dog chow and hair products, showing the world her emergency buys.

"Oh, fine—oh, Ellen!" Her nerves showed, and she immediately tucked a basket behind her leg. She looked at the rope, and then at the jumper cables beside them.

Ellen tried to peek around into Pat's basket. A cleaver and knife set had shifted to the side. "Have you seen Michelle lately? I know she misses you, wants to spend more time. She's willing to reserve time for her mother. Find a common ground to talk."

"Oh, it's fine. I know. I'm going to find her later today. You know. I just. I'm going to make some dinner, you know." If Ellen was getting into a deep conversation too quickly, Pat was backing the conversation off. "Meat. Pork chops. Hoping she'll be available." Pat backed off a bit more, the basket still cradled behind her. "It's a tragedy. You know. About your wife—about Jamie. I'm just. I'm sorry."

Ellen thought she saw wetness well in emotional eyes but could've been mistaken. "Oh, thank you, Pat. The events have been so much, really. I'm staying as far away as I can from the mayhem, but we're still married. I don't know how much time needs to go by before we are required to declare her dead, really. There's this feeling. Don't tell Michelle... Or tell her gently. I think she's gone for good this time. Taken the house and all. It's a tragedy, you're right. We've got the one body, and I'm waiting for the second, for Jamie, to turn up at a truck stop, or a back alley, or hanging from somewhere." She paused because she had said it. She knew she thought it twenty times over, but to say the words was different, difficult. "I do love her, still. Oh, my, Pat. I don't want to pile this on you." Actual tears now welled in broken-down eyes. Ellen blinked madly, trying to surface her drowned vision.

Pat dropped her basket and wrapped her arms around Ellen, shampoo, dog chow, and all. The action pulled at some of Ellen's strife. Over her shoulder, Ellen saw masking tape, a carton of milk, and black spray paint. Such an odd assortment. Still, no fewer odd things you could get in this one store.

"Oh, dear. I'm sorry, Pat. I am a wreck, and it came out now. Twine. Twine. I'm looking for string or twine. None here. Oh well. I ought to get home. Tell Mick I said hi and I look forward to him coming over. Maybe we'll have pork chops too on Friday. I have been absent for him as well." Ellen knew she revealed too much with those last words.

Ellen made a beeline for the register, then the car. Her shoes squeaked on the smooth flooring. The squares set together without so much as a gap. A cheaply constructed base made well in a big box store. The place held accessible, cheaply constructed things for the masses. Her kitchen used ceramic tile on the floor. Expensive and well made. Still, a few hard chips dotted the surface here and there. Dropped plates, whether accidents or statements, had made their mark. This cheap tile must've seen hundreds of feet every day, every hour. Her ceramic ten dollars a tile kitchen floors spoke chapters about her relationship with Jamie. Their relationships with others.

Ellen felt faint as she got to the register. She stopped mid-way at the throughway, the store's main drag in a way. People bustled in and out all around her. They all made wide arcs around her as she stood there dumbfounded, needing something to lean on in the fluorescent beating lights. A light sweat broke out. She didn't want to buy the things. The things she found, because she didn't find them all, or because she didn't want them. In an act of indiscretion, she sat right there on the main throughway. Resting a hand on the ground, she then lowered herself to the floor. She pulled her knees to her rib cage and opened her eyes wide to collect herself, assuage the increasing sweat.

The patrons, customers, walked by, continuing on their way. An old man in a brown polyester suit jacket and khaki pants looked down, shuffled to a stop, but then he continued on. No one encouraged her or picked her up by her armpits to move her along. No one, in fact, stopped more than a second or cared. Five minutes passed and she, just as she had come to the spot, lifted herself, palm on the ground, to a vertical position. She dusted her pants and picked up her things. In so much as an instant, she was galloping again on her way to the register. Nothing, nothing at all, had happened.

She relaxed in her heated seats, thinking about how she lost control in the store and dumped on Pat. She would tell Mick. Ellen drifted, wondering whether to get out or take a break from the relationship. What should be on her mind was the car payment she still had to pay, the mortgage now a month in default. She had asked to transfer Michelle's school loans the other week. Her calm and composure rolled down the hill, and the tears welled in her eyes. They now symbolized her future without Jamie, her future survival as a person with a home, a car, and a daughter.

Chapter 22

Michelle got ready for her date at a normal pace. She hadn't seen Pat in over a week. She put time in, but not as much as Pat wanted. Pat called and texted daily. Michelle responded with deadpan conversation, never giving too many details. She wanted her life to be about something other than her ma, but it always seemed to draw back to her.

Since young Michelle's early days with her ma, Ma always took center stage. Ma always complicated things. She did it on purpose every time. Michelle continued to reassure herself Ma would be back. She had to find her way back to the family. True, times would never be the same, but at least she would know they cared. They would never say enough to her about how much they cared, then and now.

Michelle zipped up her hoodie, carefully selected from alongside work clothes, khakis, and button downs. She had conversations every so often about clothes they wore to work. She always wore the same pants and button downs. An occasional tie. Never hammer loops. Michelle reserved hers, held them for weekends and dates like this. She rubbed at her makeup-less face. She certainly didn't know how to show Pat she cared through her clothes choices, her dressing up. A pair of dapper oxfords sat in the corner. They were men's, but not like any other man's, true originals with a navy-blue stripe to make them offbeat, suitable only for her in a big meeting.

Michelle got into her car, turning the ignition intentionally like she usually did. She descended into her head and thought about what she forgot. Every time she did this as a check. Tonight, wine coursed through her body and although she hesitated, her hand still on the keys ready to turn it back, she finally sat back and let the car warm up.

Michelle's car wasn't dirt cheap, but she had bought the vehicle herself. Over twenty-something years old, the car still revved with gusto. She drove a lot back and forth from her apartment, Pat's, because of their burgeoning relationship, and her mom's house. If she had to say, she was at her mothers' houses more often than anywhere else. She felt warm being in her childhood home, while others her age were off on their own, trying to be something. Her remorse grew like vines on a vacant building. She could've done something, changed the trajectory of events. The saddened feelings, the aloneness, without Ma, crushed her. She wanted to remember the good times. She wanted to capture those feelings and memories before they were gone, lost in the shuffle, the moving forward without reflection.

Crosstown traffic collided as people left work. On a Friday night, everyone seemed to be mobile, on the way to a date. Michelle swerved around a truck, who had pulled his turn too close. *They shouldn't allow trucks out on Friday nights. It should be a rule.* They probably had deadlines, needed to fill warehouses for Saturday workers came in or for the start of the workweek on Monday. She couldn't excuse the driver for any other reason.

Friday night was for lovers, in her mind. She saw someone out on a date with the top down, as she passed close to the center city. The date stood up a little in her seat, having the absolute best time. A chill pushed into her cheek, and a tingle started at the base of her spine, making her shiver slightly. She must've been warmed up for a convertible ride. In another instant, she saw another extended SUV come around to the corner, straight from the center of the city. A wedding party. Not necessarily someone who had money, but the passengers likely were having an enjoyable time.

When they spoke on the phone, Michelle and Pat had talked about reaffirming their relationship. That's what Pat had been serious about. She wanted a commitment and a symbol of their love. Pat asked Michelle to bring a physical object, symbolizing they would be together for a long while at least. Michelle got a plant, not flowers, but an itty-bitty cactus. Pat had said often she didn't like flowers because they were a waste of money. After days of work, watering, plant growth, weeding if they were outside, they inevitably died. A better gift didn't exist. Michelle could find no separate way to show she cared, or had planned for the evening and appreciated Pat's company. With her preoccupied mind, this was the best she could do.

"The suspense is more important than the food."

"You can guess by smell."

"I don't have a clue."

Pat lit a candle centrally on the table, bringing light to the otherwise shaded dishes. Only slits of the moonlight cascaded through the windows.

"Oh, we're going to have sex," Michelle said slowly, realizing the low volume of the words as she said them.

Eating in the dim light warmed her veins. The low light stunt rarely surfaced in their relationship. Candles never went with dinner. The finely glazed pork chops with a garlic and scallion sauce sat on the table with green beans baked to perfection. She snipped the ends. She must've taken care at every stage of the cooking process.

Michelle believed Pat intended to be as good as she could be to Michelle. She must've realized the consternation and anguish plaguing Michelle.

They leaned close to the plates and whispered, talking about their day and nothing more. Inevitably they would talk about Mick, Mom, and Ma, and, of course, where Ma went.

"It was a good day, for sure, but I know what you need. You need to know about my ma, the same as me." Michelle could hum about her day in this blissful quiet evening. "The thing is, I don't feel her, her presence, here or abroad, and I'm terrified."

"Honey, I don't know how to put this, but it has preoccupied you." Pat's words stumbled out. "Things won't get better if you dwell on this."

"Are you trying to say I'm not present?" Her anger bubbled and her whole body lifted from the chitchat stance of leaning and sharing about their days.

"I saw your mom today, Ellen. At Parkville's. Shopping. She had all these things, holding onto all this junk." Pat wiped her hair out of her eyes. "She cried with all those things in her hands."

"Well, did you take stuff from her?"

"I hugged her was what I did, because I love her, you." She breathed a long sigh of relief. "This is what I want to do. I want to concentrate on our relationship. Let go of Jamie, of Ma, that's what you need to do for us. She's gone, you see."

"I won't give up hope I will find Ma. That's irrevocable. You can't put my Ma before us."

"I have a feeling, you know. I think, I think well she doesn't want to come back. Returning would be too much trouble."

"I don't know." Michelle took two more bites of food and moved to the kitchen counter to get some water.

"Look. I'm not trying to break up with you. I think you should relax." Pat looked up from her plate of food, also half eaten. "Such a shame for so much care. She could at least let all your minds rest in peace."

She rose and moved toward the center of the open floor plan apartment. Some industrial poles stood in the center. Pat mopped the slick floors once a week and dusted with a wet cloth regularly. She cleaned the windows often and the bathroom always smelled fresh, but not of bleach. It was Pat's place, and she was all but begging Michelle to move in. Instead, they were moving backward. All this drama. Michelle didn't like drama in her otherwise quiet and removed life.

Pat wrapped the pole in the center of the apartment with the rope she bought at the store. The spray paint sat beside the rope. Pat didn't own the apartment, but it was clear she wanted Michelle in her presence, regardless. They both could shack up there, away from Michelle's barren apartment, with its Ikea furniture and some simple decorating. Pat's apartment was even further away, in distance and mindset, from Michelle's childhood home, where she'd been staying religiously for the past week.

Pat's attempt at flirting, at sex one more time before their relationship all blew up, was bombing. The tension pulsed nonstop against Michelle's constant preoccupation. Michelle decided she would go to the woods again tomorrow to look one more time for Jamie's body, for any clues.

"Aww, honey. Your stripper poles."

"No one ever danced at the poles, anyway." Pat ran the rope to the top and pulled the ends into a big knot she could easily remove. "This is a place for love. Look, you know I'm not an interior decorator. And your cactus is nice. Right by the sink it will go. The cactus will never die. The plant is our relationship as well. But I am—this is my act covering up the stripper pole. This will be a place for love, dammit, whether I have to say something symbolic. This is for me and you, if you want this, but I'm looking for something serious." She smiled.

"Yes, honey. Of course. This place is ours. We will be together."

"Don't go up there tomorrow. Don't go to see." Pat's seriousness showed. "I don't want you to find the ghost of your Ma floating around the place. Call the police first."

"But then we'd know, we'd have found her, and she could rest."

"Michelle. You know that's not true. She can only haunt you then. It's not worth it to try. Leave the mystique. She might be in Switzerland. She might be dead." Her words hung in Michelle's ears until Pat quickly scrambled to say, "Either way, she knows deep down you love her. Let the mystery go. It's for the best. Come to me. Let's find our way forward."

They embraced and as Pat turned for the bedroom, Michelle's hand slipped out. Pat continued on her way, Michelle standing back blankly.

She fogged over and saw her ma blankly retreating into a crowd in Switzerland. She would go there, she decided. In one year, she would go there to bring Ma home. If she left, the act was for Ma. If she came home, the return would be for herself. Whatever she was running from would be gone. She could return. They'd go somewhere, the three of them. If Pat would allow it, the three of them.

Underwear flew into the hallway, and Michelle reached for her belt and moved toward the bedroom door.

Chapter 23

Michelle stood in the bedroom's doorway and looked longingly at Pat. She ran her hand lightly up and down the jamb, calming herself. She couldn't separate the fiction in their life. Here was this beautiful woman—and she liked Michelle the person. Michelle more than liked Pat. Her heart beat. She felt the uneven rhythm every time she said her name to someone else. The tension pattered harder when she said sweet things to Pat. The only way to make the pounding stop seemed to thrust herself into this wonderful, beautiful woman. She actually did this a good deal—stood too close, felt her breath, engaged, and asked her to engage.

During the equinox in the spring, they both looked high in the sky, tracing the solar system for stars. Michelle led Pat's arm hand over hand. A glimmer in her eyes twinkled, and she ran her finger along the outline of dots to find an image. They looked up high and at the sky, searching for something—themselves. They loved the stars, but Pat said the words, the sentiment, first, "I hate horoscopes."

"Science. I think we can finally agree on science," Michelle said in the brightness of the dim glow of the sky.

They had been searching the papers for horoscopes and comparing them. They were both Scorpios and had a mission, a vendetta, to prove them wrong. If an online blurb said they were going to find a new friend, they were horrible to everyone. Purposefully, they glared—gave no one the time of day. If the paper said their lucky number was five, six, and eight, they'd play the lottery with every other number. They never won either way. On the fifth day in a row of not winning the lottery, she said those three sometimes cheap words.

"I love you," she said. "Either way, lottery winner or not." She crumpled her ticket from her jacket without checking the paper at midnight when they announced the numbers.

They had stayed up late in bed every night talking about mundane things. The few words they could say about what they'd do with the money: the car, the house, the location. The words flowed smoothly and confidently. They produced an updated version every night. They agreed on what it would be every night—even though they were far from similar.

Here she was, living her fiction again. Her mom, a vindictive soul, likely stewed in her missteps. Michelle could swear her mom's anger overtook her, compelled her to spite Ma. Dating Pat's dad Mick could only be a way to show her daughter they were all a happy family. This was far from true. Michelle felt the utter embarrassment ten times over.

Michelle felt apprehensive. She paused in the doorway and Pat came to meet her. The moment bore down on her. The anxiety, stress bled in her joints, slowing her every move.

"It'll be okay," Pat said.

"I know. But, but—what if she doesn't come back? That's all. I've lost a mother, whether or not she's alive." Michelle sniffed in apathetic to emotion, resolutely dead inside even though the act of dying and grief, her ma's, and hers, never surfaced. She never cried.

The child resorted to desperate measures. They were going to call the police in the morning. Ma had left. With Pat at Michelle's side, they would make a call. It dawned on Michelle that someone had bought their cabin. Jamie couldn't stay there now. A postcard came from Switzerland. The card was only a clue, not an excuse. No one had called the police. After three weeks of mulling, recognizing her mother was an adult and old enough to decide, and then casting her irrational, childlike behavior aside, Michelle recognized she might actually be in trouble. Something might be driving it all, or something could be beyond her control—in Switzerland.

She would call the police and put in a report. If they said they would come by for details, she would return to her apartment. Still, Michelle avoided her apartment. She decided she would much rather be with Pat at her place, in the palace of open space it was. Thick posts dotted the room linearly. More of a warehouse than an apartment, the living space gave off a hollow feel. Spaciously designed, or through a lack of designing, it appealed to Pat and Michelle. The heating system, crucial in the space, regularly blew gallons of air. She couldn't wish she were anywhere else.

With Pat gazing up and down at Michelle and then her phone from across the table, Michelle picked at her food. She wondered if she needed to go to the station to report her ma as a missing person. They might show up at her house. Her neighbors wouldn't take her for a high drama resident. They would wonder about her drug use. She would call them, then go downtown for a follow up, the required follow through. She could arrange the trip. Michelle saved the grits for last. She needed to relish them.

Pat had introduced Michelle to grits. Though originally from the South, she lacked a thick accent. She wore dark colors and clothes too heavy and warm for the weather. She claimed no Southern sports teams and convinced hiring managers she had always lived locally when interviewing for phone jobs as a teenager.

"You sure know how to cook 'em," Michelle said.

"Mick taught me how. That's one thing he's good for." Pat didn't admire or idolize her father the way Michelle did her mother. She was eager to bond, but she muttered about him under her breath. Said she knew his true intentions at any one moment and that was more than she ever wanted to know. She'd said she'd seen it all and shrugged off their awkward parents' dating situation. Everyone needed to get on board, or everyone would break up. A precarious balance started, a teeter-totter that couldn't be tipped. They both hoped things would last.

Michelle had anxiously awaited her grits and eggs. She shoveled them in spoonful by spoonful. The taste overpowered the wrenched gut. The South came through. Her gentleness as she held her eyes, asking if she enjoyed the food. The way she looked back at her while she cooked, never concentrating on the meal, only the person. Her Southern drawl did show sometimes, when they were in bed, when she was half asleep and after sex. She couldn't lose her past in those weak moments.

As Pat cleaned the plate, playing caregiver, Michelle gathered her phone, a pen, and a notepad.

"Hello, I'd like to report a missing person." Michelle leaned into the phone.

"What's your name?" A woman barked routine questions right back at her.

Because of the situational complexity, and because the person at the other end of the phone demanded details, Michelle simply said at home. She bit her tongue on hypothesis and elaboration. The officer was accustomed to emotional pleas. Regardless, she shut down every time Michelle considered elaboration or complication.

"Description."

"Is she married?" the emotionless woman emitted smoothly.

"Well, sort of," Michelle barked back, hoping to meet her lack of compassion on her own level and vocal pitch.

"Separated?" She didn't wait a beat. "Any children?"

"That's me."

"One female." She confirmed the answers.

"How long has she been missing?" she said, with unwavering speech.

"Well, I'm not sure. A few weeks, I guess. Someone saw her a week ago. It's been a while, but we're not sure how long it's been since she left. I guess. She might be on vacation, sort of."

"Listen. If she's on vacation, it's not a missing person. Confirm the person is missing. Call back tomorrow. We'll put you in contact with a detective."

Michelle asked if these questions were typical. Should she talk to a detective?

"Tomorrow. Call us. Confirm the missing date." She was abrupt and short, probably over tasked.

"No, that's about all. One missing Ma." She held the phone and, unexpectedly, the officer didn't hang up.

"Listen. This is what my mother told me when I was a kid, kid. Retrace your steps and you'll find what's missing. Go back over everywhere you, or she, were several days before she left. Trace backwards. If she was last at a bar, go to the bar. Talk to people. That's all I can answer. Retrace your steps."

Michelle could hear her tap a writing implement, pencil or pen, calm and resigned. She'd given the advice one too many times.

Michelle did the total opposite of what the officer said to do. She googled international organizations, finally settling on calling the Embassy of Switzerland in Washington, D.C. They were far from helpful, without even any trite words of advice. Obliviously, they suggested contacting her mother. When Michelle pressed her point, they seemed unable to understand why her mother would run away. Surely, she had planned a trip. Michelle slammed down the phone, resolving they must've thought her younger than she was.

"She will be back." Her voice carried a mocking Swiss accent. "Never fear. We know she will be home soon. Sit tight. What a load of crap." Michelle pictured them with red and white scarves in a sizzling summer in Washington, D.C., sipping cappuccino.

Pat came over to her and wrapped loving arms around her from behind. She swayed foot to foot. Michelle's lips dropped into an exaggerated frown.

"You're trying. That's all you can do."

Pat strode into the room confidently every time. Michelle always tried to be there to welcome her. She was never overconfident but had an honest sincerity ringing when she entered and when she lingered. Like now, she couldn't let go. Something always hung on the tip of her tongue. She would tell you one more thing to make you feel better or be softly honest about what was going on, in their lives, in her stories, in the way she perceived things. Pat was good for Michelle; she kept her balance without ever putting her off.

"I should be more upset. This was important, and the effort got me nowhere." Michelle balled her fists. Pat's continuing tenderness, and that she hadn't yet let Michelle out of her grasp, gave her a shred of hope and cheerfulness. Faced with desperation, still disillusioned, Michelle trusted events would pan out. Maybe her mother would return. Maybe for Christmas or for a hug when she passed through town. She pictured her as a deadbeat ma would appear to a young child. Here she was twenty-four and preoccupied with a postcard depicting Switzerland, hoping her mother hadn't simply moved on with her life without her.

"Where do we go from here?"

"Well, you and me. We're going to continue." An unspoken tension rested upon the both of them at all times. They never talked about the fact they both knew to be true—Mick took her mother's place. Michelle's mom and ma headed for divorce long before "Mick" severed things. A pry bar had divided the family. He only jerked at the opening. One issue might've been the fact Pat and Michelle hooked up before Mick and her mom. Another wrench could've been her mother seemed to have no problem with it. Or the reason might've been Mick was a good guy, good for her mom.

Still, the things unspoken presented an awkwardness, like her parents' impending divorce held for years. The issue drove her parents apart. They couldn't talk about—her mood disorder, her emotional instability, what they sometimes called her bipolar disorder, but only when speaking about the mental state clinically. Everyone shuttered when the words came out, unspoken or spoken in measures, entirely too softly. Everyone misheard. They didn't vocalize travesty that would tear them apart. Now Michelle and Pat felt the stress of something tiptoeing around as well—the awkward pairing of family, no matter how good, was also terribly, terribly wrong.

Chapter 24

Michelle walked briskly through the woods, a little grove they called 'the playground' in her youth. The small patch of land featured a bridge, unique trees and brush, and stones they built into cairns. She returned to this place to find her ma, to finish the damn hike. She stepped high, pulling her knees into the air. That's how everyone had always said to do things as a child. Parents must've discussed the issue after someone's kid fell and sprained his ankle. That must've been the start of the warning. On those summer teenage days when her friends would come with her up to the woods to get away with things, she would watch them. They would drink beer out in the woods. She would always watch to see who would pick up their feet, lift knees high to avoid brush and roots, who would inevitably fall. No one used proper form. Some kid always tumbled to their knees with a half drunken beer buzz.

As an adult, with much longer legs, she still kicked up her knees with extra effort. Her eyes scanned the ground. She had not come down here. *She wasn't finding herself, like she wasn't finding Ma.* She pushed away branches.

She couldn't find a piece of land that looked lived in. Fresh leaves littered the ground and a damp mud barely had prints. She crouched down to touch the mushy substance that would, in fact, take an impression of a sneaker or boot if the shoe stomped squarely on the ground. The slick mud felt like goo between her fingers as she rubbed thumb and index fingers together.

No one ever entered this place down here. Brush covered the entrance to the trail. One-half of a gate, low and ornate, stuck on a rusted post and tilted ten degrees from upright. The white spray paint chipped off, flaked from years of brushing past, of rain, wind, and storm. Where was the other half? What did it once hold? Michelle tore her jeans on the mountain laurel on the side of the entrance, the half of a gate, as she bounded down into the blank canvas of a wilderness.

She doubted Ma would've even come here. Once, when they were on a hike together, a deer passed about one hundred feet away. Ma stood frozen still for minutes, as if waiting for it to double back and charge her. In fact, we could see the breath emitted from the deer's nostrils, the glare in its eyes.

Ma confessed once and explained her occasional terror about being in the woods. She never liked to get turned around. For most people, this is true, but the getting lost manifested a panic attack, an insistent urge to find the end. Ma had recounted a terrible incident from childhood. She had wandered off beyond the family property into the woods. Turned around, she ended up sitting down and crying for hours. Someone eventually found her and scooped her up, tears, damage, and all. She never wanted to be alone in the woods again, but there she felt several weeks had passed with her alone in the woods. History repeated. Michelle witnessed it with her own eyes. More, though hopefully not too much, damage was done this time.

She stopped far enough away from the beaten trail, past the point where she might lose the trail. She looked about her and something seemed off. A moist feeling carried through the air, made her feel clammy and off. Her stomach turned as a slight breeze blew past her face.

The stench pulled through the air towards her. She reflexively knew which way to go. She saw a blur, a guess at a heinous act, before she even saw the corpse. Her steps quickened, and she caught her toe on a branch as she stepped over the obstacle. A stutter step planted her firmly. Did she want to find what she would find? Did her ma kill someone?

The wrinkled skin of the waterlogged body stuck with her the most. Bog bodies, she had heard in archaeology class, avoided decomposition in water under specific conditions. She thought back to the moment in class and the girl who said she would work in a coroner's office and be a coroner once she graduated. At first Michelle had sneered, "Aw, it's just bodies she said, once you removed all the sexuality."

They both loved the bog bodies. From there on out, they perked up whenever the professor talked about death-related things, hitting each other with one-liners after class.

Lisa's body, her delicate features and skin, infatuated Michelle more than her favorite class. The questions she asked herself. Michelle could trace her curves, but not the underlying bones. Her subtle bends and sways made magic. When the professor assigned the class to draw a still image of a femur, identifying the proximal end and its way points, among other things, she saw Lisa. Her curves clouded the dark edges of her paper as she placed pelvis to body, understanding the weight of the bearing when she arched her back in the chair, pulled her hair in a ponytail.

The girl had a much hotter body than Pat, at least in Michelle's youthful and lustful eyes, those often clouded as a kid. But with Pat, whose mind and soul turned her on while she watched, the attraction differed. She gathered her up in her arms and held her with unbending want. Frustration and torment had riddled her relationship with Lisa. With Pat, life subsided, smoothed out, and rolled over. She basked in the easy-going nature they had together and the whimsical dreams they shared.

The task at hand, her goal at the moment, was the occupation of a coroner—viewing a body. Michelle had liked the girl but had a vague sense that the smell of the dead body after a day of work would grate on her if they ever settled down. *Ha*, she thought. How presumptuous. She would've smelled rancid every night. *Humph*, she thought. Her instinct guided her.

Michelle hadn't become an anthropologist. She hadn't gone to far-off countries and hunkered down with indigenous people or even cavorted with transients in Bern, Switzerland. She had paid all this money and took away a sense of kindness for people who are different.

When she entered school, her direction took her to look to be a part of something human to find people and communicate. Naturally, she could get any job with a generic degree. In fact, she hadn't found the right place yet in the office job marketplace, let alone something that utilized her knowledge of the cladistics of Paleolithic technology or a vague understanding of ancient osteology.

What she had come away with included a keener sense of her sexuality and difference and how she could appreciate mankind. Anthropology might've left her feeling a little entitled, if it weren't for her parents who neglected every unique hairstyle in high school or off-the wall girlfriend she brought home in college. They knew she wasn't in a stage. They ignored her actions to stay sane.

Michelle leaned forward at the waist and hovered close to the body. The lifeless piece of flesh hadn't moved for several days by her guess, founded on a bit of classroom learning. The water hadn't eroded or worn away any flesh. She bent over almost as if she thought someone saw her and she would need to explain, not leave a mark. She turned, feeling someone behind her, but when she looked, she didn't see anyone. She turned left with a cold, damp body, only knowing the corpse to be dead and male. The smell leaked into her pores, and she had had enough. Pushing her hands in her pockets in a last effort to remove herself from the situation, she turned and, as quickly as she came, she bolted back up the hill to the mountain laurel gate separating where Ma had been for the past few weeks. Their secret childhood playground in the woods felt strange and familiar all at the same time.

***

Ellen relaxed in the stiff leather seats of the car. Her mouth gaped even after she spoke, and her eyes were wide. While the car stood deathly still, she held onto the steering wheel. She hadn't been called out of work since Michelle threw up all over the water fountain in third grade. She sniffled quietly and couldn't tell her what was wrong. Right now, something was wrong, and the answer eluded them both, a mystery she wouldn't or couldn't unravel.

At this moment and usually, she genuinely looked to Michelle for answers, almost as if she was the adult, the parent. Michelle would steer whatever this was—the emergency. She stretched her back constricted in the car, just as Jamie had every time she came to visit cut off from the open air, freedom.

Michelle met her at the car as she twisted, unsure of what would happen in the next fifteen minutes. "It's just my back. Cramped at work, cramped in the car. It's actually good to be in the woods for once. What is this that is so urgent that is, as you said, 'devastating.' Don't tell me you found Jamie."

Michelle's pale face screamed without words. She'd walked through the arch, down there. Crossed over and saw something. Something that would haunt her for a long time.

"Don't tell me she's dead. My god, Michelle... What is the issue?"

"There's something down there. You must come see it, so I know what I saw is real because honestly, I'm in shock. So many things are running through my head. It might be I'm confused. I don't know. It can't be real. Here on our property. I didn't say on the phone—"

Ellen bounded down the hill after Michelle said nothing more. She implored, asked for hints. What could the thing of contention be? They tromped down along the usual path, and a belabored grin crossed Ellen's face as if blindfolded. She was going to find and open a present. Michelle clenched her teeth and gritted them, dumbstruck serious.

Surprised, Ellen gasped, covered her mouth, and directly turned about to exit the way she came. When she turned to Michelle walking backwards, she egged her to come with her. Michelle gulped a big swig of air. Her eyes bulged as tears welled. She hyperventilated.

Michelle resolutely took a few photos on this, her second visit. Both thoroughly put off by the stench, gagging herself back to reality, Michelle followed Ellen back up the hill. Ellen merely looked at the body and went the other way.

"Who was the man?" Ellen asked. Happy to be involved in anything and, at the same time, somewhat disgusted, she got pulled in and involved at all.

Notions came into Ellen's mind at that moment. They were too involved in their own lives to care about who Jamie was or her difference. But a dead body had lain splayed in front of them, and Ellen, standing next to the corpse, didn't have the faintest idea of who her separated wife had morphed into—what she became under her nose.

"Mom... You don't know she did it."

"But of course, it was her. She... Michelle, I have words for her."

Ellen's anger, the acute, unbalanced hatred, bent up with decades of unspoken words. She didn't see how casual one could construe her remark. Ellen swayed with doubt, but in plain sight, cast blame for the murder of this dead body on Jamie.

For a second, Ellen thought she could forget what she saw. She could leave this old family property and say she never made the trip up. This place became none of her business. Then, she thought of Michelle, calm in her own stupor, occasionally dipping into quiet hyperventilation—still trying to cope, all while wearing a smile. Ellen would need to tell, report the incident. Someone else would find the body. The new property owners couldn't walk the trail without taking in the stench.

She sat in the car and waited. Unsure, they contemplated what the next step would be. Ellen would decide what to do. That's why Michelle had called her. Jamie wouldn't ever get out of jail, Ellen knew that much. She rolled down the window to let out the stench that had seeped into her clothing, but it only wafted in again, now slightly different. She needed to breathe fresh air. The stench, as strong as it was when she was next to the body, lingered in her nose and her exhaled breath. Proclaimed fresh air, some two hundred feet away from where she had found Jamie for months next to a campfire ring, mostly underused, was gone. The outside air couldn't clear the stench.

"I have to tell Mick," Ellen said. "He has to know."

Ellen would pace the kitchen with Michelle in mind, call out to her beyond her range of hearing. Michelle would appear chewing her own fingernails. She had found something to nag about. This happened often when Michelle was a kid.

"Mom, but Pat," Michelle said. She rolled the windows a bit more.

"I can't drive," Ellen said. She paused, chewed, paused. "Mick will need to know."

"You don't even know if she committed the crime." Michelle wore a hard scowl. She held the grimace frankly and long. A reaction, she lashed out at her.

***

Pat couldn't know. She would tell her father. Was their love thicker than blood? Michelle couldn't be sure. She couldn't turn the key on their new house—the house of their dreams unobstructed by fate and the lottery. The last dream they had talked about the night before the crumpled ticket wavered in Michelle's mind.

Pat had said she wanted a small cabin in the woods, something Michelle already had. This would've been their cabin. She would've inherited the place. Here now sold, Michelle stood in someone else's woods. And the woods had a body. The property wouldn't ever be theirs.

In high school, a kid had died by suicide down where the body now lay. They said, "Such a horrible, horrible thing." Michelle had taken part in the grief counseling the school offered. The incident literally hit close to home. She needed the support but felt constricted because she wanted to talk about Ma but couldn't. They talked for her own good. It lifted her spirits, but no one would have agreed with her. She had descended into a heavy black clothes phase. Her image presented a façade. A candy-coated smile hid behind her black eyeliner. She knew though, the phase had helped her identify with other people like her. Other goths who knew they were gay. She came out in her own personal way when the air had cleared, after everyone forgot about the body.

Another body inhabited the woods now. The person might've been thirty or Michelle's age. She couldn't tell. The parts looked male and deformed. This counted as the first time she had seen something like this up close. No one pulled her away. Back in high school, she hadn't gone down to see with the police and her mom. They wouldn't have let her if they tried. Her mom had paced in the kitchen as always, chewing her nails and looking for something to scowl about. Like mother, like daughter.

"Mom, Pat, and me. We don't like that you date Mick. You know that, right?" Michelle said.

"Oh, but we're perfect, honey," she responded.

"I don't think you'll ever know what you're doing to us, but you should."

"Honey, it's not." Mom came to a full stop. "It's true love." She gazed off.

Her mom knew exactly what she was doing. Michelle knew it too.

***

Ellen poked around in the box sitting past the bedroom door. Essentials, mostly. The square held everything she might need. Things she had packed up for Jamie when she left. Ellen had lit a fire. How could she? It was getting old, the fact she camped out in the living room, on that damn chair. But she got up and left. They had a partnership agreement, for Christ's sake. She didn't think she was in love with Mick. As much as she tried to be as they drew apart, the less she turned out to be enamored with his ways, fixing his junk, picking at his teeth with his nails, farts. That was the superficial things. Things that owed themselves to men.

Ellen lifted the carefully folded sets of outfits. Each one she drew together because it was easier to count how many total outfits she provided. Seven. Enough for a week anyway. That's what she thought Jamie mumbled under her breath one day on the recliner. One week away.

The whole thing had gotten out of hand. Mick thought he had fully pushed Jamie out of the way. He thought they would get a divorce. The more she saw Mick push, the more Jamie pushed off, adrift, and the more Ellen thought that's the way it should be.

Jamie wouldn't come back soon. Nor would she likely ever. A few cold years would have to pass until Ellen took another crack at a relationship. Mick would be on the doorstep soon, she could imagine. He appeared immensely confident in his position in her life, almost as if he had blinders on, didn't see reality. Saw it all as perfectly normal.

It must've been she didn't see the box. She didn't see the testament to their love. The care package. Thoughts went along with each outfit. The memories in the plaid flannel sat on top of the time they trekked to the woods, to the waterfall, and hiked all that way. Kissed at the top.

Her towel had been ripped from the bathroom. Jamie probably stowed it away in her canvas bag. Ellen knew exactly which one. She checked the closet to make sure she took the towel. Sure enough, she couldn't find the damn thing. Jamie was traveling. Jamie was in Switzerland instead of those goddamn woods.

Her towel, the one with her monogram, had been in the trash for weeks. Ellen remembered the fabric clearly. The Valentine's Day Jamie bought the set Ellen had gotten dishes. They were really for her, though. It was all their money, both of their money. It mostly came from Jamie, despite how unstable and crazy she could sometimes be.

The towel rested half in and half out of the trash. As Ellen stared at it, she recounted the day she saw it there. She didn't know. She wasn't sure Jamie had been in the house, but she guessed she had come home for a shower. *Why oh why not the cabin shower?* She must have. Must've used Ellen's towel, taken her own and left. The brown lump on the floor was the towel she had used since that day, taken from the hall cabinet. A retired towel, unsavory to everyone, even visitors, who usually cast it aside.

As she walked down the hallway, she tripped over a lone hiking shoe lost in the scuttle to leave. She gazed back to see the box not taken, despite its perfect organization and packing, despite its suitability for travel. Maybe Switzerland required different clothes for a different season. Either way, she would have shoved this and that in, all without making a decent choice.

The hall was long and narrow. Michelle's room was on the right side before the office. Michelle couldn't hear Ellen and Jamie yelling from her room. That's what they always said to each other. "Oh, she can't hear. She doesn't know we fight so much." Despite the muted tones they often used, there were also roars. All out fights. Michelle would never know all of it. She would always be a bit in the dark.

Ellen moved toward the window in the office to see. Maybe to see if Jamie was coming up the road, back from the neighbor's house, back from her escapade. She looked and made her eyes go fuzzy, but no one approached. Love was free. They had agreed on the idea. With life so short, they should never want something else without talking about it, finding a solution, finding a taste.

She scanned the office, the disarray. She had gone through and taken out the incriminating things. Ellen was sure. Was this her taste? Was this what she wanted to know, a criminal life, easy money, the like? They had always agreed they would never pry into the love affairs, let be what was. Despite it all, the criminal intent or not. Whatever Jamie was mixed up in, she didn't want to know. Not at this minute. Not rummaging through her things to find the truth. She wanted words, deserved words. She shuddered and left biting back a yawn.

Chapter 25

When Michelle was young, fifteen, in 2014, young enough to be impressionable, something horrible happened to her ma. The disease got her. It was the age where things stick to you. You know you'll remember. In between the high school parties, still without liquor and drugs, there was an incident. Michelle remembered the incident when the anger rose as she thought about her ma and where she was. She would later turn sad and remorseful for what she had done, what she racked her brain about to absolve. But now, in the moment's anger, she remembered why she hated her.

She drove around at night. The listless mornings turned into listless days and then she had enough energy to drive at all hours in the pitch black. Who knew where she went? She said it was like sleepwalking, but Michelle imagined much worse. In the suburban neighborhood, neighbors would wake. Lights would go on as she started up the car, as the garage door opened, and as she pulled into the driveway. Ma careened on the mountain roads in Michelle's dreams. Decidedly, when she was awake, she settled on that in fact being the best image, the best possible scenario. Michelle's pretty little head, tucked in bed, would wonder about her veering off.

No one could quite put their finger on the word that captured her behavior, her dissatisfaction. While she thought drinking or drugs caused all the problems, the issue was likely her thinking. She wasn't meeting standards at the job, suffered stress, descended into depression. She relaxed for days without looking for employment. Her newspaper sat folded, regularly untouched on the coffee table, unshared. All the chairs around the TV were askew. She sat in the same chair. The juts of her hips became prominent in her slowly thinning body. Michelle had felt the boniness of the hips and winced at the angles and her ma's general state. She could not bear to speak when in her presence. She could not compromise how she would react while drawn into herself, lashing out at night on open roads.

Michelle stayed up late some evenings and watched Ma get in her car, head down. She rustled with things in the back, talked to someone else, someone not there. This behavior was new to Michelle. She swore she would never become her, never run rabid in the heart of the night. Her guesses were someone else's guesses. What she could become would be someone else's pain. That's what she remembered.

When Jamie broke into a late-night restaurant naked and made herself a soda, everything became clear out of necessity. She had slid right over the counter and got a cup. No one bothered her, no one held her down and, as the newspaper recounted, no one told her to stop. People laughed, as they had laughed at Michelle in school. In her general direction, around corners, and in her face.

Michelle's ma naked in the restaurant. They could all see the scene. Michelle felt marred, marked for death—social death. She never entered those house parties at the end of high school. Kids laughed at her in the hall and talked about how she would have mental problems like her mother. They labeled her mentally unstable, despite a track record of teenage normalcy, doomed to be like her mother.

The boys had teased too, almost like girls. They pasted custom made stickers from graphics class on her locker, all kooky faces, crazed eyes, off balance figures—all with the restaurant's emblem lurking somewhere on the image background. The stickers adhered to the locker firmly, and when an authoritative administrative staff member, a secretary, or some other staff member, not the principal, asked her to remove them, she had to tear at them with a tiny pen knife. Strips of the bonding and base layer still plastered her locker when a teacher took the penknife from her without discipline. She had started every school morning looking at the white shredded gooey material for a few seconds. She had opened and then shut the door stone-faced without even a curse.

The cops showed up while Jamie put her clothes back on in the car. They had arrested her and she sat in the back of the car on the way to the station. Then, a psychiatrist ordered an evaluation, and the court required her to see a psychiatrist. The events unfolded in a regimented way, as if everything had happened before. The key points unraveled like the lawyer told Michelle's mom, like Michelle's mom told her. She wouldn't mince words, no talking back, no what ifs from Michelle. She sat still, in the same stupor she had anytime something happened. Many things stuck from there on out. Incidents, emotions, facial expressions. They were all burned in until Michelle had little space left for it, little patience.

Jamie had a bipolar episode. They gave the illness a casual name. When you're up at all hours of the night, though, you do strange things. Michelle would learn about this behavior in college. But a bipolar episode seemed to be more serious, an explanation. She would take that with her wherever she ended up, for safety, for defense.

Luckily her job understood. She was a good worker, valued. They didn't even make her take time off. Instead, they offered her free counseling through the job. Everyone got the feeling it couldn't happen again. This one chance was the last chance.

Jamie had to see a psychiatrist every week, then every month. Michelle found herself more of an adult, always at arm's length. The sleeping pills helped. The mood stabilizer helped. Michelle only found out about these through research, thoroughly rummaging through dresser drawers. She questioned herself every time. She was sure her time would come.

When Jamie started seeing Doctor Prince, the whole family took deep breaths sometimes together, practicing Jamie's breathing exercises with her. The time gave Michelle a hiatus from the tension, the expectation of impending disaster.

Dr. Prince was an awkward man, with an ill-fitting black suit and off-beat tie most days. He swayed from foot to foot. He was slightly overweight, but the bulky suit jackets he wore wouldn't allow a true discernment. Michelle and her mom both remarked he was quirky when others asked about him. Mostly because he constantly clicked on the end of his pen, twirled it twenty times in a row, and balanced it on the end of his finger. Each visit he showed off a new trick. But also because he checked on her mother at the house. He made house calls when her mom was having a panic attack.

"It is odd, isn't it—he shows up here? I mean your ma is a patient and there are offices for patients. That's how it normally is?" Mom paced with arms crossed. Her arm would go up and then right back down, clearly resisting the temptation to put her hand to her mouth. "She could be in a hospital if it's that bad. Right, honey. Would she be better in a hospital?"

Mom would pet Michelle's head, smoothing the hair back and picking up loose strands when she pulled her hand away.

Maybe her ma should've been tucked away in a hospital. It probably would've settled a lot of debates in her ma's head and left them without all the anxious, on-edge suppositions. A deadbeat mom at worst. She handled herself though. She moved along fine as she worked and engaged with others.

Years passed, and she worked herself into recovery. Incidents lessened, and she got a new job, a corporate job. She made good sales at work and Ma twice earned a promotion. Mostly only family had hinting suspicions about Ma's sanity, leftover gouged memories, and anxiety about what could happen and how she could make them feel. Mostly, they were sure her health had improved.

When she lost her job, tables turned again. When she stamped her foot because of who Mom fucked, things got worse. It was the least she could do as she told it.

"Honey, the job wasn't quite right for me." Ma had winked at Mom. Michelle could see her countenance from the family room.

"You know we can't survive without two incomes. We're already overextended," Mom said. She had shuffled utensils around in the kitchen. With a full utensil holder on the counter and a drawer that never closed, Ellen always evened things out.

"Do you want me to be happy?" Ma spoke in a sing-song manner.

"Because I'm with Mick... Jamie, I can't," Mom said.

The day before, Mick had entered the room and all three of them stared at each other for a solid three minutes. Michelle once again sat on the couch. That was her refuge, the only place she could find out what was going on and attach herself to the situation. The yelling, the bickering, the unkind words seeped in.

A sponge, she listened and reacted in silence. Only her face, her arms, her feelings devastated, emoted her genuine reaction. She shifted in her seat, scrunched up her face like the yells were hitting her, and plugged her ears at every opportune moment. The mothers never noticed her anguish. The angst rose and walked out the door with her when the moment presented itself during a lull in the breaking waves.

Mick broke the silence in a happy, almost gleeful mood. He started talking about his day, almost as if he had two wives and none at the same time. He made himself a sandwich and talked about his day, then the weather. Michelle's mothers gawked at each other, waiting for the next person to break the silence. Mom rushed over to find the sports drinks from Mick. She had recently added them to the fridge. Mom never would've bought something like it before.

Ma had doubled back into the family room, as she had done the day before, and sat with Michelle, witnesses to the light squabble. One that would determine their lives from there on out. The divorce started that day. Ma had sat on the couch a certain way for the first time. She wouldn't willingly leave the couch for several months.

"Jamie. Is it over?" Mom asked.

Michelle wanted to know, too. She never raised her voice. In an instant, she got up and left though, so they might discuss and finally produce an answer.

When Ma went up to the woods, after all the weeks that lead up to the departure, the whole family knew something was awry. The separation didn't wreck her. She and Mom had been fighting for years. The cause could've been the way Mom smothered Ma with her anger. That drove her into the woods—to camp. She had wanted the attention and for someone to care. Michelle's mom's words were lackluster, but at least the actions showed she cared.

After Ma left, when Mom cooked, Michelle froze. Anyone in their right mind would leave the room or go out for the evening. The drama will unfold. But she wouldn't leave her mom. Her absence wouldn't have been safe for anyone. Mom's temper tantrums could be as destructive as her ma's behavior. Her voice could kill. Michelle watched every minute until she moved out.

Then her parents started the divorce. The process tore them all apart as a family, but it had been the right thing to do. Michelle knew Ma knew that. She couldn't control her hatred, though, or her resentment. Michelle watched it peel away at them both. When Michelle had left, the stopper lifted, and life formed in the void left by three souls washed away. The lingering efforts of her mother; her stubbornness wouldn't allow her to leave the recliner. Then the vacation to their family cabin had caused her mom to snap back into a woman with blood and vengeance in her eyes, all while a sweet, caring grin pushed forward.

That's what pulled Michelle to the crime scene that day. She couldn't have wanted any more interaction or involvement with her ma. In Michelle's mind, she should want to brush her hands together and call the ordeal over. The only thing left was ruminating. That is, about the mystery, her whereabouts, and the body she left behind.

"Honey, we don't, really... It might not have been her. Right?" Mom muddled the words together, chewing her fingernails. "She, she, was crazy. That's for sure, but it couldn't have been her."

"I don't want to handle this. I don't want to explain," Michelle said.

"No need. Absolutely no need, honey. We sold the house and came back to reminisce. No one knew she was up here. No one knew."

Michelle's mom played the absent wife. Her anger would've overcome her and put her almost ex-wife, the woman who sold their property without her knowing, to the fire. Even she knew, Michelle guessed, it would be a horrible thing for everyone if they suspected her.

"I'm going to call Mick and get him to phone this in. Let's both go, and I'll say you came home. You came home, and we were going to go to dinner, but this thing happened. Mick called the murder in because you were too distraught. That's it. That's what we'll do. Let's not be here for whatever it is they have to do about the gross, degrading body in the center of the woods."

"Are you sure? Rethink that, please," Michelle said.

Ellen let out her breath and paused. Her motherliness came out full force.

"There's no reason we should be here. The woods are a crime scene. Who knows what demented soul did this and is still out there?" She coughed a laugh, likely thinking about her wife, then said, "Remember the suicide up here so many years ago? That's it. Yup. Could've been a copycat. Who knows? It's not something we'll worry about."

Michelle sniffed in and grabbed her nose with her index finger and thumb. "Mom, can we go?"

"Well, get in your car. Follow me. We'll go back to the house first."

More than anything, Michelle wanted her mom to take her back to her house, but then, of course, her car would be at the crime scene. The car would ruin the story. She slipped out of the car, closing the door softly. Someone, she guessed, could hear it and notice them. Why were they trying to clean up her tracks again? When she started her car, her mom was already gone.

Chapter 26

"You're going to have to come out here." The officer's voice sounded muffled over the phone, like he had a chin strap holding his lower jaw to the upper.

He must be tense, Ellen thought. A radio sounded off in the background. He called from his car. Ellen, more than anything, didn't want to be involved. A dead body lay uninvestigated on her old property. The body, a mangled mess, rotted as the cops took their time. Too preoccupied to explain her wife's actions on the property—her quasi-ex-wife—she bowed out of the investigation as best she could as well. They were still married. Is that what she would say? She was, in her opinion, as removed from who she was as the property. Ellen and her daughter had decided they would not talk about Jamie and her spiritual journey near the cabin. She was sure that's what they decided.

"Look, officer. I'm reporting this. It's not our property. You should talk to the homeowners. My daughter was hanging around her childhood woods. A little reminiscing if you will."

"Your daughter should come out here too," he said. "We need to confirm the incident."

"I don't see why this is necessary, officer," she said. She abruptly bit her tongue in a hard stop.

"Ma'am. It's procedure. We need a statement. We'll be over in an hour, if that's more convenient."

"Sure, sure," Ellen said, hoping they wouldn't show up. She planned the conversation over several times in her head. She would say as little as possible because she didn't wish to be involved.

When he showed up, Ellen remarked she had expected him to be the chief.

"A detective, ma'am," he responded. "Not that this case isn't important."

Officer Hillman wore a crisp suit with shiny badges. He navigated the interior of the home with his eyes looking for where he would stand. "I'll come in for a second, if that's okay." He folded his hands and stiffened them at his waist. His demeanor, respectful and plain, painted him a professional. When he entered the house, he removed his hat and ducked in under the threshold.

"Ma'am, what was the circumstance of events?"

"Well, my daughter found a body in the woods, and she called me and told me she found someone down there. Then, I called you. That's the story." She relished the attention but knew to keep things brief. She hoped her desire for the attention didn't overwhelm her desire to keep this to the point and concise.

"I'll need to speak to her, ma'am."

"I'm not sure. I don't think it'd be the best. She's pretty upset." She had all but finished closing the door and she looked at it now, where a crack of bright light showed through.

She paused, took a deep breath, and said above a low roar, "Michelle. An officer is here."

"I don't want to upset anyone. I have a few questions." He took out his notepad and jotted down a few brief notes.

***

Michelle was, in fact, at the top of the stairs. She had been listening, but she did not agree with everything her mother said. She balked at the deception, the need to not wake up the neighbors. *What would people say?*

"Hi. I'm Michelle," she said, reaching out to shake his hand.

"Hello," he said and looked back down at his notes. "How did you come about finding the body up on Wright Mountain?"

"Well. I was hiking. Like my mom said. I went up to walk around my old stomping ground, you know. I hike every Saturday or Sunday and I wanted to hike around the old property, you know. It's where we grew up. Then I came across the body, and I screamed. I called my mom, and she came out to see what I found. Then, we came home and called the police straightaway. That's it, really." She finished and scrunched up her face in a way asking the officer if her statement was okay. "The whole... This is extremely strange. Do the police have any ideas about what is going on?"

"It's too early to tell."

"Mrs. Richmond."

"Yes," Mom answered with wide eyes.

Michelle's concise description poignantly differed from the plan she and her mom made up on the hill. Michelle decided, made it simple.

"You were at the crime scene too," he said. His gaze stayed on Michelle's mom. When hers dropped, he looked back down at the paper.

"Well. I went up to get my daughter. The story isn't mine to tell, but yes. I made the trip up there to comfort her. I guess I walked to see the body to confirm, and then, well, we chatted in the car a bit. Then, we came back here. My daughter needed some soup. She needed to rest."

"Mom," Michelle said in one loud tone.

He flipped the cover back onto his notepad and put it in his front chest pocket. "Thank you both. I'll let myself out."

His emotionless gloss left Michelle's mom worrisome, and she grabbed at her lips with her teeth.

"Look, honey." She turned to meet her daughter and glared at her. "Not that we had to lie. It's easier if we don't get involved. Let's keep the family at a distance. That's not our property anymore. Well, the owners could come after you for trespassing."

"If they have questions. I'm going to answer them, mom." Her stare did not move. She scratched her head without losing the tension of the moment. "You can't lie. If she did it, she did it. There's no reason to not cooperate. She's my ma, yeah." She sniffed. "Your ex-everything." Her emphasis rested on the 'ex.' "Don't ask me. If you're going to ask a favor, don't ask me."

Michelle gathered up her coat and backpack. This rest, pit-stop, on a bumpy day, she made for her mother had been her way of coping, to disengage, and helped her get through events. But Mom had attempted to confound things all the time. She added to the difficulty of any situation.

Michelle remembered the scene, the little burrow, even the arch she had ducked through to get down to the stream. The entrance had been demarcated with half of a gate seemingly as old as the landscape, set against the far right-hand side of the lot, near a grove, wall, of mountain laurel. Wholly impassable, the bush cascaded throughout the area. *The gate was put in after the mountain laurel took over to tame it.*

She remembered she and Ma had arched and woven branches together with twine to create a more formal entry, utilizing the gate. One that was theirs, real and fabricated. The branches ended up growing into the arch. Although the string deteriorated, the trees kept a distinct threshold, a magical entrance to the woods, the playground. Still the half of a gate stood. Michelle had entered the woods on her reminiscing hike, the hike to find Ma, through the archway. The path had originally been so clear. The branches now scratched her and extended in all directions, but the imprint of the entrance remained distinct. It could be no other passage. Both Ma and Michelle had known this entrance. Few others did.

When she had come upon the clearing, she stutter-stepped down to the stream. The refreshing waterway in the summer appeared muckier and icier in fall. Ma might have bathed there while she camped at the cabin. The current might have pulled Ma under if she didn't brace herself. It would've been chilly. She could've gone into shock. All these things could've happened. What Michelle could not decide was how she should notify the police, how she would relay the story of her Ma and where she could be.

She had approached a slight bump in the bank. The body extended flat, still, as water slowly coasted around the outline. Half in and half out, the corpse rested lightly, though it didn't buoy. The mass stuck in one place, somewhat caught by the jutting ground.

Michelle had tried to build a dock, a dirt pier, so to speak, as a child. She thought she could build a pier herself. With a garden shovel and bucket, she spent a full day filling the bucket, dumping soil on the bank. Some of the dirt had rushed quickly away. She had sculpted the peninsula in the water, pulling fill and placing soil in a three-foot-wide swath. The land would never quite be the same. After all these years, the bump in the landscape had turned meaningless.

Their times together down here, Ma and Michelle had been quiet, and their heads had shifted, and they had thought, neither extending their opinions or fears with each other. Tight-lipped, they had continued to wander alone.

Mom never went down by the stream. She repeated that the swarms of mosquitoes in summer and the thick mossy goop were a bit primitive. At least, as a child, Michelle had never seen her go down there. She would come to the entrance and call for dinner or time to come in, but she never ventured past the arch. Michelle never saw her do it.

Then when Michelle found it, Mom had confidently stridden, listening and not speaking. Something serious occurred in the woods and they had descended to check on the body. She had known right where to duck under the brush at the open gate. Unexpectedly to Michelle, she had, in one sharp move, pushed the brush out of the way, not a true woodswoman, but a woman who might have gone hiking and seen a few skinned knees and knew how to handle the land.

"Mom, have you ever been out to the stream?" Michelle asked.

"Oh, rarely honey. Very rarely." Mom turned to step out of the chill in the room.

When Mick rolled in through the door, his presence relayed he had returned home for good. He stopped inside the doormat, dumbstruck, and pushing his gut out, waiting as if asking if he had to take off his shoes. He gave them a healthy smile, looked left at Michelle, and then beamed right at Mom.

"Honey, did you lose this?" He held up a bright necklace. The jewelry glistened the same as the one she lost two years ago. Michelle had bought it for her.

"Where did you get that?" she asked, cooing.

"It doesn't matter. It's here now." He handed the jewelry to her with pouty, twinkling eyes.

"You bought this? The thing looks like one I had years ago. Oh, I told you about the necklace the other week. You did…"

"Where I got the thing doesn't matter. It's home now, honey. I found it for you." He kissed her sweetly on the cheek and headed for his chair. "Hi Michelle," he said with a rhythmic downbeat. "Anything new going on?"

The stifling air made Michelle choke. Michelle didn't want to get involved with this thing. What was going on with her mom and this guy who now tried to take over her ma's old recliner chair? "Oh, you know, the regular." She would leave it to her mom.

"You sure you're okay? You sound a bit off."

Mom reacted to Michelle's attitude on Mick's behalf, which was typical. She would send an obstructive phrase in her direction when she didn't like how she approached her. Michelle suggested her mom see a therapist several weeks ago. Her mom latched on to the idea, and Michelle encouraged her more strongly. Michelle wondered herself, until this happened. Someone else needed a therapist now. Ma was actually quite adjusted. *She did yoga for Christ's sake. That time, that retreat she had tried, hadn't she?*

Chapter 27

Michelle sat in the same porch chair staring out, dreaming about a full year before. When she waited after school for her ma to come home from work, she found different rhythms in the way she swung her feet back and forth, separate, together, offbeat. She made them match the songs she learned for piano lessons, age nine through thirteen.

When she came home from college, she would sit in this spot and read. While she read, Ma would show up, surfacing from the bed on Saturday morning and come out and chat. Or she would come home late from work and stop making time. Michelle would be out on the porch, book in hand. Ma yawned widely, covering her mouth late. She always seemed tired. *She worked hard.*

Now, the autumn wind blew in and brought through all the old memories. The cars out front zoomed by at a normal pace. No screeching, peel-outs, or drunk crashes. Only the quiet streets of a suburban home. In this same place, all the noise occurred behind closed doors. Michelle took to the porch. The "noise," the cars, sounded softer than the clattering of pans shaken in malice and the issued words meant to startle and injure.

This dreamland neighborhood, susceptible to dysfunctional family syndrome, plagued them. The neighbors may have heard in their castle only one hundred feet parallel and incorporated the drama and sounds of the neighbors into their own culture of family. Michelle heard their fights clearly, the same as her own parents. Was it truly the suburban disease?

When Michelle had left for college, she recalled the anger, an octave one too high. Her city campus apartment bustled with cars, but she hadn't even noticed. Traffic didn't bother her now; she decided this was because she spent years of her youth sitting on the porch listening to muted hums from pleasant, polite cars. The quiet scenery drilled calmness into her head, so the raucous noise of the city didn't overly jar her or even exist. Yet, in the back of her head, the unwieldy clatter of mothers arguing stayed. She couldn't close her eyes without remembering the yelling and arguments.

The breeze gushed by on the Thursday they left for the yoga retreat the first week of Michelle's two-week annual leave break. Michelle put her packed bags on the porch steps. The impending rain made Michelle nervous. She had the constant feeling rain would pour down and drench her bags. She teetered on the edge of her seat, ready to go to the car.

Ma showed up and plopped down next to her in the free chair. She sipped at a Long Island Iced Tea. She said she needed the drink this time. The alcohol wouldn't affect her driving.

"I'll drive," Michelle said. "I think we better get going soon, though." She got up and got herself ready at a canter pace.

Ma didn't want to leave. The sun turned the corner on an exhausting day, and she wanted to relax. Yoga would be much better if she were calm.

"We're doing this. You will find focus," Michelle cooed.

"Focus-shomocus," her ma popped back. "You want me to be nice to mom."

"We're doing this together."

"She just… Michelle… She demands too much. If I'm honest, she's the one at fault. She's the one who has the temper."

"Ma, you have a temper. Admit it."

"I. I just—"

"Admit it now."

"Well, we have been fighting more. I like to think I can strike a few words that hit a nerve."

They careened down the road. Ma's hand extended out the window, swishing up and down in the wind. With the top pulled down, she raised her head, and the gusts pushed her cropped hair back. She said, "meditation," and the words rumbled out into the air, the wind distorting vibrations and tone.

"Why does meditation have to be silent?" Ma asked intonating like a child talking to an adult.

Matter-of-factly, Michelle responded, "I don't know. I guess you have to find quiet. That's the first step. And then feel what is around you. Oh, Ma, we'll learn in the classes."

"And yoga is… like… you have to be quiet to concentrate. The things seem opposite really. You find concentration in yoga, but your mind wanders in meditation."

"Maybe it's a combination that makes yoga and meditation great when paired together. I don't know. Like I said. We'll see." Michelle stomped on the gas and a great energy rose in her body, a gleaming grin. The happiness was entirely for her Ma. "Let the breath out now, Ma."

Ma took her cue, screaming at first, plain yelling. The vibration vibrated everything around them. A reserved yell, held back a little, came through, clear and high-pitched. Michelle smiled on.

"I love life." After the choppy words, Ma had nothing else to say.

Several hours later, of singing along to eighties music and having philosophical muses about the practices of yoga and meditation, they arrived at the retreat ready to unpack bags and rest.

A peculiar man greeted them, bobbing his head from side to side. He bowed instead of shook hands and extended himself with a gracious smile. He spoke in brief curt sentences, and he jumped in the car and showed them to their parking space. Then he moved with them as they carried their own bags toward the housing.

Ma's goals for the yoga retreat were to practice calmness, think about how to react appropriately around her wife, and learn to be present in conversations with her daughter. When they led the way to her apartment, which wasn't more than a college dorm room, they asked her to recite her goals. She knew them because they were her homework. She and Michelle had gone over them. After she had prefaced the recitation with details about her failing memory, the yogi simply cut her off, nodded, and then continued on his way. She never recited the goals.

"Trying to be quiet this weekend. This is for reflection."

Michelle's ma never stated her goals to the yogi. The clamor inside her must've been too much. The yogi could probably feel the destructive energy. Michelle could feel the negativity.

Michelle chimed in with her goals. "Find time for family, listen for true feelings for my partner, and bond with my mothers." She set herself to getting her mother the help she needed, urging her along, but she had a few things to work on by herself too.

She lost her words. Michelle said them, but they felt empty. She held her mother's goals much closer; those were also hers. She had eyed her every so often during the car ride, glancing at her out of the corner of her eyes. Now here, she tried to keep the same bead on Ma as she drifted, moved beyond vision and looked dramatically away from her. She couldn't see, as often as she tried, if Ma was being sincere.

***

Days before the retreat, Michelle had come home to a fight. Ma had been drinking a similar Long Island Iced Tea. Michelle liked to think each one tasted little stronger than the other, the sole drink she drank the day of the retreat.

Michelle's ma had hovered in a corner, trapped logistically and emotionally. She had braced her arms against the armrests of the recliner for support. She had cowered with her responses. The incident had truly shaken her. Broken dishes were all over the floor.

Someone had lashed out. Michelle understood her ma, understood she couldn't move for many reasons. They had to work out the tension. Sudden movement might set her off. She had lurched.

When Michelle had entered, her ma's voice audibly had cracked, and she sat like a dog commanded by its owner in the kitchen side chair. Michelle's mouth had gaped. She did not move, but that had not even conveyed the deep concern she had in the moment.

"You always think the wife throws the dishes. I mean, in the TV shows, the woman is always throwing the dishes," Michelle had said. Ma had cowered at the words she spoke. She didn't mean to make a joke, but the humor was all she could give rather than black out of the moment.

"Look, honey," her ma had piped. Mom had sat stiff in an electric chair pose across the open room.

"Well. You all have some explaining. But I'm not sure it's to me." She stalled. If she were ten years younger, she would run and banish herself to her room. But she was an adult. More adult than her parents at the moment. The only one not having a tantrum.

"Look, honey, there's no bruises," her mom whined, supportive of her ma.

"Well, I would hope you wouldn't defend Ma's actions, her episode." She said the last words with emphasis. She meant them. However much Ma's disorder was a disability, when her emotions directly affected her mom in this way, the effect was bad for them all, especially her. "You can't enable her. It's co-dependent."

"Honey, you don't understand..."

The words became Michelle's adult cue to go to her room. The role-reversal flip came back to her.

***

They were at this retreat quietly burying or silently working to correct the things she had done. How would Michelle know? How would she confirm to her mother? Silence solved nothing really, did it? The loud protests of the age brought down change. They were family secrets, not entirely secret to the neighbors or the trash collectors that emptied sets of dishes into their truck. Loud, raucousness caused this. Her ma's behavior and her many erratic moods, each a different shadowy figure, had spread turmoil through the family unit. Quiet relaxation had to kill it all.

As they ate breakfast, yogurt with granola, her ma's favorite at home too, they nodded hello to the person across from them. He gave an arching wave back.

"Here for the women?" her ma spit out, giggling and choking on her yogurt.

"No. Here for lower decibels," he said, full and proud. "Money well spent."

"You've been here a while?"

"Yeah, three weeks," the man said.

"My wife did this to me unbelievably. I'm a little touch and go sometimes. I tend to overreact."

"Ma! he's not your psychiatrist," Michelle said everything almost as one word.

"It's fine," the man said. "'What are you in here for?' is a common conversation starter for some reason this year." He chewed his food and paused. "I'm a health nut. Raw food eater. I moved out west years ago, but I come back to see family and go on this retreat once a year. I met my wife here."

"Oh," Michelle's ma said.

"Cancer. I mean, that's why she's not here. She died." He sighed and set his eyes back into his bowl.

Michelle's mother broke many rules. If she knew what the rules were, she broke them. If she didn't, somehow someone had to remind her not to do something. They were here for quiet introspection, and she became best friends with the health nut. Pretty soon, they'd take off for the bar, or at least a juice bar, considering the guy.

Ma always rubbed against the grain with the force of her being. She teetered on always saying the wrong this, or doing the wrong that, or broaching the wrong subject. Religiously, she ended up turning the other direction when something wrong happened, assuming people would forgive her. Michelle always forgave her. Mom always forgave her.

Chapter 28

"I can't see anything in this brush area over here, but maybe?"

"Check everywhere. Get a stick if you have to."

Mick took a long stick from the ground a few feet away and rustled the branch halfheartedly in the bushes. "I don't mind helping, but I'm not sure she's up here. There's the postcard for one thing. She's not here anymore. She fled—er uh, moved on. However you want to look at the crime."

"Well. This is routine Mick. You must know. We do appreciate the help."

"I think I saw her come out to the woods. As far as I could tell, she stayed at that campsite, but the cool water rushed around the corner. She must've come down here. I saw her with some wood for the fire. Likely got it down here."

"Good. That's good. If anything is awry, it will be much more important." The officer left Mick to talk to some other people and the dog handler.

They had removed the body almost at once, probably took the usual photos and swabs. They mimed the crime scene activities at the absolute least. But they made the investigation quick. They wrapped up their work and an additional search started at once. Mick offered to help. He dated the suspect's wife, and they were all somewhat close, but the police disregarded the information—in favor of justice, he supposed.

Ellen was a wreck. He had seen her hours before. An effort to keep his distance from her was about the least he could do. She was erratic and easily put off, subsuming Jamie's moodiness. Mick gathered as much of the complaint as he could. They were still married and bound in many ways.

Mick saw an officer hovering a piece of shirt over the dog's nose. When they sent the dogs out, everyone stopped. The quiet place only let in the rustle of paws. They all listened for the key to a mystery. Maybe they were linked. Maybe Jamie killed that man, Rich, they said his name was, and she fled. The possibility existed, too, that they were both casualties. Mick waited for the dogs to turn up another body. That's where his bets rested as he recounted his thoughts meekly to the officers.

When the dogs didn't turn up any scents, when they moseyed back to their handlers for a treat, the search ceased, and the police officers huddled up out of Mick's earshot.

An officer moved toward Mick in earnest.

"You going to pat me down Officer Pete, is that it?"

"Yeah, Pete. No, Mick, we have to evaluate what's going on here. You were up here when she was up here, right?"

Mick knew Pete from the shop. He came in like several local police officers for Mick's mechanics to work on his personal car. Mick and Pete had chatted each time he came in. They had chatted quite frequently.

"Yeah," he leaned in, "I mean, women don't kill people, do they—often. It's less likely."

"We're not ruling anything out, Mick, that's for sure."

"She was alright? I mean, she had problems, right? If she were a child, you'd call her troubled, right?"

The property owners kept their distance. The man held his arms around the woman. They stared out at the distance; the people combed the place. Occasionally, the man would whisper in the woman's ear and hold onto her, give her a tight pull at the waist.

"What were they doing all the while?" Mick asked, eyebrow raised.

When the officer went over to the couple, Mick stayed out of reach, close enough to hear.

"Edward. Hi. It's a pleasure to meet you."

"Hello," the officer said. "A few questions, if you don't mind." He opened his notepad and reached for his pen from a front chest pocket.

"What was that woman doing out here?"

"I was going to ask you the same thing." The officer continued searching for his pen to no avail while the other officers gazed up now and then to look at the officer and the couple whose property they were searching. The couple at present remained unshackled.

"We come up here a lot to explore. But, really,"—Edward's eyes were imploring—"we only came up on weekends. Well, we took a few days to get settled, move stuff in. We're... Well, we might need another a week to get things in order."

"I see." The officer held his hands in a fist below his waist, leaning in every so often. He replaced the pad in his chest pocket, the pen lost.

"We came up here a good bit to hike. We were looking for a cabin."

The woman pulled at her cuticles with her thumb. "She was kind of off."

"Honey. Let me," Edward continued. "She camped outside, but when we bought the house, not much was wrong with the site. She had a few contractors take a day to fix up some windows, but that was the only problem. Strange she camped out here. I mean, everyone loves to camp, but she had a cabin right there."

"That's all we wanted was a cabin." Edward bowed in apologizing to his wife. "Look, it's none of our business. She sold us this house. The place is ours now. Paid for in full. She was a pleasant woman, really. She left a week or so ago when the sale finalized." He bobbed, nodding his head up and down.

"Well, I can see you're a wholesome couple. Too good, really. I can tell you're good people. But you didn't see anything?"

"Not really. I mean, you can't see from here really, right? The brush is fairly thick. You can see over there in the field where they are now, but not past the mountain laurel back there. I mean. We didn't know. We have plans to explore, but we're worried about the cabin right now."

The officer returned to Mick, caught listening. His preoccupation, his cover for listening with an acute ear, had included eyeing his phone. His eyes darted here and there, while others combed the area. Mick turned to greet the officer as he approached.

"How many times did you come up here?" the officer asked.

"About four. I dropped off food. She was always in the same place. Warming the spot, I suppose. I mean, you find a comfy spot on the ground. I guess that's the best you're getting, you know?"

"Why didn't she go in the cabin?"

"I don't know. We all thought the cabin was in some kind of disrepair. She didn't want to, I guess. The house needed some work for sure. You know, the place needed to be winterized. I think they winterized it." He cupped his hands in a mocking gesture of whispering and said, "She probably wanted to camp out. I mean, people like to camp out, right? Why not?"

"This is a little irregular, Mick, and you know it." The officer stretched his back and twisted his torso. "Thank you for your help here today. We'll be in touch—as we get information, of course. We'll be in touch with the spouse."

Mick drew down over the hill towards his car. The police and a few civilians, helpers, continued to comb the area. He got in his forest-green convertible, its soft top up. Not quite camouflaged in the surroundings, he revved his engine. Then he was off.

Chapter 29

"Mr... Dr. Prince. You were at the location of the crime, correct?" The officer tapped his hands on the door molding next to the doorbell camera.

"Yes, of course, come in officer." Dr. Prince held the door open as the police officer entered. Dr. Prince's wife was in the kitchen. The officer looked past him, and he assumed his wife had caught the man's attention.

"She knows when it's business. She'd rather not get involved." His tone changed to a lighter, airy quality. "I guess she is sick of all this drama. This death somehow is connected to me. I mean, Jamie was my patient. People might see me as partially responsible. Is that what you all see, officer?" His voice lifted lightly, inquisitively.

Dr. Prince showed the officer who smiled meekly to the living area. He showed the officer in a crisp laundered uniform to one of the two short guest couches. The officer remained standing as Dr. Prince eased into his preferred couch further away. He tilted his head up in an introspective glance, still awaiting an answer to his question. The officer held his knees stiff.

"We don't have any hard and fast suspects at present." The officer tapped his pen on the pad, just as he had on the door frame before he entered.

"It's doctor patient confidentiality, you know. We can't divulge, so to speak, the details of the patient. We can't extrapolate on their condition in any way."

"I see. But if the patient is dead?"

Dr. Prince shook his head.

"Well, tell me about when you visited the site at least. When you went to the cabin. The date. You went to visit Jamie Richmond there. We're interested in Jamie... Jamie Richmond... and finding her."

"It was a month ago to the day. I've been thinking every day about the patient's condition. About what she is capable of, but I cannot tell you anything about her behavior. Let's say the behavior is erratic. That's all—I can't say."

"What were you doing at the site?"

"Checking up on a patient, really. Giving her the talk. When a doctor is needed, they are most certainly needed. This is hard for us all. I should check on Ellen. Have you talked to her yet?"

"We're going to see her next."

"Well, tell her I'll be over then." The tightness in his cheeks dissolved with the officer's expression of surprise. "She needs someone to talk to. Of course, I'll bring any evidence to you, but I need to communicate with Ellen, you see. She is probably hurting."

"Is there anything you can tell us, Dr. Prince? Any telltale signs about the suspect. Something that would let us know where she is, or where she is going. What she might do next?"

"Officer, really. Have I seen you before?" Dr. Prince adjusted his butt in the seat. "No. I mean, she was a patient. Erratic, yes. You've seen behavior. I can't say she ever told me about killing someone, but—" Dr. Prince looked down and scratched his knee cap. "I don't know. They say she's in Switzerland. That's what I believe, I guess. She hasn't contacted me, that's for sure." He bit his lip viciously.

Dr. Prince drew the officer to the door. He moved swiftly, without compassion. The officer's solid and stern chin revealed nothing, but the wink he gave Dr. Prince as he left told them both much more.

"Dr. Prince. Let us know if you leave the area. Okay?" The officer turned to leave and let himself out, shutting the door behind him. Dr. Prince watched him go.

Chapter 30

Ellen restlessly pushed the vacuum around the room. She wanted to find Jamie but, at the same time, she didn't. There would be many questions, many airings, and few answers. She knew Jamie couldn't handle the questioning. Ellen couldn't manage much. The feelings she had for Jamie compounded. Ellen needed Jamie to get through this, though she knew they couldn't handle the situation together.

She finally got a much-needed break from Mick. Being super busy, as he told it, she let him go. Let him think he didn't have time for her. But Ellen felt fed up, sick of him, all his pompous statements and overt boldness. Finally free and finally stuck.

"Listen, I don't know where she is," Ellen said. "I don't care, in fact, but if you want me to pretend like I care for you, I will. Is that what you want me to say?"

Ellen wanted to know everything that had happened up on the hill, by the cabin, in the clearing beyond the brush. Mick didn't have any business up there, in Ellen's opinion.

"It would be in your best interest if you cooperate with the cops," Mick said.

"Right. I know. All is well. We weren't getting along. And she is, well, impulsive."

"Others have mentioned she has bipolar disorder. They won't discount that, this incident, even if she is. It's important we get to the root of the crime. The cops need to know."

"Couldn't he, the victim, have fallen or something?" She was impatient and way too loose with words, considering she was among the people being questioned. A suspect or, at the least, a person with information. "She was erratic. That's what I know. What did you say exactly? To the cops?" Ellen was as impatient as she got, as impatient as if Jamie were in the room and they were ready to fight.

"I saw her up at her campsite, by our cabin... which sold somehow." Mick's voice became louder and more pronounced. "She lived outside our freaking cabin, for Christ's sake." Her mouth gaped open. He added, "You know—wouldn't take a shower."

"Are you saying you think she murdered that guy, then?" Ellen covered the phone, pursed her lips, and held in a tight breath.

"Do you?"

"No, no. Absolutely not. She was emotional, but relatively harmless, unless the death was partially an accident. Most people with mental illness are relatively harmless, unless pushed and shoved. They don't mean to be themselves, have their illness. Jamie was no exception. She was embarrassed of it all." Ellen was firm with these words and these words alone. "Did you say she left the cabin ever? What did you say about her mental state?"

Ellen moved to the couch. The same lumpy couch everyone refused to sit on. Jamie had slept on the cushions many times before she lost her job. The family all avoided the room out of awkwardness. Someone would inevitably have to sit on the lumpy couch. They all looked out for each other. Their last bit of kindness reserved for deep depression. That's what Ellen told herself as she sat there on the phone with Mick, trying to decipher many things.

"The campsite. Hardly. Not that I know. She always said she was going to do this or that, but then everyone said she never did. She had a makeshift tent blow down in powerful gusts, a sleeping bag, and dry food for the time she spent up there. The vacation hardly counts as camping. More like vagrancy."

"The cops are going to do what they are going to do. But if she shows on her face... Comes back from Switzerland or wherever the hell she is... she will have a lot of questions to answer. She is likely the prime suspect—but I couldn't say."

"Mick! You know she didn't do it. You have to know... You know who did it. I'm sure of that." Ellen hung up the phone.

Chapter 31

When they pulled the body out of the water, pulled the mass out of the woods, Michelle knew something serious was happening. The events, what they were calling a murder, most definitely involved her mother. She conjured up these preconceptions alongside images of her ma naked in the darkest moments of the night, mixing orange juice and milk. The medication had changed her sleep pattern. She sleepwalked, restless, every night at best.

Jamie had recounted the time she opened the door and let the dog out. She swooshed him even, saying he needed to be free. Was the dog safe with her? Was anyone safe with her? Those questions had plagued Michelle and as she reflected, she was embarrassed she had even had the thought. There was much more she could have done to help. Talking, bonding, even helping her seek treatment. They were all things she could have done. The guilt bubbled as she knew it had after the fact, in a lucid Jamie.

The police officer showed up at Michelle's door, entered slowly, and scraped his boots across the doormat politely. He entered with a big step over the threshold to a house usually in disarray. Today was no exception. Blankets from the night before floated across the furniture. Michelle had taken to sleeping in her ma's recliner, gripping the arms every night, as she imagined she was hugging her mother.

The cop, in the freshly laundered uniform, dropped his hat to acknowledge her and sat, unprompted, to ask his questions. He had no room for small talk. Michelle gathered he had been through this before, though she had not. She approached the situation with caution. The cop might think she was also involved, or she was an accessory or not trustworthy and covering for someone who could only be seen as a victim of mental illness.

"One more time, ma'am." He coughed directly after what could only be seen as a statement of why he was here. "Why were you"—he cleared his throat again—"in the woods that was not your property? Were you looking for Jamie Richmond?"

"Well, sir,"—she tried to put the snideness aside—"I was looking for my mother. She suffers from some depression and takes to camping out on the property." Michelle looked down, already realizing she said too much, and much more had to be said. "She, well, the property sold, and we reported her as a missing person."

"The same day of the report of the body, correct?" He tipped his hat up a bit.

"Yes, the same day," Michelle said. She tried to be short without being rude.

"Hmm, Okay. It was private property at that point, but you were looking for your mother." He sheepishly lifted his head.

"It's hard to remember your childhood sometimes, but you should always revisit it, you know. I went to the property, our old property, to look for my ma, mother. I thought she might be there, you know, reminiscing. We hadn't seen her in a bit at that point."

The officer continued to discuss the timeline of her events, and where she had been in the weeks her ma was missing. Why did she pick that time of day? She accounted for the night at her girlfriend's and told him about the call and then her outing to what would be the site of the crime.

"Or the site of crime, I guess," she relayed. "I love my girlfriend, but she didn't need to come to the woods and watch me get all sappy." The officer relaxed as Michelle gave detailed information. She ran her fingers through her hair, trying to show her charm but not wanting the cop to get the wrong idea. "I packed a lunch, really... Oh, you know, I think it's still at my mom's house, Ellen's, well I mean Jamie's too, but... I never ate the food. The peanut butter sandwich, coke, and carrots are likely still in this small multi-color bag. It's mostly greens and oranges." Michelle took a breath and bent her head sideways.

"Did you know any people who would want to harm Jamie or who didn't like your family?" The officer was unfazed by Michelle's retelling.

"Welp. Nope. No. Can't say."

"Well, I hope you could say..."

"No—Sincerely, I don't know."

He wanted to know the time of the incident and even what she had for breakfast.

"Eggs and grits... if you care." She shrugged. "And 3:38pm or so."

"Exactly."

"No. I mean, when we called. The time was right after I—well, I called my mom and then she..."

"Was the sandwich made at your apartment or this house?"

She strained, smiling meekly with a cockeyed eyebrow, saying, does this matter? He got it.

"Answer," the officer said.

"My girlfriend's. I said I was at my girlfriends," Michelle's impatience increased.

"How many days was it until you realized she was missing?" The words bit into her. The police officer sat awkwardly on the couch, a place for relaxing. His stiff, oversize, polished presence hung over the worn and lived-in couch, at the end of the cushion. He bent over to look closely at his notes.

"A week or so." It had been almost three.

"So, you didn't know where she was for a week? And reminiscing made you go look?" He crossed out some words on the pad. "The property owners don't want you up there again. They're incredibly stressed out, you see."

"Do you have any leads on my ma?" She almost didn't want him to have any information. Whatever it was would be bad. She was dead—bad. She was still missing—bad. The police wanted her for murder—unbelievably bad. She likely would be under investigation.

"No ma'am. I'm sorry. We were hoping some new information would surface on your end. I will say that, if you find her, we will want to do some questioning. She should come down to the station right away."

"Hey, I heard some witchcraft took place up there. One of my friends from high school said some locals would go up there. I guess they would be my age, and they cast spells and things. Maybe cut up animals?" Michelle introduced the information and shook her head furiously, left to right.

"Your ma ever mention them?"

"No, officer, but I'm sure... It wasn't far away."

"Welp. That'll be it then."

He flipped his notebook closed. "We'll continue to touch base, come by... or call." With a mosey out the door, he lunged for the knob before Michelle could even think to move towards it.

In a flash instant, after the police officer left her precious, disastrous home, Michelle launched into a hunt for the good doctor, Ma's psychiatrist. The man had seemed to help, but was untouchable; a lure in cockamamie plans to make money tempted her fate.

Outside the blocky gray building she couldn't see inside, she pretended to sit and read her phone. Unsure of the premises, she made careful steps. For thirty minutes she watched two people filter out in that time span. Four cars littered the lot. When she approached the building, she peered in through the hushed, tinted windows to a point where she could see an odd man sitting, staring at his computer in boredom. She backed away quickly and entered the building.

The board on the wall listed several businesses. One of which was the doctor's office. Second floor—210. With relief, she breathed one long breath in, held the gasp, and then breathed out slowly. She did not repeat the exercise. She had found the right place. Double-checking, she held her index finger to the name and pushed it to the right, matching it with the correct office number.

"FedEx? Nope. No, you're not FedEx. God, they never come on time." The bored man at the computer lurched over to chat. His short sleeve white shirt, damp at the armpits, bore some of his lunch or breakfast. The fabric, a slightly off shade of white, looked similar to a jersey material. He scratched at his love handles and looked at Michelle quizzically. When Michelle didn't respond and shook off his weirdness, he said, "Do you have an appointment? You know this isn't a public building. I mean, it's all offices."

"Yeah, I know."

"Strange people always hanging around the lobby. You know Mick, heh." He turned and slunk away, back to his den.

"Mick who?" Michelle stepped on her toes, raising her body in his direction.

"Oh, weird guy. Hung around the office lobby now and then look-ing for the doctor. Is that the name you were fingering when I came out? You need an appointment, you know."

Understanding Michelle wanted more information, he said, "Tall guy, rough around the edges, stubbly face... Navy Carhartt jacket."

"Hmph. Nothing. I think I know him."

"Well. Doctor patient confidentiality, you know." The office work-er moved again back toward his office.

"You're not, you know, a doctor...?" She egged him to say what he knew.

"Look, the doctor is in cahoots. If you know him. I mean, patients go straight to the second floor. Don't lurk in the shadows, waiting, stalking." With four more steps he was in, slammed the door.

***

She parked her car alongside the road, looking up the hill two days later, against the officer's orders. Well, she wasn't on the property, she thought. *What I'm doing should be fine.* She cried the tears of a widow. Her mother was fragile, mentally frail. People had taken advantage of her, turned her into a pawn unable to defend her best situational interests under pressure. Michelle drove around with no purpose, feeling this place as best she could.

She went straight back to the arch and the clearing, the only area where Michelle had ever played. Despite the body and the madness, she wanted to revisit her memories. She found the only place she called her own. Such a coincidence she left the body there. *Who else would have known about her secret passage?*

The cleared-out area looked entirely different. The police took the tape down days ago. Now a picnic table sat not yet stable in the mud positioned in the field. The archway of trees had grown significantly larger. Someone had taken an edging tool to the entrance and cleared out the entire area. The gate no longer served a makeshift purpose. What was beyond the gate was no longer a secret place. Still, the gate stood.

She twisted a branch at the entrance, pulling the limbs and tucking them behind the wrought iron, and looked in. A wide swath of land was now visible. It was unrecognizable, demolished beyond conception. She split the thick green leaf in half and rubbed her finger against the ooze, lightly wetting her index finger. She turned to leave.

A sense of place, the ability to be, remember, and imagine, is important. It surfaces emotion. Michelle felt her ma. She imagined the good things to come if she was only back at last safe. The loaded memories, the remembrances, morphed in her mind. They were no longer burned in images of her mental state, incapacitation, or irrational nature. They were of her easily raised smile when Michelle said hello; her glazed blue eyes when they said goodbye. Michelle's way of seeing, the way she found this place and fit into it, looked at through a specific lens, was a way no one else would see or sense.

The fog, a cloudy mess to Michelle's clarity, had overcome Ma. No other woman, no other man, would see this place as Michelle felt this place. But in the misty morning, in her car, imagining the places they were and the feelings they shared, Michelle felt her presence and felt, if she could ever be psychically linked, that Ma was alive. She knew it, sensed it in her bones.

PART IV

Chapter 32

Here I am in your place. Your den. Is that what you said? Jamie shivered inside the cold, unheated room, smiling through chattering teeth. November seemed no warmer in Switzerland. A fire outside the concrete-like doors beckoned Jamie, and she moved closer to the opening.

Outside the door, an encampment buzzed with people and action. Sparks flew. Residents clanked on cans. He called the place an encampment. The cove of ten tents of varying sizes and shapes all showed wear and tear a bit too much. Several fires had been lit, one in a stereotypical drum. Others hovered small in rock circles or in small metal pots or buckets. People held pans over them at two in the morning.

Clothes of muted greens, dirty reds, and worn oranges wobbled in the firelight. She hadn't thought it through. Did she come here in earnest to reunite with Gerry or run away? She flopped to her belly, anxiously waiting, and pulled her body in tight to generate body warmth. The valley's mild breeze sent a chill up her spine. What would the mountains be like?

In the stale air of her abandonment, she hoped for Gerry to appear. Jamie had left, but only because Ellen had left her. Wallowing guilt and sadness drew inside of her. A piercing cold stirred within. Why would this person care anymore for her with her irrationality brought to light? He had banished her from a lot of places.

A stranger poked their eyes in the tent and wiggled their fingers. "It will be time to celebrate." The broken English carried a clear, upbeat mood. The intention pulled a grin onto her face.

"Gerry will be back," Handle had said. "He'll be here. You'll love him," they said, as if Jamie and he had never met. The pale moonlight glistened on the water, topping the edge of a 55-gallon drum. The night skies of Switzerland shed clear, crisp air. Jamie took in a deep breath.

Several lucid souls had greeted Jamie the other day and said she could stay in Gerry's tent. They poked her to see if she'd run when he first arrived. Their distorted, dirty fingers prodded her. When she giggled and said stop, please, playfully, they accepted her as knowing, somehow aware of who they were, and that they could be friends.

Gerry returned, showered and clean, and his charisma and calm came through. He must've had ways to survive, Jamie thought. She had spent the last of her precious money to find a cheap hotel, one where she didn't even shower. Gerry, hard on his luck, smelled like roses and held three rolls of sushi. His beard was grown in full, but trimmed, and he stood taller, more self-assured.

Jamie hardly had any money left. Dr. Prince had taken the money from the cabin transaction, even though Jamie thought it was going to be all hers. He showed up with a gun, a pen, and her checkbook. He said it was to cover Jamie's butt for leaving her inventory of transactions with doctors at the scene of a murder. Mick must've left the piece of evidence there. She had carefully destroyed all the documents. She knew she had. Jamie kept a bit of cash here and there in the house, hidden away in several places for emergencies. This mostly happened when she had an episode and thought her family would hospitalize her and take over her checking account.

Jamie missed her family. She could still say that. She missed them all a great deal. Their eyes and their love. They had warmed her heart, however cold the weather now was, when they had brought her things onto that hill.

She stayed there as long as she did because of the warmth. Hiding out until the murder they framed her for boiled over. They never did come after her, though. Out of sight, out of mind. It was plausible, in part, to be a showpiece for Jack, in the organization, to show to his pawns what happened when you didn't comply. Mick left her list, her signature list, at the crime scene. That's what he said. He said to get out of town. That's what Jamie did. But the cabin wasn't far enough away. Away from Ellen.

"It's a long story," Gerry coaxed her along.

"We've got time. I want to know about you, your life. What I missed out on."

"Well, you could live in a tent alongside me in a tent camp in Bern, Switzerland. Of course, you are at present."

"I enjoyed being up on top of the mountain for those months. You know?"

"Ha. Camping out for fun. Sounds like a dream." The last word trailed off. Gerry took a long hit of a cigarette and coughed into his hand.

"I only had one thing to think about up there. You!" Jamie shifted in the crossed leg style, putting weight on her butt.

"Be in love with the woman. The woman you found."

"I found you, though. Isn't it the same? Isn't this where we are?"

"I've aged." A short cough appeared again. "This isn't the life. You have the land of opportunity. So much, right?" Gerry didn't know the whole story, but he knew enough. She had told him there was a house. There was a person.

"I've got a home here. Could you stand it?"

After a pause, he coaxed out, "No." Smoke blew between them. "And I have a woman. But I've been preparing for you." A sheepish smile lit up the encampment. "The three of, well, maybe, but this isn't for you. I'm fairly sure, my dear." He swallowed and grinned, bearing grime on his teeth. "Com'on. You love her. Do you want this? Do you get why I made you come here? Get her?"

Gerry bore his muddy back and the scar across his hip.

"Casualty. That's what it is. You will get cut around here. I'll give you tonight, ten days at most, to decide, but you are candy. They will eat your innocent American self. If you want, really want to, you can stay. But it is not good. The area is not safe." He laughed big and strong, then clutched his belly, which had grown since they last saw each other.

"Is it so bad?" Jamie asked. "Do they haunt you? You know, mess with you and your stuff?"

"It is all ours, even my cunt. I have Ash, that's all that's mine, Ash and mine."

"Where is she?"

"She went, my dear"—Gerry pulled a finger across Jamie's forearm—"to another encampment to see how their supplies are. See if they need anything. She will be back tomorrow and then you must decide. She still gets jealous, you see. You can't dawdle on emotions with her."

For a moment, they were silent.

"Com'on. You love her. I want to hear about her, Ellen." He rocked on his crossed legs and leaned in. He looked excited for her, his old friend, a three-week lover.

"I do. But Mick,"—Jamie sighed—"Well, I stayed as long as I could. I lived on an easy chair."

"Sounds mighty comfy to me." He belted a laugh.

"She was everything. All the time, she snapped at me. She showed force and control, probably because I had none. Given a long leash, you know, the dog will run, break free. She tried to hold me in command. She tried to temper my emotion, and it only tempered her soul."

"Yeah, good." Gerry clapped and spoke. "I love, love, your love." He sighed. "Sometimes it's better, no? to have only one? I say this, and here I am with the whole world."

Jamie remembered the nights in the hotel and being trapped—the suffocating joy. She had left renewed, a different person. Here she was, trying to find something. Something to be again.

"It's that fucking Mick. That's why I had to go to our cabin."

Jamie fell back in her mind to the place on the hill, her place. Her home existed in parallel to this place. No shower, people helping people. Jamie was only a taker, though. Gerry was only a giver. As they related, some people only need to take, that is their job. They both agreed that Jamie was capable though, strong and fit. Jamie should contribute, whether or not that meant taking care of Ellen. Stepping up, being a sound person, living the life she could and that Gerry could not.

"It's my incapacitation, my weakness in the world that keeps me here. But I know the place. I know the ways. This is the only life for me. I wouldn't survive with a tie. Could you see me with a tie?"

"Aww. You don't have to wear a tie all the time."

"Maybe if it was years ago, if my teeth weren't ready to be pulled and the tear in my shoulder didn't need attention, I would go with you."

"That's ironic."

"That it is. You'll be alright without me. Get Ellen. Get Mick," Gerry said.

"I wish I could. You know. It's the scheming. I don't know where I am in the relationship at all. What's at stake? Someone died. They shot my contact. The distributor. They said they'd blame a murder on me if I stepped out of line. And that was to leave Ellen for good. Mick would take care of her. Oh, the whole affair gives me such a headache. I had nowhere to go." Jamie bent her head and played with the nylon floor of the tent. "She loved me. She must've if she showed up to bring me food. See me?"

"Fuck that Mick."

"He came to see me too, I guess. His visit was scary as hell. I thought he'd shoot me."

"I'll come with you. I'll shoot him. We must take care of that Mick. They'll come after me." Gerry, riled up, said, "I can leave for that."

"I actually have no money. There is no way for me to get home, really."

"I'll get you home."

"They'll kill me."

"You must kill Mick? Get a gun? I can't go."

"I can't show my face there. They think I've killed someone. I was framed and I'll be arrested. I'm sure it's sealed up. They're professionals. I'd fuck the plan up, as I always do."

"Get a gun. Tell Ellen the truth—Mick was holding you hostage so he could get what he wanted." Gerry paused. "Around here, if you show force, people listen. Even the mob. Really, you need to give them some crazy eyes and they're good. We've—out here—we've got nothing to lose."

"It's not like that. There is no way I could—" They spit back and forth, learning more about each other than they ever had. Jamie chewed at her nails because she knew Gerry was right.

"I must get her back." Jamie leaned against the piled up sleeping bag, neither in it nor using it as a pillow. As sleep egged on, she could do anything but stay awake figuring this out with Gerry as she had figured things out—she had needed a one and only, a genuine lover many years before.

She bobbed awake now and then to recount what had happened and think, unfruitfully, about what was to come. She could not imagine or picture the scene when she returned. Her future vision lacked clarity. She was not a seer of any regard. She was, in fact, stumped on how to handle the police or Mick. As a last whisper, Jamie swore she would get Mick. Justice or not, she would have Ellen back. She never, not even for lack of foresight, had let that idea go.

She loved Ellen but had fallen to bits. There had to be a way to put the pieces back together, to see themselves through this ferociously long episode Jamie was having. They had put their lives on pause for too long. If only the truth mattered. All those months Jamie had tried to think of a way to get back at Mick. All the while, he had her locked up as the culprit in a murder and then another.

A flash came through to Jamie, a memory about her wife. Ellen had put a pile of rope on the kitchen counter one day. She brought the heavy mass down the stairs, almost hiding it, but no effort could.

"What's the rope for?" she had asked. She lifted her whole body up in the air to see over the couch into the kitchen. The object was absolutely none of her business, and yet it totally was all of her business.

Ellen, in a stupor of anger, did not respond. Mick had surfaced sometime later and grabbed the pile of one-inch tightly bound and waxed rope. No one said a word. Jamie did not ask.

It hit her now. Ellen must know. She couldn't have incidentally, unknowingly aided and abetted. Ellen must have known. Known all along. If she didn't. Jamie could make her see, talk the reason into her about the entire ordeal.

The truth about Mick could make her see. Jamie knew so much. She was sure.

Chapter 33

Jamie hung by the phone, waiting to board the plane. In a casual manner, she motioned with her hand, beckoning someone over to ask how to dial out to the United States.

"Are you alright? You don't look good."

The woman, about Jamie's age but much different, spoke in broken English. She didn't even attempt to begin with her native tongue. Which, by Jamie's understanding of accents, could be literally anything European, maybe a French-speaking country. She hunched over a bit. Her age showed in her eyes, and it seemed like a thin layer of dirt or dust, likely makeup, coated the pale skin on her face. Her cheeks didn't show even a hint of color.

"I'm fine. Trying to dial out."

"Oh, get out. I see." She pressed a few buttons with sharp fingers. "Don't you have a cell phone? No... no, you might not." She corrected what she had said, clearly taking in Jamie's condition. She frowned as she looked at her and nodded her head. "Let's see." She grabbed the credit card Jamie held in her hand. "You're lucky they have this one. It must've been difficult to find. I think it's the only one at the airport."

She finished dialing the numbers and swiftly picked up her bag by the handles and moved away, her steps a little off kilter because of the bag or the arch in her back.

Jamie had given the women her wife's credit card. This had been her emergency card for the ten weeks she was in Switzerland. Jamie had not used the card once. A charge would show she was in Switzerland. Regardless of the fact no one would make the trip, even the local mob, to Switzerland for someone implicated in a murder they handled. The court would find her innocent if rationally investigated in the United States. DNA swab, alibi, motive, the truth of the chain of events. All would render her innocent, despite being tangentially associated with the organization. Jamie was safe from being implicated, but she was out of reach for investigation. She worried for her life back in the States, as evidenced by the constant threats she was getting from strong arms right before she left for Switzerland.

This phone call told the good doctor she was in Switzerland, out of his hair, away from the action, reserved to be the guilty one in the primary plot. Jamie held the butt of the phone in her hand and dialed. The metal of the wall that held the cradle was consuming. Cold, harsh like a prison cell might be all she could think. Then she looked herself in the eyes in the mirror reflection. Her short grown-out crew cut was about to classify her as a long-haired butch. When she got home, she'd have to clean up, use some money, some of the cash she had left, to get herself in order. That hotel everyone had always mentioned she would like. That would be her first stop.

"Dr. Prince." Jamie adjusted at the hip, lowering her bag to the floor between her calves. "Is that you? I didn't think I'd get a hold of you."

"Jamie is that? Jamie?" His words got big, greeting her.

"How are you?" Jamie could imagine him on the other side of the phone, squinting his eyes.

"Yeah, it's rough here—Switzerland."

"Sorry about this," Dr. Prince said. "I'll have to tell the police I spoke to you. This is beyond doctor patient confidentiality. We know you did it, you see."

"I didn't—"

"Jamie, I have to tell them." He paused. "Unless you think it was Mick. Jamie, are you coming home?"

"Oh, no."

"Because, you see," Dr. Prince said. "Mick might have done it. The cops don't suspect. But he might have."

Jamie could envision Dr. Prince scheming, twirling the cord around his finger.

"What do you mean, he might have? He absolutely did." Jamie realized her trouble, and the trouble she would get back into if she went home. "Dr. Prince. I wanted to see. I wanted to guess at what it would be like to come back."

"I know you love Ellen, but you have to let her go. But me, us, we could still have a place for you. You know? If Mick was dead—"

"I'm staying, Dr. Prince. That's what I'm telling you. Tell Ellen I love her."

She hung up and made for a padded airport seat close by. She eyed the massager stationed in the middle of the room but knew she didn't have enough coins and shouldn't use the credit card again.

Jamie had plotted in the woods, trying to figure out a way to get Ellen back, punish Mick. But he one-upped her. Mick had only made things worse for Jamie, as long as she was there. She worried about what he would do next.

Jamie tried to ruin the plan she got stuck in the muck of and throw a wrench in the entire thing by planting the inventory sheet in Mick's car. Jamie knew he was up for questioning in a body found in his car lot. She put the inventory sheet in his glove compartment at Ellen's house. That's what triggered his rage. He put the item, with Jamie's signature, at the crime scene. Jamie had spiraled. They would implicate her in the end.

The time away, the time she eased off the distribution, the bad guys told her she would have to pay the debt off in her hide. She would still owe the money, whether or not she collected and distributed. "You know these people need their pills. You have to work, Jamie."

Bull crap. That's all Jamie could think while she tried to find herself next to a vacant cabin in the woods.

She relaxed into an easy chair set in a section of four. Jamie didn't have any change, the euros, to make the thing work. She had a few American bills and that was all, leaving as she came. She wasn't sure how she'd take a cab once she landed. The leather was thick and loose, and the folds moved easily over the cushion beneath. She couldn't discern the foam from the dense cotton or the like. The fancy gadget stitched with care felt even and smooth, extra cushiony.

She hadn't a clue what the next day would bring, but she knew she couldn't last in Switzerland. She had no control. No structure. When she lifted from the haze of serendipity, in a haze of disillusionment, she thought she could stay in the country where she knew no one, hadn't even been down all the streets. She would panic. Scenarios were never good when Jamie panicked. Ellen and Michelle knew this best.

A person walked past Jamie, brushed her arm with their elbow, moved past, and then came right back. They bent at the waist without showing their covered face. A ripped hoodie with several holes and a fresh, clean scent ducked past the arm of the chair. A scarf unraveled and the yarn cascaded. The person's jeans were well worn, torn in a fashion statement in almost equal sections down the length of the legs.

"A friend of Gerry's." The chair vibrated.

Handle's muffled voice had bubbled as if from the depths. Their oversized sweatshirt engulfed them. Only two beady eyes could be discerned. They backed away, the mass of them, the large pants and extra big sweatshirt, hovered ominously. As if a ghost, the mass made its way to the door. Little bells jingled from the fringes on their jeans. They whipped their scarf back around their mouth.

Jamie remembered the face, now much older, from the bar, many years ago, when she had met Gerry for the first time. They had come in chatting loudly, almost angrily, and sat on the other side of the bar. Jamie never saw the person again. She never saw them at the tent encampment and hadn't expected to see them ever again.

Jamie thought back to the encounter on Wright Mountain when they stopped in to check on her. She realized now that Gerry had sent them to check on her. Gerry was always around, even when he wasn't. That night in the hotel, the way they bonded, the things they spoke. Gerry would always be with her, look out for her, whether or not he loved another. Gerry would always think about her as much as she thought about him. Their lives and souls had intertwined, as it would be, forever.

Handle had tested her to see if they could walk among her and, if she would not respond, not give them away. They would protect her, a person for a person. Their task became primarily to see Jamie home.

Chapter 34

Over a month ago, Jamie had snuck a peak into events that were unraveling before her eyes. The doctor's office walls were thin, and Jamie stood, lingering close to the wall and the crack of the door. It was one you could rap on, and it would echo not dampen, not require a fist as heavy as the door itself.

The words bit like an October chill. "I'll kill her." The word cut, and Dr. Prince could see saliva grow in Mick's mouth, leak out the corners as a rabid dog usually does.

"Look. It's not for you to—"

"I'll smash her skull into a fucking wall if I ever see her again."

Mick sat down at the table and pulled in his chair. Out came a prescription pad, and the doctor lifted the pen situated strategically alongside the large blotter on the solid wood desk. His eyes looked down as he wrote, moving in sequence with the words he wrote intentional and deliberate, meaningful.

"I hardly ever use this, you see. It's all the pills, or vitamins we should call them. No prescription needed. But you are right now. You need this. Take some time. Spend the day in bed, then get these."

"I won't spend any fucking time in bed." His rancor would not settle. "You don't get to say this is over. You kept this from me."

"I didn't know they had sex. I didn't know their intentions. The relationship was casual; I'm sure. They're married for Christ's sake."

The doctor was so still he shook, afraid of the possibilities. The words turned true. "I'm breaking doctor patient confidentiality. This is not to be taken for anything." He stiffened again.

"She fucked her? That can't be true. Yeah, right." Mick paced in the room, following his footsteps, foot over foot then turn, foot over foot then turn. "Oh, she'll pay."

Mick hunched his shoulders then straightened them.

"I'm angry, doc." He grabbed the paper and moved toward the door. "This does not involve anyone but that woman and my girl-friend. I will kill her if I don't ruin her life. This patience with her sleeping on the chair has worn thin. She will be gone. I will move in. If Ellen even thinks of choosing her, I'll kill them both. I'll kill them both. That's what I'll do," Mick reeled. Grabbing the small piece of paper, he quipped, "I'll sell this, but thanks." The oxy didn't matter.

Mick moved for the door. The doctor could only say "don't" as Mick popped out the other side, slamming the door.

Jamie had lingered in the waiting room for long enough, long enough to know he would kill her, long enough to overhear him learn she and Ellen had sex while Ellen and Mick were together. When Mick's boiling had reached spilling and sizzling on the cooktop, she had moved for the hallway. For now, everything would stop. That's all she could think. Ducking into the bathroom next door, she composed herself, and a door slammed down the hallway, smacking with delight for future actions. Those actions would involve Jamie.

She knew Mick's anger, gathered from the last bits of the conversation, that her life was in danger that she would need to hide out, find a peaceful place, get the fuck out of dodge. Most of all, Ellen would be off limits. This would be the least Jamie could do to protect her best interests.

With laser eyes, Jamie caught Mick in the car outside the good doctor's office, acting as if he was waiting for Jamie to leave her session. When Jamie doubled back toward the office to see what his intentions were, and to figure out the full discussion between Mick and Dr. Prince, she knew trouble would ensue. What she guessed, but did not know, was in three minutes, her life would be in danger for months and years to come.

She slunk up to the office, wondering if Mick had listened through the paper-thin walls as she did, accidentally, unavoidably.

A therapist's office should be soundproofed, locked in, capturing voices and resonating them only for the people in the room, for their purposes. She hadn't needed to lean in when Mick got angry, when his voice rose above a roar. She knew only her life was in danger and Mick would kill her in an instant.

Backed up against the sink, Jamie wondered how long she should wait. Obviously, she needed to hide in the bathroom, a schoolchild with a cigarette, at least until Mick left. Hopefully he would not see her car, but she couldn't stay too long, not the months and years she now needed. She had to act.

Jamie and Ellen had slept together in what others might call sin if they agreed on certain other conditions. They had a long relationship, raised a girl up to her twenties, and they deserved to rekindle with passionate sex if they wanted. She needn't worry about a boyfriend, a simple tryst with a man who didn't have the clarity such a long relationship had provided Ellen and Jamie. Their bond was solid. Even if they pretended it never happened, they said to each other, even if it were never a light in their life flickering until the end, they would remember they had love even after departure and divorce.

Mick and the doctor associated, commingling. Together, they plotted mayhem and doom all along. Jamie, now a witness, as Mick's chokehold on her grew tight, felt the heat. She now had no job, for sure. The doctor gave her another assignment at her appointment. The one now fifteen minutes ago, where she told Dr. Prince she slept with Ellen. She'd said that it was good and they might get back together, but now she had to get out of this madness, this scene of crime, petty crime.

Dr. Prince had ordered Mick to clean up a crime scene and drop a gun off at the site. A body lay over a ridge in his contact's parking lot. Plant a gun.

Jamie could do nothing now but think about Mick and his link to it all, who his contacts were, what level he was in the scheme. His role consisted of keeping tabs on Jamie to make sure she exited the scene.

That afternoon, at the end of October, Jamie left for the cabin. A place in the woods. She concocted a plan to hide out and let things boil over, consider Jamie's love that she gave to Ellen in the face of a relationship with Mick, who had a job, albeit a sinister one.

She would hide out, that's what she decided, until things boiled over, until Jamie could rescue Ellen and they could flee.

When Jamie moseyed up to the cabin, she had two choices: sleep inside or out. She chose the uncomfortable and did not know why. She wouldn't ever be able to say. The only thing she knew was she felt like seeing an old friend turned to crime that she met in Switzerland. A place that now felt like a decision. Her absurdity landed her near a fire ring. Up went caution tape. She didn't have to explain her irrationality. On the contrary, it triggered.

She thought about her options for her departure: Ellen or Switzerland. She thought about them every day, knowing full well Mick would act. When he came up the hill with chips and soda, what some not communing with nature might call groceries, he wanted to kill her. He would do it on the spot if he wasn't such a worthless criminal.

Gerry or Ellen. Gerry with his speckled cheeks from too much sun. His careful caress. The gentleness became nothing less than care. Gerry had planned Jamie's future, set her up for excellence, imbued in her the confidence she needed to find herself, find someone, not necessarily Gerry. Jamie, in fact, found someone different in the end.

Gerry had locked her into a hotel room many years ago and set her free at the same time. Without inhibitions, without the weight of a relationship, she was free. She never cared about the nightlife downtown, the gay clubs that might be there. She didn't care about the cute girl who might be at the chocolatier, or a five-minute stare at a clock tower, something three hundred years old.

All she needed overflowed in the room, and maybe the fruit, the sparkling wine, the tiny bags of pretzels, Gerry, amounted to what she needed at the moment. She needed a locked room away. Imagining herself in the room, safe. A liege at her door guarding the imminent. She had to get out, had to be and to not be. Only Gerry could give her these things.

As she drifted with clouds of the past, of ecstasy in a fluffy bed, she felt she was there in that same space, feeling love and tenderness. As much as she loved Ellen—another surfaced. They were the only one who could be her savior now, after all these years. She knew, Gerry knew.

With quick steps she climbed up the hill and ducked into the secret entrance, the one she had helped her daughter form many years ago. It was their bonsai tree; they joked. They still tended the tree every year through a meditation seminar or yoga retreat. To find peace. They both agreed they needed the growth and tending.

The way Jamie talked to her daughter about her mental illness, her disadvantages, had illuminated so much. They discussed it once, separated from those words—mental illness. "Mom. Let's go find peace in the woods," Michelle would say. "Or let's go for a peaceful drive," and she'd swing her arm clear around from her butt to her opposite shoulder, endearing, heartwarming, loving.

They didn't discuss clinical symptoms or emotional responses. They tried to avoid using language like "triggers" and "coping." All those words surfaced for the doctor, who never seemed to achieve a lot of results from Jamie.

Instead, Michelle and Jamie spoke about what they could be. It had been Jamie's idea to work on the bonsai. They'd think together. That's all they needed. Jamie didn't need to take an adult voice or scold or tell her how she could act. Ellen often took that stance. Together, Michelle and Jamie spoke about calmness and envisioned waves together for fun. That's what Michelle had always tried to get at. Simple, loaded activities to find peace like an expert in meditation might. Like the books said.

When the body appeared through the mountain laurel, she smelled the stank in the stream down the hill, still on the property. A deal was awry. She needed to see it, and now Mick's words came leaking into her, resonating with the full force of his fury, his anger at something that happened.

Jamie had got her money and turned the amount over to the good doctor, a deal to get out. Out of this madness. "I can't protect you from Mick," he said in warning. Basically, saying get out of town. So she would. That body, the last incident, marked doom. Incriminating her would pull stress off everyone else. As a scapegoat or a reason and without protection, she found herself in danger. Jamie didn't know which. She only had a few contacts. Mick banked on her, a perfect setup. She couldn't link herself to others. He cast her, mental instability and all, a viable candidate for wanton murder. Even Jamie agreed with that.

She went down to see the body, to see the evidence planted there on her behalf. She scoured the scene and did not see her clothing, hair that was hers, or a trace she had been there. Her boots in the muck set in an alcove of trees. The only thing. The only thing she guessed the police needed. Because she had been there on the hill and would leave now, see someone else, she was the culprit. The cops would choose her. Jamie would never come home. She would never find Ellen again and live without fear. Her pestering, only otherwise called devotion, dissolved. Her pining, only otherwise called pleading for love, would never be received by the one she intended it for. Jamie would move on.

Lest she ID as a culprit, Jamie left the scene in two steps. The body and the muck. The footprint in the mud. They would all wash away with the next rain. How much time would pass until they came for her? How long until she was in jail? She would try to explain her story, but the authorities would never listen. She'd never quite assigned the blame the right way. Surely there was a ripped cloth on the lump of the mangled body for a reason. It was hers.

She moved back to the height of the property and then descended five driveways down, closer to civilization. The bus would come to the small, covered shelter on its regular route. Jamie would take it to the closest town. She could transfer to the airport. Then she'd be gone. The events would cease. And she would wipe her hands of a cheating wife and unpleasant situation. She would've done it sooner, and Mick knew. A body pushed her over the edge.

Chapter 35

"Honey, I... I'm home," Jamie said. Then the phone call ended.

Ellen sobbed, trying to sniffle up her composure for the day. So much worry released and somehow, she still panged with guilt. She missed Jamie and the glow of her face. She had fallen ill with sadness, found depths of her own, even though she knew she could not compare it.

She picked up around the kitchen halfheartedly. Jamie had always put things in the sink, at least. She couldn't even be half as much a Jamie in some ways. She had left and come back. Brought herself back to Ellen. Found the truth. Ellen would get another shot.

In her galoshes, she thought. What is better? Knowing someone, even if they are off-base, or the unknown with someone who appears perfectly sane? Ellen liked Mick; They almost said I love you before Jamie left. But when Jamie left, Ellen found herself empty-hearted. Erratic and distancing herself, as Jamie leaned out, all the more Ellen had leaned in. That was, in the past, she drew closer to Jamie to save her. This attempt to let Jamie go hadn't made her any less rational, and she began losing her person, her first love.

She made her way to the driveway, leaving the house, leaving her and Jamie's shared space behind. That's where she stayed, waiting for Mick until he got there fifteen minutes later. Like a cold penguin bopping around, she waited, silly almost. Here she left the house, embarrassed to go back in. Her first move proved correct. She wouldn't double back.

A neighbor waved to her.

"Is it chilly?" she asked from across a long patch of grass.

Ellen nodded and smiled, crossed her arms, and made a shivering motion, a cartoon character agreeing.

She would not tell Mick. She would not bring the issue up. Jamie would be back, she knew, but all in time. A crime had emerged, a supposition. Ellen wouldn't turn her in. Jamie had not done what they said she did. She knew this only to be true. Jamie, afraid most days to kill a fly, couldn't possibly do certain things. She couldn't even skewer beef. The feel of knives on meat made her cringe. She looked away at the murder scenes in movies. Her anger never rose above a certain roar. Even Ellen's could get louder, more raucous. Jamie's pale face would have nothing but innocence painted on it. But likely surfacing pale and afraid, she might give to persuasive people. People who would test her fate.

"Hey hot cakes. What's up?" Mick pulled up to her in the driveway.

Instantly Ellen knew he did not know. She would have to keep it a secret if she wanted to get Jamie back. She nibbled slightly at her lips. But Ellen knew, knew it in the gut from those five short words. "Honey, I... I'm home." Her breathless words had dripped with anticipation and frustration. Ellen knew she couldn't talk because something must happen. She knew she was not yet free. She also knew, as she had supposed since she saw the body, Mick framed Jamie, who could go to prison for a crime she never could've committed.

"Hello, darling." She put on her best slightly disturbed smile, hesitated, then smiled boldly as a ruse. She got into his Chrysler and buckled her seat belt. They would go for a drive.

Mick never questioned her snooping, her casual questions. Ellen knew this much: Mick dealt with the mob and had roped Jamie into some activity. They could've implicated her, sent her to jail, or shot her. Ellen hid in the shadows, looking for details, trying to find Jamie a way out. She didn't want to interfere. When she finally tried to cut it off with Mick, tell Jamie she had to bow out on her own if they would ever be together again, Jamie had left and there a body rested in her place. She truly wanted to help. Somehow with Mick again, she tried, this time, to get out herself.

Mick's nose ran, and he sniffled in big heaves. He wiped his nylon jacket sleeve against his nose. Loose at his wrist, it slid and slipped as he wiped, pulling the cuff around his fist for greater precision.

"Oh, honey. You're being gross. Let me find you some tissues." Ellen pulled at the glovebox handle as Mick's eyes darted at her hands.

Ellen jumped back in the car seat; her seat belt still buckled. Her hands outstretched, open palmed, clearly said she did not touch the thing in the glove compartment.

"Ellen, it's a little handgun. No biggie." Mick shoved the glovebox shut.

"I mean, honey, you said you had a handgun, but in the glove compartment?" Ellen opened the glovebox again and pushed the gun with the tip of her fingernail in disgust, and then ran her skin over the metal. Stout, thick and secure, the ridges on the handle presented as a thin rubber applique. She didn't know the brand or type, couldn't even guess at it. She thought somehow, better not to ask, not to know.

"I know, you're thinking dangerous, right? Sexy maybe? I might have some handcuffs in the back. Am I right?"

"Wow. Off base," Ellen shrugged and held her biceps arm over arm, squeezing and shuttering. "Do you use this? Have you ever used this?"

"Honey, you know I have a boring job. I manage a mechanic shop and car lots and vacant buildings. Well, there are some sickos in the buildings, you know, the mentally ill. Sometimes someone will try to start something in a parking lot. It's for protection. For intimidation, really." He sniffed with a pouting face, clearly trying to gain sympathy. "You want me to be safe, right?"

Ellen had, in fact, found the rope he made her get from his trunk the other day. The bundle of rope sat irregularly out of context in the trunk. Ellen avoided talking about it. He had never given her a reason he needed it and dismissed her every time she asked. She didn't want to snoop, even though curiosity, a need for answers, overcame her. She didn't know Mick well, but she had come to like him. He had a way of putting his fists under his biceps when he talked, looking tough. He had been a typical man, something she craved in a way. She had unending curiosity about him and his place in the world. A strong, sturdy man, he served his purpose sexually. Her interest rested in a few small character traits, some checkboxes in a way. Almost, she joked to herself. He made do so she could meet a quota. Any man would've been okay. Not that she wanted to get back at Jamie. She needed another experience with a man. She spent almost her whole life with Jamie and, off in the far distance, she saw the other side. It begged a visit but not a stay. She wanted to see, so she took Mick.

At first, he was conceived as someone to be thrown away, but as she pushed Jamie away, as she decided they couldn't be together, he sufficed as a good stand-in. He created a buffer between them. Only lately, Ellen realized she missed Jamie, despite how much she had to care for her. The sometimes nurse-like qualities of their relationship, the interventions and stern conversations, and the talks to bring reality back. Still, it made her whole. Their banter kept life interesting for sure, but most of all, Jamie was her person. She had abandoned her person, and nothing she could do would bring her back.

She had stood in the corner when the postcard had come. Ellen slunk in the corner, her person no longer hers, but still her daughter's. Still legally bonded, they shared basic things. At that moment, she was spiteful and remorsefully reminiscent. Jamie was still out there, she knew, in Switzerland. She knew. She knew because that's where she had been before she came back to the United States, before she found Ellen.

"It's better than the killer girlfriend, wife, you had," Mick spit out, clearly reacting to Ellen's hatred for his occupation. Ellen marinated on his words, and he backtracked.

"You don't know she killed that person." Ellen clucked. "You don't know what Jamie is not capable of."

"I know what she is capable of. A lot. That's for sure." Mick reached for the gun. "She is crazy. Let her go. She'll kill again. Probably while she's disassociating; she doesn't know what she's done. I talked to the doctor; he's told me. Said he'd order her confined. Don't worry, he'll lock her up in a mental facility. She won't go to jail. He'll attest to her mental state. Brutal things are going to happen if she ever shows her face again."

Mick went to get out of the car, but Ellen stopped him. "You've been talking to her doctor? Her psychiatrist? Dr. Prince? Mick you shouldn't." Ellen rustled; her turmoil boiled through. Yet, she relaxed as easily as she could in the face of someone with a gun. "That's illegal."

"Listen, honey, this is the part where you decide if you're onboard or not." He got out of the car.

Ellen watched him move toward the abandoned building in cool, empty steps. His steps broadened. He moved determinedly, as if he had done this before.

Rushing to unbuckle, she got out of the car. She moved to the hatch of the car to check on the rope she had seen the other day. A tarp. There had also been a tarp. What else would you use a tarp for but a body for wrongdoing? For leaves, for covering something from the rain, for laying down over mud. Ideas, excuses ran through her head, and she knew it wasn't true.

Gunshots rang out in the abandoned building.

As she noticed the dots of blood on the tarp, smears on the rope, despite the large men's boots that seemed clean, she could affirm. As she realized the murder, her intermingling with a murderer, she lifted her arms, almost as if someone asked her to raise them. He had, for sure, asked her to decide.

She grabbed the rope, slammed the trunk, and ran as two homeless people emerged from the building.

She moved swiftly, and her breath quickened. She couldn't remember why she hadn't worn sneakers today. Late on a Saturday afternoon, she was usually planning for a night out, but even with Mick, she wore only low heels on their dates. She stretched her brain for memory. Maybe they had planned a sporty date that night. She couldn't remember. Even if Mick took her mini-golfing, she would have worn low heels.

The unplanned pit stop, Mick sounding shots to scare homeless people out of a vacant building, ran terror through Ellen's veins. The boldness devastated her. She never expected he would clue her in this much. Surely, he didn't even plan for her to see him in action. She knew the extent of the dilemma and Jamie's involvement in it all.

The scratchy beards and string belts of homeless men who surfaced showed they were beyond begging on the streets. They had lain down in that empty building to die, to be, to sleep. Mick just as quick would kill them if he liked, find them death a little quicker, but she knew somehow this time he intended to only scare them.

She rushed to the strip mall, a protracted line of outlet stores and small shops, and pulled herself into an establishment selling clothing. Pants and button-down men's shirts lined the walls. She moved to a dressing room and pulled out her phone, calling direct to the lead officer on the case.

"I'm... I'm in a dressing room. I'm sorry. But I need to chat with you. I'm not involved, but there are certainly my prints on this rope, but..."

"Ms. Richmond. Please slow down."

"Can you come meet me? I may still be in trouble." Ellen gave the address of the store and he said he'd be down directly. He said two cars would come.

When she met them, she stood still, an embarrassed mess, relieved by the sense of safety.

"Officer," she said. "Mick is responsible, you see. This rope. This blood. The DNA must match the victim. I know that much."

"Where did you say you got this?"

"Mick Kitters. The restraint came out of his car." Ellen's straight and even tone resounded confidently.

She attempted to implicate Mick, to turn him in. Otherwise, Jamie would go to jail. An innocent soul, her forever lover, would perish at the hands of the criminal justice system. She made her choice. She had never pulled Jamie out of the criminal activity like she had hoped, but at least she could save her from prison. Her sentence would be minimal.

"Lady, how do I know..." The officer grabbed his pen and notebook, looking only half serious.

"You trust me. That's how," she said, giving up one half of her that loved Mick for the other half that knew all along, knew she was still in love, always would be, with Jamie.

"I'll have the rope put in for testing," he said.

The second officer turned to the lead and mumbled, "He bound him, right? Toxicology tested blood at the wrists?"

The lead officer nodded.

"Do it right away. This test is imperative." Ellen lunged at them with her shoulders, trying to spook them with the truth.

"We'll send some officers out to follow him. I'll tell you that, but I also need you to wait here."

The police officer put on latex gloves then bagged the rope. "Lady, next time leave the evidence at the crime scene."

"I... I had to get away." Ellen now sat hands in lap in the police station. She lifted them and rested them, staring straight down at her lap the whole time. In fact, she wanted to go nowhere else. Her safety required strength to sit still. But Jamie, where could she be? Could she possibly know the trouble she would come home to? Ellen posed the questions. Then she answered herself with the obvious. Jamie sure as hell left for a reason. She could perish either way.

Ellen took a seat on a bench, bowed her head, and waited. Ashamed in a way moreso that she had fallen for a criminal, but also that she had left, almost left, her distressed, endangered, wounded wife.

Chapter 36

Jamie lurked in the house on an inopportune day. She tromped directly upstairs and gathered up some paperwork to be burned later. Incineration. She would overly enjoy it. While she fiddled with the file cabinet, again trying to get behind the barrier that held a wad of money from shifting to the front, Ellen walked in. Jamie could hear the echo of her steps, the particular way they clapped on the floor.

Michelle would be at her place, surely. She would have stuck around her looking for her good old Ma, but not forever. She wasn't, in fact, there today.

Jamie pushed her arm through the file cabinet, almost reaching for another place, somewhere out of where she was. She worked the leg of a small stool to pry it open. The dark metal, bent to a point at the opening, cut into her skin and drew blood. A quiet "ouch" emitted under her breath. She couldn't reach the money.

Ellen clomped around the kitchen mumbling to herself, and Jamie wondered how she could feasibly make it out of the house, and, once again, how in the world she could prove her love to Ellen.

Jamie opened the window in a move to throw the damn thing down two stories, crack it open. Her urge to try anything required thirty minutes of planning. She needed the money. She snapped back. For once she thought about the things, the neighbors, Ellen's footsteps followed by her chastisement, her final swearing off—of Jamie, of their life. Jamie didn't act, or preemptively act on things that involved Ellen. She didn't pick her up in a horse and carriage, didn't bring her home a new car. Nothing impulsive because she knew her impulsive instincts always fucked things up.

Jamie smoldered in the house, the root of her troubles. She didn't even know where she would go when she got the last bit of cash. She'd probably find herself a hotel. Flowers wouldn't do, and Mick would kill her. Jamie couldn't think, couldn't decide, whether to go down and meet her wife, Ellen, or flee until she could compose herself. She let her arm trail on the railing as she descended, still indecisive about turning to go back up and hide.

"Look, I don't—"

"Oh, Jamie. How could you?" Ellen's voice wavered. The words formed not in anger nor as wailing, but close to crying.

"I love you. I can tell you that."

Her instinct told her to flee, but Jamie held herself there for things she had to say. She pulled her composure together and smiled. She drew a long hard smile as she put on a guise of confidence like no other she had ever given. All wrapped up in the immense insecurity of the moment.

"Mick is trouble. I mean, I'm in trouble too, but Mick is in deep. I'm not sure how you don't know, but it's the truth. He's done horrible things, Ellen." Jamie looked down at her shoes, not intending to show shame, but sure it showed anyway. "I've done crazy things the last year. That's for sure. But I love you. All the things I've done, all done somehow, for some cockamamie reason, because I love you."

"Jamie, I, I don't know what to say. When you left. There was so much... And Mick..." Ellen embraced Jamie with full force. "They got him. I was, as you said, stupid about two things."

"And the good doctor?" Jamie's hope rose. The shameful dust subsided.

"Gone—Fuck outta dodge."

Jamie's easy chair still sat out of the arena, the playing floor for Mick's minor struggle. The quiet scene, a theater set, displayed similar qualities as it had before Jamie left. Emptiness, an eerie quiet. Flecks of dust shown in the light cast by the setting sun. Jamie looked past Ellen's shoulder to see if a tornado had surfaced on the horizon.

Ellen had watched the police officer slap handcuffs on Mick right there in the room. His "Wait, what, explain this to me," dumb faced inquiries got nowhere. They had enough evidence on him to lock him away for a good bit. Whatever the body Michelle found floating in the water at the family cabin did, Mick took care of it. And in a stone's throw, got Jamie on the run as well.

Mick, when the officer turned him around, looked right at Ellen. Ellen had hid her actions to implicate Mick until she lured him back to her house. The officer then grabbed him in one sweep. Mick became incensed, obnoxious, aware of doom. Part of the reason Ellen had liked him was because he could subdue her. Ellen always wanted an alpha dominant partner in a relationship. With Jamie, Ellen had been the yeller, the power, the person who put them both in their places.

As she rushed away, Mick slammed the car door and shuffled to the front door behind Ellen, who had scrambled around and gone inside.

Mick has probably come over to put things right. He would want Ellen to keep quiet. Even the neighbors bobbed their heads down as he approached.

She wanted the argument, his raise in temper, the potential repercussions of her noncompliance to sound off thick walls, be contained. Ellen had to hush the beast until the cops burst through the door.

Mick did, in fact, raise his fist before the cops entered. As the scene melted and the clamor of police officers shook up the place, Ellen blacked out. The sense of time, place, and words eluded her. Ellen had chosen between crazy Jamie and seedy Mick. The gavel dropped with a final decision. Mick raised his fist and Ellen ducked. His flavor of anger, a spitting, bitter cocktail, tasted so much different than Jamie's blank faced self-sabotage. Ellen could be a casualty either way.

When he lifted his head against his shoulder and looked back at Ellen, his simple, "Bitch" rang with so much hatred, so much effort to demean, to cause harm. Landing punches he had wanted to throw but never had.

Off-kilter, he collapsed on the chair, that same plaguing recliner, handcuffed and twisting in his mess. A few tears formed in his squinting eyes because, surely, he knew. He struggled in the chair and the police officers let him. They wanted to know about any abuse, additional charges. Ellen did not say he beat her. "He has this anger, the aggression. It can be scary," Ellen said.

They drugged the beast of a man away for colluding with other criminals. Criminals who cared not about a body in the woods, a pittance, but who others knew for revenge. They might come for her. Wouldn't she rather be in Switzerland?

Jamie sat subdued, calmed as never before. The darkness cast down now evenly, spreading peace throughout the dimly lit room. She whispered about the money. She still needed to get to the money.

Wrapped up in this same lie, Jamie knew trouble lurked close by. She had aided and abetted in so many ways, because of her illness or not. They would question her without a doubt. She had trafficked for them, albeit at gunpoint. She delivered product and collected money, wrapped up in a live or die scenario. Jamie would be on the run or fess up.

Jamie didn't know if Ellen would stay with her or not. But coming home to the roller-coaster ride in the suburbs meant she loved her. Jamie hoped she saw that.

Ellen helped Jamie. She got the pry bar from the basement. A weapon of choice for Mick, she thought. He could also have found the implement in her basement. He hadn't stolen the damn thing. Ellen used the metal bar to pry open the filing cabinet.

When they returned to the living room, Jamie rocked on the easy chair, happy to be home, back in her place, even if their relationship, their love, was no better. They both stared at the money, the wad of hundred-dollar bills. "A new car? I always wanted to buy you a new car," she muttered under her breath.

"Nope. Straight to charity. Straight to the homeless shelter." Ellen picked at her fingers. "Either way, honey, we have to move. We have to start over somewhere."

"Well, not the family cabin. Not Wright Mountain. I know that much. I fucked up."

They looked at each other, dumbfounded. Ellen sat in an armchair no one ever sat in. A clean square surrounded by dust became the object of attention. "I got rid of it. No one liked that thing, anyway."

"If that's the only thing that's changed." Jamie looked up into Ellen's eyes and sniffed in hard. "We can...we can be together?"

"Jamie. There's so much. It's going to be hard. But I've said the words a thousand times. You're my person."

Jamie moved to the edge of the recliner and clamped down on Ellen's outstretched hands lingering over the edge of the table. They both rose together, and Jamie pulled Ellen into her. Jamie got out in a lucky twist of events, but someone could still compromise her safety. Implication was at bay, albeit falsely in a murder, or actually in fraud and laundering, though they wholeheartedly deceived her. She knew what she had done in several ways.

Most of all, Jamie didn't want to lose Ellen. In their embrace, she whispered quietly in her ear, then nipped it with her lips, "Forever and ever."

Ellen was her reason to live. The life she wanted to go on. The whole time she stood staunchly trying to bring her back, even though she might never have guessed her intentions. She could whisper in her ear every day, "I love you," or force it down her throat. She did, with all her power, try to show her love up on the mountain. The actions were misconstrued. The words, the decisions, never came out quite right. But here she was, through serendipity again, and she whispered the words because the sentiment could never be truer between them, the words held by them both. "I love you."

Ellen whispered her response quickly and buried her head in Jamie's neck. "I love you too."

"Honey, let's buy a van or a motorhome. Take a road trip, early retirement. We can do it. We'd have enough for quite a while. Something impulsive for once."

Ellen laughed for quite a bit at the end, pushing out the laughs so Jamie would smile along. "We'll pick a place, live there?"

"I don't know. The money isn't coming in anymore, and the cabin is gone," Jamie said.

"Honey, I noticed the check bounced on your primary account. I poked around the accounts while you were gone. You wrote out a check to the doctor?" she said, in a quizzical but knowing way. "The money. The whole lot of it he never withdrew."

Jamie shook Ellen in her arms slowly back and forth, rubbing her emotion in. "Honey, I'd love that. It would be perfect. Us... finding a place, any place."

Chapter 37

Jamie summited the top of that same damn hill. She shuffled easily over the newly paved drive. Rocky, rumbling gravel no longer rolled underneath her feet. When she had camped at the top of the hill, the sound of the rolling gravel had struck anticipation, sometimes fear, into her being. Her car, soon to be sold for something better, rolled to a stop. She squeaked the brakes ever so slightly to test out the surface below her.

The postcard said to come up to the mountain to enjoy the sights one more time. The writing promised no dead bodies. It warned she didn't own the property. She went on the expedition one last time, hesitant but curious.

Dr. Prince might've tried to cash the check, but the money never went through. She double-checked with Ellen and her bank account. None of the money had changed hands. Eventually, she had stopped the check. Peace of mind consisted of a fifty-dollar service charge. She didn't rethink it.

Hands on the wheel of her soon to be sold car, she took in a deep breath. She would escape this place yet, the silly memories of sleeping out in the woods, composing herself to see what would transform her soul.

"It will embolden you," the postcard from Gerry said.

She ducked out of the car and took stride to make it up the hill. She would have to knock on these poor folks' door one more time. Come snooping around with suspicious behavior and crazy antics.

Halfway up the hill, a Swiss flag poked out of the ground. There had never been a flagpole there before. She immediately shrugged her shoulders and shrunk back into herself. She couldn't believe it. This only meant they, Gerry in spirit, his organization, hovered close, a beacon, a barrier, a warning.

She watched Edward, the same man who had wandered into her camp months ago, who had come back to her for a quick sale, stick his gardening trowel into the ground right outside the archway. An ornate trellis made of the same gate, which had been part of the archway down to the stream, now acted as an ornamental feature, vines tangled through it.

Edward sifted through the dirt, and Jamie turned to descend. Perhaps they would never know she stepped lightly on their smooth pavement. She moseyed back to the car, not caring if the Swiss flag meant their soccer team won. She arched her back and flexed her muscles. As Gerry explained, her mental coping skills, a strength not purely physical, had grown. Her safety cost nothing. No one would touch her. She knew it.

"Old friend."

Barreling down the hill, Handle met Jamie as she opened the car door.

"Ah, Jamie. Hello. Ready for the hug?" Handle lit up bright and shiny in the dewy morning.

Then again, as before, they looked at each other, sized each other up, and collapsed chest to chest. The strength in Handle's grip proved much more powerful than before. They could crush limbs.

"So good to see you! And Gerry? Together? Surely you both will ride into the sunset?"

Jamie put her arm around Handle's neck, an act of friendship. "I will never love him more than Ellen, nor Ellen than him. It is all different. For all pairs, it is different."

"Or threes? Right?"

"Yes. Absolutely. But not in this instance." Jamie winked.

Handle coughed and moved to the side, creating distance. A new topic surfaced. "I bring good news. The people who bought your house are Swiss. They are Swiss and they are with our organization." Handle stared Jamie in the eyes, confirming she understood. "They will kill Mick if you'd like."

"Wait, what?" Jamie balked at the words.

"We're saying that the Swiss will be making a presence in your hometown. Do not worry. They will always protect you. It is now confirmed. The couple we sent over... ah... Edward and Elsa. I just met them, but I'm going back to Switzerland tomorrow."

"Yes. Gerry knew. But I met them in the fall when I camped here."

"Yes. They will live there and make a presence. That is simply it for now. A warning. I ordered it as a favor, and they will stay there. Your check, ah, the doctor check, is not cashed, and the money will be yours."

"I mean, yes. I thought. They were quiet mostly. Wanted to take care of business."

"I saw to the transaction. The transaction was quiet so as not to startle you, create a fuss. I am glad you came. I'm glad to see you. Gerry cares for you, Jamie. He feels this is best this way."

Handle had to be on their way. He rushed, saying he had to get to another house. Jamie was only a cog. More moving parts churned,

Handle relayed. In parting glances, they each reiterated their favorite cheeses.

As she turned over the car, she saw Edward move to the top of the hill. He squinted his eyes with his head wavering and jutted forward. He batted an arm, neighborly, seemingly saying come by anytime. Jamie promised herself she never would.

She returned home to Ellen. Chewing on her nails like a six-year-old, she said nothing at first. She puttered around the kitchen. "We're safe," she finally said. "Don't ask me to explain, but we're safe."

Ellen leaned on the counter with her hands behind her stiff elbows. The counter had always been low. "You mean..."

"It has to do with Gerry. That's all I really want to say." Jamie knew Ellen knew she rarely talked about Gerry, if at all. Only that Gerry had given her a transformative experience.

No more words needed to be said. Somehow, Ellen didn't understand. Her ways, her controlling persuasions, disengaged. Gerry and Jamie had a bond, and Ellen should only listen and know. The danger was gone.

Chapter 38

Michelle got ready for the day at her mother's house. Her lease would be up at the end of the month, and with everything going on, she thought it would be best to stick around a bit more. She had all but moved back in. She wanted to help as much as she could.

Michelle heard them downstairs, talking, laughing. Ma's big belly laugh could shake the house. She hadn't heard the booming glee in so long. The laughter had certainly been absent months ago on the couch. For months Ellen had pined for Jamie as best she could, tried to show love. Then Mom tried to help Jamie get out of the madness she had fallen into behind her back to show her sincere love. The family would forever call those months the "couch era" among family.

Their open relationship, Michelle, didn't quite get. She didn't quite understand the dynamic how it could be okay to date others but not have rational agreements. The act appeared wholeheartedly wrong. Ma didn't want Mom dating Mick, yet still they trudged on. Ma didn't reveal everything she knew about Mick because it could implicate her. She didn't know what Mick would do was what Ma had said. Jamie, Ellen, and Michelle were still a family, but in a way, for several months, they had only held onto shreds of themselves and things they agreed on. The series of events and incidents were unhealthy for them all, though things had been, for the most part, healthy in the past.

Michelle rubbed some adhesive off the corner of the book she held before going down to greet her mothers. They made books about this stuff now, she would tell them. It's easy to have open conversations if you're on the same page.

In the family room, Michelle didn't quite get out as many words, but she handed the book to Ma and Mom the same. They reached for it equally and they both laughed, a belly laugh from Ma and an "Oh, darling" from Mom.

Michelle turned the ignition on her car and sped down the highway to meet Pat. It all had come down hard and Pat had witnessed it. She tapped on the steering wheel, making erratic turns, wanting it all to be done, to go back and check on Ma and Mom. She couldn't deal with it at present, and she meant to end it when she got to the park. They couldn't go on with everything behind them and, at the same time, in front of each other. Words escaped them. They at least needed a break.

When their parents had started dating, Michelle and Pat tiptoed around the issue before Ma ever even got involved with Mick's mob connections. But now they had to worry about added charges, or who might come after Ma or Mom for turning in Mick after all that soft stepping, all the avoidance of the easiest thing to do. Mom had tempted fate from the beginning, and it had only gotten worse. A chill washed over Michelle as she moved toward an encounter with Pat she would never forget.

"Where's this leave us?"

"I mean. My dad's in jail. Do you think we could smile through that? Your mom is back with Jamie, your ma. Do you think I could disregard that?" Pat's words stung.

Pat moved toward Michelle, looking ready to embrace her. They edged closer toward each other on the park bench. This had been an intermediary place, one between both of their apartments, almost equidistant. The agreed upon location said then what they both knew. There would be no fight, makeup, sex. And Michelle would not move in. Pat and Michelle met, at equal yards, bringing into full view what they both agreed was true. They could never be together.

"Pat." Michelle edged away from this last and final attempt at an embrace.

Michelle gave Pat a tap on both arms, a slight pressure at best.

"Pat, do you need me? I don't think you do."

"Of course, I need you. I totally understand why we can't be together." She pulled out, sniffling.

"We shouldn't. You know. We shouldn't see each other."

"I thought you would move in. My dad. It's a boatload of trouble, I know."

"But none of the drama involves you. You weren't culpable in any way."

"I'm sure there's something. I gave him a ride somewhere or took some cash off him. They'll come for me." In a sharp moment, she said, "Maybe?"

They wouldn't. In fact, the only actual loss was Michelle and Pat's relationship, a casualty of this entire ordeal.

They sat on the bench a while more. Michelle aimed to calm Pat enough so she could leave her and not worry, not always think about a distraught, crying face she left behind in the park one afternoon.

Michelle pointed at the person throwing bowling pins in the air. Juggling. "Who juggles nowadays anyway?"

"I know, right? If you're going to busk, play violin at the least, or organize a card game."

Michelle left the conversation, left the fight, their break-up. She pushed Pat out into the world to find something more, something that compelled her.

"I know you love to people watch, Michelle. But, the squirrels, nature, that's where I'll go. I'm going to go on a hike, Appalachian trail, take some time away. I wanted to ask if you would come with me, but of course you won't."

Michelle took a moment and composed herself. It would end here, the absurdity of their relationship. Their odd connection. The mismatch had somehow worked. She let go. "I...I can't Pat."

"Well, I'll be going then. Hopefully, I meet some people who don't know this mess, who are far removed from anything I've ever known. I'll have space at least. The very least of it will be I can scream into the woods about it all." She traced a heart on the bench and stood. "I'm leaving, Michelle. We both knew it wouldn't last. But now I'm unbound. Nothing could hold what we had together. What we had in the universe, this ludicrous world... Love ya." And she left, stepping larger than average steps. Her gait increased with distance.

Michelle walked casually back the way she came. With the lover gone, she could prowl for someone new. Instead, she casually looked into windows, hoping for an object, something she could buy. When she got to Mack's TV and Appliance, she went in.

An absent seventeen-year-old greeted her and simply waved and returned to his phone. Michelle moved toward the thing that had caught her eye in the window. The afternoon news. She collapsed onto a couch to watch the news carry on the conversation about—who was he? Her quasi-separated bisexual mother's boyfriend, a revelation in mid-life there might be something more.

Michelle wouldn't be here if her mom weren't bisexual. They wouldn't have found Ma together. Mom cohabited much better with women, Michelle thought. So levelheaded, rational, and sane. When she had almost married George, during the elopement after three months, Michelle had acted out, brushed off everyone's words, kept to herself in her room. Michelle had no right to tell her how she should live her life at that age. But she had grasped the severity, the change in attitude. When she latched onto Ma, it made Mom sane. In the weeks and months that followed, Ma's irrationality only made Mom stronger, more a person.

Butt saddled into the car, Michelle shimmied into the seat. She paused, hands on the wheel. Michelle hoped she might find love again, with less drama. She mused about Switzerland and having enough money to go. She would get a second job if she had to. Switzerland rested in her dreams. She had set her mind on a trip months ago. Now, with Jamie at home, with money, the dream morphed into reality.

She had decided when she saw her mom, she would go with her to Switzerland to look for Ma, for Jamie. She would remember what they had and the good she had brought to them both, but especially Jamie.

Michelle laughed and looked up. "Do you remember when Ma—" She looked over. She laughed again and remembered when Ma had tried to build a pool in the backyard for them all. The finished pool was to be shallow so they could wade in the water. She worked at constructing the feature so they would all have something to do in the summer and sit around the pool.

"Talk, swim, peel oranges in the summer sun," she had said. She had never finished it and the remains of a ditch, odd tile, and bags of cement left out in the rain still went undisposed.

Michelle wanted her Ma. She wanted them both back. Together. She would at least ask if Mom wanted to go with her. Retrieve Ma one more time from her trouble from the whatever sort of mess she got into.

She tally-hoed home, not even embarrassed she had talked to herself. Perfectly normal. She laughed several more times on the way over to Mom's, remembering.

When she entered the door, they were both there, gathered around the coffee table, discussing. Michelle couldn't believe Ma was there and wrapped livid, gleeful arms around her, stretching up to kiss her on the cheek.

"You're back."

"Yes. Of course. Of my accord, you know," she said, laughing at her awkward language.

"I've taken her back." Mom swayed her arms together in front of her, swooning over Ma.

"We were waiting to tell you. We were waiting for things to cool off." Ma held herself steady on the wooden, carved end table near the entry to the living room. Lightheaded, she closed her eyes.

She had exited the recliner. In fact, when Michelle entered, Ma sat in the chair. Mom stood in a shadow. It foretold so much.

"Honey, we're worried they'll come after Ma. That they'll come after Ma for some trivial things she did for them. They used coercion. Because her life was at stake. You get that right, honey?"

"Right. You didn't need to hide. I'm happy Ma is home. That's all I can say."

"Honey, we're going away for a bit. Camping, so to speak. You're welcome to come. It's a little early vacation, a test for retirement. We're going to get a camper and go cross-country for a bit, let things blow over. We'll leave the house for now. If you want to stay here, that's fine. Or come with us. We're going to be a family. We're going to rebuild." Mom hung on the ends of sentences, as if crying and satisfied at the same time.

Ma pet Michelle's head and held her to her chest. Ma had moved in when she was six. They all relaxed. The room paused, still waiting for even a slight sense of action. Everyone stood on their toes. What in the good green earth, out on the road, would Ma do to make it all absurd again? What would she do to get them all in trouble or ruin what they would build? They left for their rooms to pack.

Chapter 39

Michelle entered the gray and tan camper van finished in typical fashion with typical small appliances, and a typical table jutted into the center. A typical twin bed occupied the back, with what you would expect, no space on either side. She ran her hand on the leather, cushiony cockpit seating. The controls and stick drive shaft separated them enough to give them both their own space and comfort, but the distance might not be enough room to prevent bickering or the rising heat of an argument.

Ma dressed plain in her usual clothes, albeit relaxed comfort for traveling. The same sweatpants she wore on the recliner night after night now fit her body a little looser. Mom wore a typical Saturday outfit of skinny pants cropped above the ankle. Mom might be a little taller than Ma. Still, they were typical, typical together. What you would expect.

The map on the dashboard held a course routed precisely, with highways, stops marked with red dots, a hotel, and yellow, a tourist attraction or place of interest.

Ma handed Michelle a map. "Here. I made one for you." As she often did, she had carefully planned it. She followed in usual form with, "We might make alterations, but this is the initial plan."

Concocted or not, they had a general course to follow. The course would take them down through Kentucky, over to the southwest, up through California, and back across a northern route.

"It'll be time to decide. One more time, decide if we should be together and if this madness of mine will ever wear off."

Mom embraced Ma, holding her tight. She motioned for Michelle to subsume into them. They all embraced, a picture-perfect family, what you'd expect from them. They displayed to the world a window into everything, including normalcy.

Chapter 40

Ma lifted the stick with a marshmallow on the end into the fire. This must've been the twentieth attempt at a perfect golden-brown color.

"I swear I practiced."

"But what, you say you made a fire? More than once? Truly," Mom rebutted.

"It took me a while but, in the evenings, after I got my hands on a lighter... The magic happened. I perfected the art."

"Never to be duplicated," Michelle said.

Ma pulled the gooey mess from the twisted twig, a witch's finger, and wiped the extra remnants of goodness, those she dared not lick, onto the cuff of her pants. She breathed out happiness. In the revel of the pleasant moment, she beamed a smile, crouching into her posture. Everyone felt the air, the smile, and Ma's calmness, unique in all its glory. If only Michelle could hold this emotion for her, hug it into her if she needed, and never let it drift too far.

Michelle had run out minutes before to get some graham crackers. What seemed like a simple assignment had taken longer than expected. The mini market didn't carry them, so she drove further to the grocery store. Slamming on the brakes, she cursed the poorly orchestrated traffic of the parking lot. When Easter had passed, everyone jolted forth with spring fever, active on Friday nights, and ruining Michelle's assigned task, completed sober.

"Drunk asshole," she yelled out the window as she pulled past the single entrance to the store.

This wasn't a part of town to get shot in, she thought as an afterthought. If she were in on the east side of town, yeah, she wouldn't swear out the window. But Ma and Mom lived in a decent part of town, where privilege got the best of otherwise cookie cutter people. They always moved casually on their way after an affront, somehow armored by their wealth and assets.

Jamie, Ma, had been on the other side of it all, fallen of one kind of wagon or another. Finally back among the living, she'd lived to tell a tale, so Michelle counted her blessings. The future suggested much pending doom for her wayward Ma.

The two had fully packed the van with food, even without the threat of a snowstorm. There wouldn't be a shortage of food. Similarly, Michelle didn't expect her ma to freak out, panic, or create a nightmare of a situation anytime soon. She had calmed down. Her pills worked, took hold. She had a new doctor. Things improved in the short term.

When she picked up some Reese's Peanut Butter Cups in the aisle, she saw a child kicking and screaming in the walkway. He yelped about the soda, which set on a rack in the next aisle altogether, but this child conjured up or had inklings in his short-term memory of the thing he wanted so much but could not have.

Michelle would've given him the soda.

The mom dragged him by the arm, making the tantrum officially a scene. Michelle relaxed; it wasn't her place to say. She kept her distance. The person who knew the child the best could resolve the issue. If she acted in response to the abuse, the potentially dislocated arms, or leaned in to quiet the child, it would all be the same. She would cause the scene, the reaction.

Michelle understood her ma to be like a child and like an abuser. In both regards, everyone said the fault didn't rest solely with her. They talked about it not being her fault. But, their responsibility, whether it was hers or her mom's at any one time, muted culpability, and managed it as best as possible. That's the way it was, for the world.

She returned to the scene of the anti-crime; what Michelle had named it. Where nothing was an assault, a dig deeper into the world of mayhem and guilt. Their simple fire would last. They'd hold it close in case anyone ever fell into an absurd abyss again.

"I also got peanut butter cups. Mmmm, melty." She smiled a quiet smile, hoping in a way to not wake the beast before they left on their trip.

"Well, that's a little wild." Ma said. Everyone leaned back, mice still tiptoeing.

Before Mom changed the subject, Michelle said, "I get it. For once, I get things. Don't worry. This trip will do us good, I mean."

"Yes, Michelle, we'll be fine," Mom chanted. The exhaustion had left her body, and she sat a little straighter.

"Ma. Did... Should I be scared?" Genuine fear rose.

"Honey. I'd twist his nuts off slowly with pliers," Mom said. She held the stick before her with stiff tension. Despite not applying pressure, it seemed like it might snap in an instant. If only Mom twitched her eye.

"Honey, you're not in the middle of a ring, but I am. There's a network of workers and I hardly know any of them—the people, that is." Ma stared hard at the twig in Mom's hand. "But your mom could break any alibi Mick gave. She documented hundreds of nights when he went out. The time she found blood on his clothes. The time he left a gun on her couch. Oh, and when he had appointments."

"Sloppy Mick," Mom said. "Men often are." They all laughed.

"I locked his calendar, the records of his appointments, the places he visited, his distributors, all his contacts—I locked it up in a safe deposit box. It's being opened with our will."

Mom snapped the branch as if she had been waiting for years. With clarity, she barked, "Men are sloppy, Michelle. Leave them be."

"Oh, Mom, you don't have to worry about me. For real. You're the one—"

"Honey, I knew something about Mick, the doctor, was not quite right. Thank God, I could recognize it. Mick was nice, and a man now and then, well…"

Ma begged for a continuation of her story, the saucy details. Not a smidge of jealousy pervaded the air. "She saved us really, Michelle. Us both."

"Once she got close enough to Mick, she reeled him in, got the dirt on him."

"But you?" Michelle choked.

"I'm bisexual, but yes. I had sex with him. Honey, I had to. It was the only way." Mom cuddled up to Ma on the wooden bench made from two stumps and a thin piece of log. "That's the long and the short of the matter. Miscommunication, yes, along the way."

"Switzerland amounted to a miscommunication, to say the least." Ma shut her eyes hard in angst and to feel the warmth of the body beside her, the comfort and security leaning into her.

They would leave the next day. Their extorter was locked up and the daughter safe by all degrees. They would exit the scene with only a slight apprehension of the future, a daughter left behind, left to grow up, and the traces of crimes would kick up in the dust.

After several giggly hours and way too much motherly advice, Michelle bid them goodnight, pushing them into the world to grow up and be adults, love each other, as they had let her find herself in college, helped her arrange her dorm room, but didn't stay the night. Her family would move on, but Ma and Mom had to find their way alone, find a place, a home, a new home. Somewhere out in the world's wilderness.

Chapter 41

When I said I loved her, the sentiment meant I would do anything for her. I would always be by her side. Nothing changed when I needed to save her from the deepest depths of disaster.

Ellen wrote heavy handed in her journal, the one she had started as soon as Mick went to jail. To hash out the details of the affair, the months of trying to salvage a relationship by putting the root of another behind bars, Ellen wrote in the journal her feelings, and the chain of events. No one could say she made it all up. The record would be complete by the time they got back from their trip. She would enter enough evidence into the ledger, everything she had gathered from the months she waited for Mick to incriminate himself or fuck up. Her feelings would be there for Jamie to read. They would resound in her ears. They had to.

Jamie had bought her a fancy pen with silver and gold embellishments at all the edges of the pen and cap and a bright bullseye, silver with a center of gold, dotted the bottom. Smooth to the touch, it felt weighted, but it wasn't a telltale sign. If you picked at the base, one-half inch up, and stuck a bit of a nail in, it would come loose. A small knife would appear, ready to stick with purpose, with something so small you had to be sure, into a target. This, by all means, was her failsafe if ever attacked. It tucked gently inside her pants pocket, the metal pen cap flange on the outside of the pants, the pen, the knife, within.

Jamie had dwelled underwater when Ellen found out when Mick stepped into her life. Michelle had introduced Pat's dad to her moms at a dinner one evening. As an absent parent and spouse, she had dipped into depression. Her hard-to-managed condition had manifested as doubled-edged mania. She had acted nervous all the time. They drifted apart and Ellen, as much as she pried, hadn't known the reason, couldn't have known, what drove the malfunction in their life.

After all of the mess was over, Jamie relayed her thoughts and feelings in an open way as they did when they first got together. Back then, their relationship took off so quickly because of their equal frankness. Jamie told Ellen the full story, details she had kept bottled up. When Mick had sat down at the table, Jamie immediately recognized him. She proved defensive and anxious, sweating within a minute or two of his entrance. By Mick's actions, everything could continue as normal. Michelle and Ellen looked at each other with darting eyes, markedly concerned for Jamie's wellbeing. They asked if she felt okay, if she drank or ate something bad. They lay her down, but not before Mick shot out, "Hey—You are okay." The entire room noticed it. He acted as if they met each other somewhere before.

Ellen knew Mick was a trigger and finding out more about him had meant finding out more about what troubled Jamie. A bump in the landscape, pale as a ghost, as if she had a gun to her head, Jamie had denied it all at the time, denied ever having seen him before.

"Oh, yes. What was your name? Mick? Oh, yeah. Mick, I'm fine. Really. You said it." She spoke. "I must've eaten something bad." She motioned to the peak of the stairs. "I'll sit this one out."

Ellen had continued complaining about Jamie at the table, letting out some frustration under a few glasses of wine. Mick had taken a liking to her. When Jamie said she had work again for the next three weekends and Ellen mentioned she wanted to go to a flower show,

Mick stepped in with his number and an offer. She had been home for so long, doing nothing. Then, she had worked all the time, odd hours.

Mick took Ellen's number, a ruse of a gesture of friendship. They got close. Mick had tried to kiss her on the first date, and Ellen let him, hoping for the weeks to come she would find out more about her wife, about what bugged Jamie and what she had dug herself into. As much as it made her ill to be with this man, a composite brute and sports bro, he left clues.

Casually he made her aware of his ventures, parking lots, casinos, multiple streams of money. The deeper she got, the more she guessed Jamie had involvement in the same things, but she wasn't sure what, or if she could get out of it all. Jamie's nervousness said she was stuck, and Ellen looked for evidence. She found logs and receipts for both their actions. She counted money left in collector cookie jars along a top shelf after Jamie had moved out. She took photos of multiple different guns she had found in various places. Placing her thumb firmly on Mick, she waited until the events were solid, provable by law.

When Jamie finally went missing, when they found the body, Ellen had known she had to wait. Wait for Jamie to surface. Jamie's innocence would shine through. Ellen didn't doubt truths like this. But when Ellen had the evidence, the ropes and blood, she confirmed her hypothesis.

Jamie returned, a godsend to them all. Mick and the doctor would go to jail. To keep Jamie out, she had to step back. She had been lucky through everything and stayed that way throughout the investigations. How far they would go was up to the police. She had been questioned and let go. It was in Jamie and Ellen's best interest to take a vacation, take some time, before heat from associates or the police rose.

Their honeymoon was their second awakening. They would find love and lust, and put what was done, the man and the crimes, out of their minds. They were together again, despite the muck they had raked to get back to that place. Their true love would last.

Ellen rubbed the wax over the old camper van, hoping the shine would gleam. A new product on an old piece of metal. She surely didn't confirm if it would work as expected. This home would shine, or it would be the death of her. Her elbows ached, even so, a woman who was usually the chef, rubbed. The work on the road would be equal parts. The physical labor and the emotional. Jamie grabbed for the wax to do a job she would usually have done. Ellen snapped the wax away, asking only if she didn't think the cladding already shined as well as a brand new boat. To this question, Jamie only cooed back. It was beautiful.

Her diary sat on the dashboard, warming in the sun with the wax. She wouldn't share it with Jamie until they returned. She wouldn't let Jamie in on it all until they found common ground on their own, got over what had happened with Mick, and told her with her own words. The journal, the stories, would double the words down. For now, they needed to move swiftly through it all with calm words, care, and tempered emotions.

Chapter 42

The voyage day had arrived. The cruise would set sail. Ceremoniously, they cracked a champagne bottle on the camper van, creating a sticky mess on the wax job, and grabbed a few more things from the house.

"Only a few more things. We're coming back here after all." Ellen chased after Jamie with a yell.

Jamie fiddled with a drawer in the kitchen, seeking a few things that had popped into her head. Riffling, she remembered all those angry dinners. The smoke and hollering. She remembered picking on Ellen for not telling her she was stopping at the grocery store, making dinner later than expected. "So unthankful, selfish."

But it had slipped out. She hadn't meant it angrily. Her butch voice wavered men on occasion.

Jamie wasn't convinced it would be a perfect journey. She guessed they would fight. The measuring cups taken from the drawer were the same ones Ellen had thrown two nights before Mick first showed up for dinner. They were all silver and rang when you pinged them with your nails.

Jamie shrugged away the thought earlier and wrote "Just Married" on the back of the camper van. She grabbed a brand new progressive pride flag and headed back outside.

Finally, with a turn of a key, they were on their way. The door locked, and they commenced their ride, which would last for months.

By the time the commotion subsided, their house would be cleansed. The air would have no casualties, only the drifting stale air of dinners with voices above a roar and memories of a few breakable things thrown across the room. If it was too much, if the house was in ruins, they would buy a new one or live in the van. It didn't matter which. They were going on a epic journey together to see the world, share the world and the things outside of their home base, the home base that was damaged beyond repair.

Ellen had loved Jamie through everything. She understood, somehow, the love was a motherly love, the kind Jamie occasionally needed. When Mick showed up though, their relationship had seemed much like it was over, like Ellen had flipped a switch. Mick came into her life, and no matter how hard Jamie shook her head, nothing flung off the sense that told her Ellen was suddenly crazy for men, as if she had always been. Jamie had dug herself into the deepest of all depressions. Yet here, she owed her life to Ellen for her sacrifice, her innate ability to date men, for whatever devious reason that Jamie could not attempt to fathom.

All while bitter about the switch, the hell that appeared because of the situation, stuck through things for the pure hope and faith their relationship would last, Jamie showed her love. She would not leave, the only way Ellen could see and push through her sudden desire for men, to realize they were still in love. Jamie needed Ellen to still be in love. She would not waiver, sticking to her guts that told her what they had was still right. Their marriage, the rings, the child. And they had made it through. Now they saw the irrelevance. Whether or how Ellen wanted Mick, had sex with Mick, had bailed Jamie out of a problem. They soldiered on, knowing each other and where they had been—no secrets for the faithful.

Ellen, after all, called on the police when the body surfaced. She might've discussed it with Michelle and never mentioned it. Let life move on. But they had turned in the evidence, let the police rifle through their house and question them with blunt words. Had they proved Jamie's innocent, or did she shrug and give up and let what would be, be? If Jamie had been responsible, would Ellen have stood by?

They set everything up to make Jamie look responsible, yet Ellen had turned in the hard evidence of life. To Ellen, truth in the matter of life and death was more important than their relationship. As it should be, Jamie guessed.

"That was the last straw. I'm telling you the truth. If you were gone, really gone, what would it have mattered?" Ellen pushed the measuring cups into a small cubby above the pull-out table. "You could've been the body. You could've caused it. Or they could've framed you. I bet on the framing, the fraud—Mick—and hoped with all my heart the body was not you."

In the next instant, Ellen climbed from the rear of the van into the driver's seat.

"Honey, in or out. Now's the time."

"But I forgot the matches; You never know what you'll need."

"The door's open. In or out. Buckle up. This is going to be a wonderful trip. You don't want to miss the journey." She smiled as Jamie climbed up front, the door shut, and rested a loving hand on Ellen's thigh. "Wouldn't miss this if it was a choice of life or death."

THE END

Acknowledgements

I would be remiss if I didn't take the time to thank some of the many people who helped me with this third work. First, my wife, who said she wanted to read a finished one this time and hasn't yet taken a peek, who gave me a hug and kiss and said you're the writer not me, who gave me a whole room in our house for all writerly things.

When I came out to my mom as an author, she was excited to read whatever was put in front of her. The dedication to my next book, beta read by my mother, is forthcoming. Mom, I hope you enjoy this one too. And to my dad, who loves mystery and thriller novels of a certain air. Who I truly always have tried to impress. And my brother and his family for ordering each book without hesitation and offering support and unending kindness about it all. And my mother-in-law, who would fistfight my brother on release day to get her hands on a book. She wants every one signed.

To Erin and Marie who said, "Sure, I'll read it." And I said, "Errr, it's a bit…" And they said, "Sure, I'll read it." I analyzed every word and comment. They each made a difference. I'll ask for the rest of my life what I can do. I hope the gummies made up for it. I hope I make it to Oklahoma this year. I hope I can sit around a campfire. I hope you ask me for something.

And to Spectrum Books, Andrew and of course Carl, who plucked my book up and gave it a shining spotlight. Thank you for your attention, direction, vision, and sincere assistance.

What really would we be without the people, friends and loved ones, who offer their time, thoughts, care, and sense of you and what you have done?

ABOUT THE AUTHOR

S.E. Smyth is writing away as much as she can. She is inspired by history and stories that have not been told, pulling words from true events, her lived experience, and education in history.

S.E. has published has published two novels with NineStar Press, Hope for Spring (2023) and Criminal by Proxy (2022). Recent short work can be found in Scarlet (Jaded Ibis Press 2023). She writes the stories that are hard to tell. Her accounts are never exactly how they happened, and she firmly believes it is reparative to reimagine.

Excellent LGBTQ+ fiction by unique, wonderful authors.

Thrillers

Mystery

Romance

Young Adult

& More

Join our mailing list here for news, offers and free books!

Visit our website for more Spectrum Books

www.spectrum-books.com

Or find us on Instagram

@spectrumbookpublisher

Made in the USA
Middletown, DE
04 November 2023

41752178R10156